BEWITCHING HEARTS

BEWITCHING BREWS
BOOK 3

SHERITTA BITIKOFER

Cover Design by Patrisha Badalo (Art Muse Graphic Designs)

Ebook ISBN: 978-1-946821-50-8

Print ISBN: 978-1-946821-51-5

Contents

Dedicated to all those who believe in magic, miracles, and the mystical power of a good cup of coffee.

Chapter 1

Alexa let her lips curl around the Latin words as she wrapped up her morning ritual. The language never mattered so much as the intent, but there was something about the ancient tongue that seemed more potent than plain English. And these days, she needed potent. She needed that extra boost to get her through the day.

The incense smoke rose from the altar, the ambrosial aromas of herbs and oils swirling through her senses and seeping into her spirit. Her fingers deftly rolled the carefully selected crystals in her palm. She channeled their energies, feeling the smooth, cool texture of their surfaces. Behind her closed eyelids, she envisioned her chakras aligning and strengthening, ensuring that her intent was fully manifested as she did every morning.

"I am strong," she chanted. "I am confident. I am joyful and whole."

Beneath her feet, several grandfather clocks chimed on their hourly cue. That was Alexa's sign to finish or she'd be late for work. She opened her eyes to take in the dull gray light slanting through her bedroom window. This cool January morning was full of promise. That's what she told herself every day, whether she believed it or not.

Taking one last, deep breath, she set her crystals upon the table by the window, positioning them perfectly as they had been before the ritual. With a few extra invocations, she closed the rituals and snuffed out the glowing tips of the incense sticks with her wetted fingers. Miss Macy, her landlord, wouldn't allow an open flame in the apartment Alexa rented, but incense was never questioned. The old lady liked the way it fumigated her antique shop, so it wouldn't smell like dust and mothballs.

The studio apartment above the shop along Johnson Avenue wasn't much. She couldn't cook there, she couldn't light her favorite candles, and she couldn't own a pet like her friends, Krystal and Valerie. But it was enough. All she needed was her bed, her dresser where all her rituals were held, and her small collection of books about the craft she had been studying all her life. The floor beneath her woven rag rug squeaked in response to her hurried footsteps, and the faucet in the bathroom across the hall didn't always spew out hot water, but it was home. For now.

Alexa inspected her hair in the small framed mirror next to the window, smoothing the stray hairs in her blonde curls until they were just right. A quick adjustment to her cardigan, a bit of twist to her skirt to make the flowery patterns face forward, and she looked ready to take on whatever that day had to throw at her. Still, she didn't turn away just yet. Alexa checked everything a few more times. Her hair, her makeup, the way her clothes hung on her petite frame, for any twisted strap in her heels, or underwear lines bulging through her blouse. Blue eyes searched for anything out of place, anything that might suggest she was ill-prepared for those challenges.

In the end, she knew there was little she could do to truly be ready. And yet, she continued to try. After securing her tiny sachet of crystals in her skirt pockets and grabbing her designer purse from the floor, she hurried toward the door. She was almost there when she realized she had almost forgotten something. Her heels made a loud thud on the floor as she stopped dead in her tracks and spun to the modest fish tank in the corner of the room.

"Sorry, Mr. Fish," she said as she rushed for the food container. "I expect you need breakfast just as much as I do."

The orange goldfish wiggled its way to the top and chomped at the flakes Alexa sprinkled into the bowl. Miss Macy might not have wanted her to have pets in the apartment, but like the incense, she found a loophole in the agreement to suit her. Life would have been even more lonely than it already was if she didn't have Mr. Fish.

Alexa smiled and resumed course out of her room and down the stairs into the antique shop. The entire first floor of the old building was packed from wall to wall with knickknacks and donated heirlooms. Rusted farm equipment, vintage furniture, oil paintings, marble sculptures, chipped dishware, carved statues, beaten steamer chests, fragile dresses, and every other sort of trinket imaginable found its temporary home in Miss Macy's Antiques.

The incense had done its job again and Alexa could hardly detect the scent of aged wood and musty upholstery. Picking her way through the darkened labyrinth, Alexa passed some of her favorite pieces. An onyx statue of a cat with topaz eyes, one of the many grandfather clocks featuring a wide-eyed owl perched upon its top, a blue velvet wingback chair that needed more stuffing. Her slender hands brushed each of them as she walked by, feeling their texture and individual energies. Her mouth tugged into a new smile at the memories they must have carried with them into this shop.

She exited out the back way and bypassed her yellow Volkswagen bug, since the coffeeshop was just a few blocks away. Though it was still cold and her toes would be nearly frozen by the time she got there, Alexa could never resist the journey.

Much of Goldcrest Cove was still asleep. The crowds that were drawn in by the holiday season had died away, leaving the town to its locals once more. Snow mounded on the few cars parked along the curb and coated the streets in a fine, unbroken sheet of white. The trees that bloomed in spring were bare and tall, multi-armed skeletons reaching to the overcast sky. And yet, Alexa could somehow sense spring in the air. Tomorrow would be Imbolc, the halfway point between winter and spring. It was a day of hope for those in the past. A day to remember that the hard times were almost over and the sun would shine warm again.

They didn't need those kinds of assurances now, but the traditions always gave Alexa something to look forward to. Something to hope for.

She neared the coffeeshop and found its lights casting a welcoming glow onto the sidewalk. Another reason to smile. The blast of aromatic heat hit her face as she swung open the door, a clear sign that Krystal was in an excellent mood this morning. The place would have been freezing otherwise. The cheerful ring of the bell above the frame echoed through the shop, bouncing off the distressed wood floor and brick walls. The chairs were still turned over and sitting atop the tables. Krystal hadn't been there long.

Her best friend's long coat hung on the rack near the counter and an empty ceramic mug styled with leaves and vines sat on the counter by the register.

"Krystal?" Alexa called out.

"Back here!" shouted the owner of Perfect Books and Brews.

Tossing aside her own coat and purse, Alexa skipped to the hallway that led to the bathrooms and offices. She found Krystal Hayden – soon to be Krystal Daniels – sitting at her desk, turning over reports and pages lined with numbers and figures.

"You know that's my job," Alexa said teasingly with a hand propped on her hip.

Krystal delicately pushed aside a long strand of her bangs from her eyes. "I know," she mumbled absently. "I'm just checking it all over."

A slight rush of panic swept through Alexa. There shouldn't have been anything wrong with the reports or the finances for the store. She had gone to school for accounting and would have known if any calculation was off. Nothing was amiss. They were actually doing fairly well after the big holiday rush. Why would

Krystal have any reason to doubt her? Then again, maybe there was every reason to question Alexa's competency. They had before.

"Does it seem like the traffic's been down lately?" Krystal asked, turning her dark eyes up to her friend standing in the doorway.

Alexa shook her head and shrugged. "I don't think so... It's probably just the wind down after the rush. You know how it gets this time of the year."

Resigned to that excuse, Krystal stood and sighed. "I guess. It just gets me a little worried when we seem a little less busy." She shook out the wrinkles on her boho skirt to make the rippling folds drop down to her ankles. Alexa always admired Krystal's earthy style, from her flowing cotton blouses with bell sleeves to her patch work skirts and dresses. If she didn't love bright colors so much, she might have copied her. She wanted to be like Krystal in almost every other way. She always had since they were kids.

Alexa gave her longtime friend a sympathetic smile. "We're the only coffeeshop in town. We're never going to go out of business, if that's what you're thinking."

The bell over the door jingled and the two girls looked to one another skeptically.

"Valerie?" they called in unison.

"What?" By the snappy tone, they knew it must have been her. And, as usual, she was not in a happy mood. Mornings were never her thing.

Alexa and Krystal quickened their steps down the hall to see the third co-owner of the coffeeshop sling her khaki jacket over the hook of the coat rack near the counter.

"You're never here this early," Krystal remarked.

Alexa examined her friend, but found no dark circles under her glittering green eyes. Neither did she look like she had just crawled out of bed. Once, Valerie had been running so late that she didn't even bother to change out of her pajamas. But today, she was dressed in her usual attire. Jeans and some rock band t-shirt that Alexa hadn't heard about. The amethyst pendant hung around her neck, neutralizing all the woman's negative energy that couldn't be contained.

Valerie pulled down her black mug from the shelf where all the customized mugs were stored. "Yeah, well... Caleb's been keeping me on a bit of an exact schedule. The man wakes up so early in the morning that it's hard not to get woken up about the same time. Might as well get up too, you know?"

A devilish look came over Krystal, the one that a year ago would have never made an appearance. Devin Daniels, the newest cop on the Goldcrest Cove police force and Krystal's fiancé, was bringing out the more playful, easygoing side of her every day. "I've found it's a little hard to go back to sleep after my man wakes up too."

Valerie didn't even blush as she pulled back her dark hair into a ponytail. The burgundy streaks popped in the light. "There's that too," she replied wryly. "Goddess, Caleb can be a real beast in the bed."

Alexa giggled, glorying in this talk of sex and boyfriends – or in Krystal's case, a fiancé. The transformation in her friends over the last six months had been nothing short of magical. If love and Twin Flames could do that for them, then it gave Alexa hope for her own future.

"Maybe because he *is* a beast?" Krystal offered.

Valerie waved away the sly comment about her boyfriend being a werewolf. "Oh, that's hardly it." Another wave of her hand toward the espresso machine on the far counter made it whirl to life. "Has anyone had their coffee yet?"

Alexa pranced behind the counter and snatched up her own mug, the most vibrant one on the shelf with its purple and pink fairy designs glazed into the sides. "Not yet."

"Girl, you don't need coffee!" Krystal joked. "You've got enough energy to run half of this town." Using her own magic, she turned and made every last chair in the coffeeshop rise from the tables and turn over. A unanimous clatter shook the floor as they all dropped into place at the same time. It was a good thing no non-magic folk were out on the streets yet, or they might have seen the whole thing.

"And with coffee, I could run it all!" Alexa replied, holding up her mug as if to toast to the very idea.

The other two witches laughed as they all went to brewing their favorite drinks. A chai tea latte for Krystal, a mocha for Valerie, and a macchiato for Alexa. They had been together ever since they were children. They learned the craft of magic together, they struggled through life's challenges together, and they started this business together.

Through deaths in the family, through drama, through trials that no non-magic folk could possibly understand, they had always stuck together like sisters. Most recently, they defeated a demon, a necromancer, and a serial killer under the influence of a charm. A twinge of guilt struck at Alexa's heart for that infraction, which she knew she would pay dearly for in the future. All evil would be paid back to her seven-fold eventually. But despite it all, they never faltered. Never shied from the fight, and reaped some worthwhile rewards. All except for Alexa, that is.

Krystal and Valerie had found their Twin Flames, their fateful lovers for eternity. Getting into a relationship with a human and a werewolf was controversial enough to tear families apart. And yet, they were as tight as ever. Maybe even tighter. It gave Alexa the impression that nothing could keep them from being friends. What was best was that they were happy. Both of them. Alexa strived every day to be happy for them in return. They'd found love and connection. That's what the Mother Goddess wanted for all of them, and one day it would be Alexa's turn. She had to cling to that hope or she'd lose it for sure.

Seeing them so happy, seeing the coffeeshop thrive and prosper, seeing their town once again blossom into a beautiful place of joy, it all made Alexa's heart burst. She never wanted any of that to change. With maybe one exception.

Slow your pace. Amble a bit. Soften your face. You probably look like you're fucking constipated.

It took all of Wesley's effort to relax. On most of his missions, he could blend in with ease, but this place was different. He had studied Goldcrest Cove for weeks. It's street layout, the names of the business owners, its history, everything that would help him. His commanding officers praised him for his attention to detail, but no amount of studying could have prepared him for how this town made him feel. Damn his sensitivity to energies.

There wasn't a proper way to describe this place. It wasn't like the magic-heavy places he had scouted before, but there was certainly an electricity in the winter air. It made him wonder if the Council had underestimated the problem here.

There had been some suspicious activity in Goldcrest Cove. On record, there were six witches living within the city, and now one werewolf had been registered. That alone should have been a red flag. Pouring over the reports, Wesley couldn't see a connection and neither could the Council. But too much had happened and it warranted a visit.

The tricky part was making sure that none of the witches knew why he was there or why the Council would make him pay special attention to Perfect Books and Brews.

Wesley greeted the townsfolk he passed, making sure his smile reached his crystalline blue eyes. Many nodded and returned his smile, but there were a few who realized he was not from around there. A few advisors from the Council had warned him the town was insanely inclusive, but he hadn't wanted to believe it. News of his arrival would probably be all over by now.

Might as well have dropped into Mayberry, he thought to himself.

He neared the coffeeshop and could already smell the fragrance of roasted beans and espresso. He picked a time at peak traffic, so he wouldn't be noticed, but something didn't seem right. From customer reviews, one common trademark of the place was the line stretching out the door and onto the sidewalk. This was their busiest hour of the morning and there was no trace of a line.

Wesley entered the shop and found only three customers queued at the counter and a small handful in the lobby. Couples talked softly across the table from each other, college students typed away on their laptops, a few older people quietly read to themselves and sipped from ceramic mugs. He had learned that every regular customer had their own mug and Wesley glanced behind the barista station to see the eclectic collection.

The aesthetics of the place were homey. He'd seen coffeeshops like it in the big city, but they all lacked one thing. Magic. And it was everywhere in this place. Unlike most magic-folk, Wesley had trained himself to detect the lingering traces of charms and hexes. It proved useful in his training as an Enforcer and made him an invaluable tool to the Council. Which was why he was here. To see if there was anything amiss. And there was plenty. It was his job to see how it was all connected and who was using their magic illegally.

Then, his eyes fell on the witches. His mind immediately switched gears.

Krystal Hayden. Twenty-six years old. Youngest daughter of Gordon and Catherine Hayden, elite members of the Council for the northeast district. Engaged to be married to a human – of all things – as of last Yule when he proposed at a family gathering. The diamond engagement ring on her left hand sparkled in the mid-morning light that came through the front windows. Black hair, brown eyes, five-foot-seven. Her dark magic entailed fire manipulation, a product of discovering her Twin Flame. That had to be the only reason she had agreed to marry a non-magic folk. No witch or warlock in their right mind would agree to such a lopsided union unless Twin Flames were involved. He would know.

According to the records, her name was listed first on all business contracts and licenses. The coffeeshop must have been her brainchild, and the other two followed her in the scheme.

Wesley stepped forward and looked to the second witch. Valerie Lloyd. Just turned twenty-six two weeks ago. Parents died in a car accident when she was a child and raised by her non-magic aunt. Lives with a teacher, non-magic also. Green eyes and naturally light brown hair, but she dyed it regularly. Five-foot-eight, she was the tallest of the group, just barely.

Out of all the girls, she had the least impressive profile, but the most spectacular and rare dark magic. Energy manipulation. That amethyst around her neck was loaded. Such a unique gift bestowed on a witch who hardly wanted her powers at all. Perhaps that was why she was currently dating a werewolf, whom she also lived with. A witch and a werewolf. It was just as unnatural as a witch and a mortal. Perhaps worse, given their age-old feud. Twin Flames had a nasty way of screwing up a person's life, and these witches were falling prey to men who would ruin their chances for a normal, magical life.

Taking a calming breath, Wesley forced himself to stay objective. He couldn't form opinions about the witches. None of them. Not even the blonde one.

His jaw clenched when he watched Alexa Boyer turn around to hand off a drink to a waiting customer. Her profile picture hadn't done her justice. She was the youngest of the three by just a year, but she might have been the prettiest. Blonde hair, blue eyes, slender frame, standing only five-foot-three. No dark magic, but like her friend, she was raised by a non-magic guardian. The poor woman was a half-witch and that explained the vibrations that radiated from her. She must have been well aware of her own deficiencies, judging by the obnoxious pouch of crystals that clattered when she walked.

Alexa was far more flamboyant than the others, her smile the brightest, her energy levels through the roof. She drew his attention so effectively that he almost neglected the moving line in front of him.

His gaze lingered on her. From the way her hair shined down to the firm curve of her ass in that skirt. Every inch drew him in like gravity. With a quick shake of his head, he snapped out of it. *No opinions. No feelings. Stay objective and on track.*

Any of them were suspects. They all had their own reasons for using magic in this place, but he had to figure out just who.

Gradually, he let his vision become unfocused, seeing the world through a hazy lens for just a moment before his second sight kicked in. Then the colors came. Arrays of greens, purples, blues, and yellows swam around the human figures. They pulsed, faded, and morphed in front of him as the customers interacted with the barista witches.

He observed the flow of energies. He watched how the aura of the witch at the cash register, Krystal, seemed to have a talent for absolving any hint of red or black in the people she met, and replacing it with her shade of emerald. Valerie's aura remained a strong hue of purple, most likely thanks to her absorbing amethyst. Alexa, bouncy ray of sunshine, was anything but. Her aura was so dim, hardly there at all.

Wesley allowed himself to stare, to analyze, but he couldn't make sense of it. The witch seemed to be bounding with energy, but all he could detect was a thin layer of white and yellow.

In all, besides Alexa's incongruence, nothing seemed nefarious. Not yet. There was no residual sparkle of magic about them or their workplace. He could usually sense magic up to two or three hours after its first use, but he found nothing here. It was still early in the day.

He was one customer away from the front when he was finally noticed. Krystal glanced his way and instantly knew he was a warlock. It was impossible for her not to know, being this close. Valerie and Alexa, too, took stock of him. Valerie's brows lowered in suspicion, but Alexa's response cheered him beyond explanation. Her once dull aura exploded into a vibrant gold, giving her an ethereal look that complimented everything about her. She glittered like an angel the moment they locked eyes. The corner of his mouth twitched into an authentic smile at the sight. It had been a while since someone's energies responded to him in that way.

Wesley stepped up to the register and the two magic-wielders appraised one another in a friendly onceover.

"You must be new in town," Krystal said, her voice pleasantly disarming. She held out her hand to shake. "My name's Krystal Hayden. Welcome to Perfect Books and Brews."

He gladly took the offered hand. "Wesley Griffith, and thanks. I got in a few days ago and finally found time to take a look around."

Valerie's aura darkened, infected with a distrusting black and gray ring, but he didn't pay her any mind. Her profile said that she would be the more skeptic of the three.

Krystal's smile widened. "Well, Goldcrest Cove is a great place to live. Very quiet and everyone's really nice. We get a lot of people that move here from the city to get a taste of that small-town life."

Wesley nodded. "Yeah, I really get that vibe here... Are there more..." His gaze roamed to the other two who were listening closely while brewing their coffees.

"Yes. Three more besides us, but we haven't had... someone like you in... well, I don't even know how long."

She must have meant warlocks. By his briefing, he already knew that. Wesley lowered his voice so only they could hear him. "That's a relief. I was told by some people that this was a safe place for people like us."

The witch beamed under the compliment. "That was very nice of them to say. And they didn't lie. It's very safe."

"Especially when her fiancé is one of the best cops in town."

Even the sound of Alexa's voice was imbued with stardust. Light, happy. His grin unconsciously widened to its melody.

Krystal, however, didn't seem amused. She fumbled for her words. "My fiancé is... he's non-magic."

Wesley feigned a bit of a shock for their sake, though he knew the whole time. "I see... Does he know?"

She nodded. "Yes, he knows. He's adjusting to it all really well, too."

Her aura didn't waver. No deception. That was a relief. At least he wouldn't have to worry about that aspect of this mission, though it was peculiar in itself. Few non-magic folk could handle the truth that there was more to this world than they could have ever thought possible.

"We do have to warn you, though," Alexa chimed in, "we have a werewolf now."

Valerie whirled around and shot him the nastiest look he had ever received from a witch in his life. "That's none of his business, Alexa!"

The sunshine in Alexa's aura vibrated and dimmed at the rebuke. "I'm just telling him in advance before he finds out on his own."

"It's true," Krystal joined. "He moved here about a month ago, but you have nothing to worry about."

Once more, Wesley had to act surprised, or at least taken aback. But not too much or they'd think they ruined a chance at having a warlock in their town. In reality, he knew that it was Krystal's father who authorized the werewolf's registration with the Council. Another reason this town had fallen under scrutiny.

"And he's a friend of yours?"

Valerie looked fit to be tied at his doubtful tone.

Krystal nodded and answered before her friend could snap at him the way she snapped at Alexa. "Yes, he's a very good friend and trustworthy."

He thought it interesting how she would openly admit that she was engaged to a human, but completely leave out that Valerie was dating a werewolf, which seemed twice as scandalous.

"I'll do my best to be civil whenever I bump into him, then." His strained smile seemed to set the feistier of the witches at ease. A bit of the black ebbed from her aura and he decided the worst was over. He blinked and willed away his second sight, returning to the world of solid lines and definite colors.

"Goldcrest Cove really is a great place," Krystal continued. "You're going to love it here."

Chapter 2

A lexa's eyes were fastened to Krystal, waiting for her reaction to the hot warlock who just walked away from the counter. The dark-haired witch turned, a crafty smile on her lips and an impish look in her eye.

"Now, that's a warlock," she said in a low tone. No other customers were waiting in line, giving them all a moment to breathe and catch up from the minor morning rush.

"You're engaged," Valerie reminded none too gently.

"Yes, I am. But my sister isn't."

Alexa's momentary hope vacillated. She didn't think about Sierra when she laid eyes on Wesley. She thought of how it would feel to weave her fingers through his dark blonde hair that looked so soft and full in the coffeeshop light. She thought of what it would feel like to be under the stare of those twinkling sapphire eyes while he leaned in for a kiss. She thought of how those lips would feel pressed against hers. She thought of herself going limp in his muscled arms, so full of power. She imagined what it would be like to drown in that delicious, manly scent that she could just barely sample from across the counter. His warmth and his energy screamed for her like nothing else. Then she thought of herself falling, hard and fast, into the bottomless void of bliss and sensual desire that awaited her, if she could be his and his alone.

He was every inch the knight in shining armor, straight out of one of the fairytale books her mother read to her as a child. All he needed was the white horse and giant sword to complete the picture. And she, with her long pale hair and sunny smile, wanted to be his princess.

"I don't think Wesley's her type," she slyly hinted, leaning to take a peek at the man in question. With his Americano in hand, he browsed the packed bookshelves along a portion of the brick wall.

"You've known him for all of five minutes," Valerie said. "How could you know what type he is at all?"

Alexa turned, one hand on her hip. "Sierra's way too aggressive for a guy like him."

"Aggressive?" laughed Krystal. "That's a little harsh."

"You know what I mean. She's... she's like an alpha wolf and Wesley wouldn't be able to handle her."

At the allusion to wolf hierarchy, Valerie made a thoughtful face and shrugged. "When you put it that way, it makes sense. If you look past the huge arms, Wesley doesn't fit the alpha profile. She needs someone hardcore. Same for Amber."

They all agreed with a giggle as they pulled up the image of the purple-haired innkeeper. Out of all the witches in town, Amber may have been doomed to singlehood for the rest of her life. There wasn't a human, warlock, or werewolf they knew who could take on her sassy ass. Only her Twin Flame, whom she never spoke of and they knew nothing about, would be the perfect match.

With a finger tapping her chin, Krystal offered, "Wesley might be good for Taylor."

"Oh, Goddess," Valerie groaned. "There may be such a thing as too much sweetness in one couple."

Alexa still didn't like the direction of this conversation. Why not her? Why suggest every other witch in town but her? Was she that invisible? Or did they think because she was a half-witch, that a warlock like him would never even consider her? The idea was like a sledgehammer to her gut, and their words hovered over her like a deadly hex with no reversal charm.

"Taylor needs someone, though," Krystal argued. "She hardly comes out of that greenhouse. She needs some companionship."

Valerie rolled her eyes. "I can see it now. They'd be half buried in plants, whispering sweet nothings in each other's ears."

"And what's wrong with that?" Alexa bridled. "I'd give my right arm to have someone be all tender and sweet to me like that."

The other two witches exchanged dubious looks. They all knew how far Alexa would go for romance.

"I'd rather have a man moaning my name in my ear all night," Krystal answered, a satisfied glint in her eyes.

"Oh, but have you ever had a man growl for you?" Valerie shivered with pleasure. "It's the best."

They laughed, sharing a moment that only happily taken women could share in. Alexa's usual cheery disposition faltered. She had never been in a serious relationship. There were boys in school and college, but nothing beyond a few dates before the guy cut it off. She was too much, and she knew it.

Suddenly, she wondered if the others were right to consider Amber, Sierra, and Taylor before her. They had a chance. Alexa probably didn't. The fantasy she had nearly given herself up to just a moment before began to splinter. She was no longer the princess in this story, but the wicked hag who wanted to tear the couple apart. Wesley seemed so calm and tame. And she'd be too much for him. Not like Amber and Sierra would be too much, but in a different and perhaps more annoying way. She always was.

The air behind her changed and she knew someone had approached the counter. A fraction of a second before she turned, she caught a whiff of Wesley's cologne, but her heart still leapt into her throat when she saw those perfect blue eyes fall on her.

"Can I buy this?" he asked, the timbre of his voice reducing her knees to jelly.

It took a second for her to realize he was holding a book in his hands. Her lips parted, mouth slackened, but no words came out.

"No, unfortunately," Krystal answered as she stepped up to stand beside Alexa. "But you can borrow it for a little while."

He smirked. "So, you're a coffeeshop and a library too?"

Alexa giggled at his slight joke, which wasn't really a joke at all, and that made her look even more silly. Still, his eyes seemed to brighten at the sound of it.

"Sort of," Krystal replied as she took out her notebook from under the counter. "The books are more for the customers who want to read while they drink their coffee. If you want to take it with you, I'll just need your number."

Wesley gave it and Alexa couldn't help but try to remember the seven-digit combination just so she could slyly save it in her phone for later. It wasn't like she would ever call him, but she could see his name in her contact list and wonder about the possibilities.

"I was actually wondering," Wesley continued after Krystal scribbled down the numbers, "do you know anyone who could show me around town? I haven't had much of a chance to explore, but I'd rather have a local help me along if that's all right."

Alexa's whole body was pitched into a war of emotions. Fear that one of the girls would suggest Taylor to take him on a tour. Excitement that she could do it herself and have a chance at the warlock first. Shame in her own uncharacteristic silence in the face of such perfection.

None of it showed on her face, but it all came out in one blaring offer that nearly everyone in the coffeeshop could hear. "I'll take you!"

All at once, she was aware of the stares upon her. But she didn't care about them. She fixated herself on Wesley and the suggestion of approval at the idea.

"Your shift isn't over until late tonight," Krystal countered.

Alexa, her heart racing, finally shifted her attention back to her friend. "I'll just switch shifts with Valerie."

The witch folded her arms. "I'm working late too. Krystal's the one who's leaving early to go to the cake tasting. Remember?"

Yes, she had forgotten about that. Krystal and Devin had been trying for weeks to get an appointment with the busy baker. This was the only day he had open and Devin had even requested time off to make it there. Aligning their schedules had been a nightmare since the engagement was announced. If Krystal missed this appointment, they might not even have a wedding cake.

"Can't you hold down the store tonight?" Alexa's pleading went unacknowledged by the witch who had covered more shifts than any of them combined. That was, before she met Caleb. Now she starkly refused to deviate from her schedule. She had a life now and wouldn't give it up.

"Nope. Not this time."

Alexa looked to Krystal, realizing she was the only one to grant this single wish she so desperately wanted. It might have been selfish to try and steal Wesley from having a chance with Taylor, but she had to know if she could have him first. If she, a half-witch, was worthy of a warlock like him. She needed to know and every fiber of her soul cried out for that possibility.

A few seconds of silence settled over them and then Krystal finally said. "Go ahead. I'll just call the cake guy and cancel."

A ripple of shock spread through the two witches who just heard their friend's verdict.

"Cancel?" Valerie echoed. "You've been planning this for weeks."

Krystal simply shrugged. "We have time before the wedding. It's not like Devin's going to dump me for delaying this one part."

Alexa took Krystal's arm to make sure this wasn't some trick. "Are you serious?"

It occurred to her that Wesley would have absolutely no clue why all three were acting like this. Why Alexa was so desperate, why this response from Krystal was so out of character. Hopefully he didn't think they were all nutcases.

"Absolutely!" Krystal smiled and reached for Alexa's purse under the counter. "Go on. If you have time, come back to work. If you don't, it's not a big deal. You know this town like the back of your hand and Wesley needs a guide like you." The uncanny assurance from her friend threw her off so much that she nearly dropped her purse.

It was as if the fairy godmother in the stories had come down to personally bless her with this opportunity. How long until her carriage turned into an overripe pumpkin was anyone's guess. But she wasn't about to waste it.

Unable to control her effusive gratitude, Alexa hugged her friend about the neck, grabbed her coat, and then darted around the counter before anyone changed their mind. Wesley's brows were slightly pinched, giving hint to his confusion upon witnessing all of it, but he said nothing with his Americano and book in hand.

Together, they walked toward the door and Alexa had to keep herself from skipping all the way. She was too happy for words to be in the company of such a handsome warlock. The first she had really ever met.

Deep breaths. Be calm. Don't screw this up.

"What was that?" he asked as he held open the door for her. The mid-winter chill struck her in the face and helped to cool her flushed cheeks.

In a panic, she shook her head. "I didn't say anything."

Wesley appeared even more confused, but said, "Sorry. I thought you did." Then he laughed. "Wow, where are my manners? I just realized I don't know your name."

Alexa pulled her coat tightly around her and gave an embarrassed laugh of her own. "I am so sorry! I'm Alexa Boyer."

He tucked his borrowed book under his arm and they shook hands. She relished in the feel of his fingers wrapped around hers. His grip was gentle, but she could sense the power behind them. He could have crushed her if he wanted.

"Wesley Griffith."

"Yeah, I heard you introduce yourself to Krystal earlier."

A little color rose up his collar. "Oh, right."

Then it occurred to her that they were still shaking hands for far too long. They let go and Alexa jammed her fists into her pockets to hide how they trembled.

"So, where do you want to go first?" she asked as she glanced up and down snowy Johnson Avenue.

"Where do you suggest?"

Immediately, a scheme took shape in her mind. A scheme that would keep them out all day. "Are you sure you want to give me that much control?"

He mirrored her smug grin. "Something tells me I can trust you. Lead the way."

Wesley grandly swung out his hand in one direction down the sidewalk. It took all of Alexa's self-control not to giggle when she turned and began walking the opposite way to lead him on a small adventure of her own.

Alexa was absolutely adorable. Energetic, enthusiastic, and an abundance of energy that never seemed to weaken no matter how long they walked in the snow or how many stores they popped into. He suffered being introduced to every non-magic folk in town, learning the histories he already vaguely knew. She helped to put names with faces and feeling to everything about Goldcrest Cove.

They walked down one half of Johnson Avenue, all of Main Street, and every other street that hosted some interesting piece of history or community interest. The school, Our Lady of Peace Catholic Church, the park, the local library, the best grocery store, the bar by the harbor, down several residential streets, and now they had come back to where they started.

It was all far more than he wanted to know, but he couldn't stop Alexa. Nothing could. And he didn't truly want to. It refreshed him to be within her bubble of light and joy. Spending all his time amongst Enforcers who took their job far too seriously had made him forget how to enjoy life. Alexa was slowly reminding him.

He had finished his coffee long before they arrived at McRae Morsels less than a block from Perfect Books and Brews. They had come full circle, just as Alexa had planned. They sat in the pastry shop, sharing a cinnamon muffin when he decided to broach upon the subject he really needed to know.

"So, you've shown me just about everything in Goldcrest Cove, but what's your connection to it all?"

Alexa's gaze darted up from her half of the muffin, a bit of a crumb still on her full bottom lip as she gave him that deer-in-headlights look. "What?"

Wesley allowed himself a smile, as he had through the whole afternoon while he watched her occasionally skip and twitter along in her tour. "I don't know much about you. Have you lived here all your life?"

As if shy that she was now the center of attention, a tinge of pink bloomed in her cheeks. "I... Yes, I have."

Wesley waited for more, knowing by now that she wasn't a girl of few words. Not in the least. But when she wouldn't come outright with more details, he pressed further. "You showed me Krystal's house, but did we walk by yours?"

Alexa pinched off a bit of her pastry. "Well, sort of. I live in an apartment above the antique shop at the end of the street."

"No big house?"

She shook her head. "Nope. Just me and Mr. Fish."

He grinned. "Mr. Fish?"

With each new question, she seemed to become more and more bashful. "Yeah, he's my fish. My landlady won't let me get a pet, but a fish isn't quite the same as a dog or cat, so she let me slide."

"No family or roommates?"

Again, she shook her head, blonde tresses dancing with the motion. How he loved to watch the way she tossed her hair in the wind, how her slight but firm body moved in time with a melody that was all her own. All of it made Wesley keenly aware of his own body in response to hers and he gloried in the distracting essence of it.

"My mom lives out of town and my best friends have their own places."

Her words brought him out of the lusty daze he had fallen into. Yes, her mother was a mortal. He remembered that from her profile. Though he knew the answer already, he asked, "What about your dad? Is he in town?"

Alexa opened her mouth to answer, but hesitated. As if bolstering her courage, she straightened her shoulders and said, "He's just not around. What about you? Where did you move from?"

Just as he expected, she had deflected. The sore subject warranted it, so he eased off for now, though he wanted to know her side of things so badly.

As he had trained, he lied. "I lived in Boston."

The weight of focus upon Alexa lifted and it showed in her fresh smile. "Oh, that's where Devin's from. Maybe you two knew one another."

Innocence. How refreshing. "Boston's a big town. It's unlikely I would have known a cop."

Realizing her blunder, her lips drew tight. "I guess you're right. I'm just so used to living in a small town, I forget what it's like to live anywhere else."

He hoped that his smile would be beguiling enough. "Don't worry about it. We all have a different way of thinking about things... Like the coffeeshop. I saw all those personalized mugs on the shelf."

Alexa relaxed and he could just barely see that in her aura. "Yeah. We try to make the place as cozy and homey as we can. We've been to those big chain coffeeshops and they can be really impersonal. We wanted to open a coffeeshop that was just like a town. Open, inviting, and personable. The regulars can use their mugs instead of getting the regular to-go cups."

Having finished his half of the muffin, Wesley sat back in his chair, the old wood creaking under his weight. "And whose idea was the shop?"

"All of us," she said, completely comfortable. If he were honest with himself, Wesley would have admitted that he had grown comfortable too. That's why it took him this long to get to the point of this interrogation. "Well, mostly

Krystal's. She came up with the idea and we all loved it. She really wanted to give back to the community that had given so much to us."

"Give back?"

A flicker of hesitation told him plenty. "Well, there wasn't a coffeeshop in town at the time and we know a lot of people that really need their coffee in the morning, so it just made sense. We don't have any reason to resent the people, even though we're..." Alexa glanced around to make sure no one was listening over the country music that floated through the speakers in the corner of the room. "Even though we're not exactly all the same."

He nodded. "So you have no prejudices toward non-magic folk?"

A bit of alarm surfaced, but Wesley knew better. No one was paying attention, and even if they were, he had dropped a veil around them to dull the noise the minute they sat down. Everything was completely private.

Alexa straightened again. "Nope. No prejudices whatsoever. We're all friends."

"And you three want to help your friends whenever and however you can."

She tilted her head and wondered if he had said too much. "Of course, we do. That's what friends are for."

Wesley appreciated her honesty and openness. His gratitude to the Gods for allowing her to give him the unnecessary tour had no limit. If he had any of the other witches take him, this wouldn't have been nearly as enjoyable or profitable.

While it wasn't a complete confession, he could extrapolate what she meant. The coffeeshop was under examination, along with its owners, for meddling in human affairs. The cardinal rule of all witches and warlocks was to not use magic on non-magic folk. If the girls were using magic through their coffeeshop to "give back to the community", then they were in violation of that law.

But he needed more proof than just a verbal admittance. He had to catch them in the act or find some material evidence. To do that, he had to earn their trust and witness it.

Alexa slipped another piece of her muffin between her teeth. Such a simple thing to do, but she made it sexual. Wesley froze, aware that his cock had begun to harden for her. If he had any hope of finishing this mission, he had to stay impartial. He leaned forward again and rested his folded arms on the rocking table between them.

"So, did you show me your favorite place in town?"

Alexa looked down to the muffin on the napkin, her mascaraed lashes long and fluttering. "No, I didn't."

"I don't think our tour is complete then."

"Oh, it is," she replied, then pinned him with a playful stare. "My favorite place isn't in Goldcrest Cove."

He feigned disbelief. "How sacrilegious, coming from a girl who praises the town's coziness."

As desired, she giggled and dipped her chin. "Oh, be nice. I love this town. I really do. I couldn't imagine living anywhere else."

"And yet your heart lies somewhere else."

Wesley came dangerously close to flirting now, but his mind could hardly stop his mouth. Or maybe it was his own heart running away with him. Everything about Alexa demanded his full and undivided attention and devotion.

He cursed himself for wanting that trim body plastered against his own. He hated himself for wanting to slide his hands over that supple, purely feminine body. He wanted to hear her screaming his name and begging for him to do all the things he secretly longed to do. One afternoon together and he had lost his head to her completely.

He'd fight her for as long as he could, but who could resist her spirit?

"It's not my heart that's somewhere else," she admitted with a simper. "It's my stomach."

He narrowed his eyes in a question.

"There's another thing that Goldcrest Cove lacks and that's a good sushi place. There's a town about half an hour away that serves the best sushi ever."

His brows arched. "I would have never pinned you for a sushi-lover."

Alexa smirked. "I'm full of surprises." Then she did it again. Took another pinch of the muffin and seduced him with the way her mouth curled around the morsel.

"Well, are they open?"

That caught her off guard and her eyes widened. "What?"

"This sushi place. Is it open?"

Alexa seemed to scramble for an answer and it was as if a switch had been flipped. She went from playing the temptress to the awkward little schoolgirl who had never spoken to a man before. "Well, I... I guess they are. I'd have to check their hours online, but I would think they are. It's Friday after all. Most places are open on Friday."

He checked the clock on the wall. It wasn't quite dinner time. It wouldn't be for a few hours, which would give them the chance to prepare. "How about I pick you up from the antique shop at six and we go there. Tonight. Just you and me."

Dumbstruck for a brief moment, Alexa simply stared at him like he had just proposed marriage. Had she never been asked out before? What did she expect? How could she not have taken the clue? How could she not be asked out every day by every free man in town? She should have been used to it.

"Six... Six sounds good."

Wesley nodded. "Six it is then."

Just for shits and giggles, Wesley let his vision relax to see her aura. A halo of cheery gold and passionate red framed her upper body. Her hair blended in perfectly with the bright, shifting shades, but her eyes stood out in sharp relief like glowing beacons calling him home.

He returned her gleeful smile, knowing that he had been the one to put it there. In the back of his mind, he knew he was playing with fire. This wasn't part of the plan and if he drew too close, it would ruin everything. But it felt so right to be in Alexa's company. Like she sucked all the tension and stress that had continued to build over the years of training and responsibilities. And somehow, she negated it like a charm gone wrong. She did it so seamlessly for a half-witch, that it seemed damn near impossible that she was real.

But she was real. Completely and totally real.

They must really be in love.

I wonder if this is their first date.

They look so cute together.

Wesley snapped to attention and turned to scan the crowd inside the pastry shop. A retired couple sat in the far corner sharing a piece of cheesecake. A younger girl with a library book nibbled on a scone near the counter. And Mrs. McRae with her round belly and frizzy hair stood deep in the back kitchen, her sleeves rolled up and flour dusting her apron. They all looked away when he had met their gazes.

It was the same as when they were leaving the coffeeshop earlier. Their voices, so distinct, rang in his head with an eerie echo. Not like he heard it with his ears, but in his mind. Now that he let his aura vision dissipate, the ghostly voices were silenced. All that was left was the tapping of forks on plates and the country music drifting through the lobby.

"Are you okay?"

Alexa seemed genuinely concerned, and she had a right to be. This was the second time this phenomenon surfaced and he couldn't explain it. There couldn't have been anything wrong with his hearing. And they were all so far away from their semi-isolated table that he might not have heard them anyway.

"Yeah, I'm fine. Just thought I heard something."

He shrugged it off and blamed it on the lack of sleep. Perhaps in preparation for his date with Alexa, he might shake up his routine and take a nap. There's something he hadn't done in ages. Take and nap and go out with a girl on a real date.

Chapter 3

Alexa tugged at the off-shoulder collar until more of her smooth skin showed in the mirror. The hem of her black dress only reached halfway down her thighs, but the high velvet boots made up for some of the exposure. Outside her apartment window, she could see the fresh snow flurries drifting in the breeze. At least she had long sleeves. Hopefully it would be warm at Emperor Jimmu Sushi and Hibachi.

If this had been a girls' night with Krystal and Valerie, she would have dressed more appropriately. She would have smothered herself in frumpy knitted sweaters and a snug pair of jeans. But this was for Wesley. All common sense left her and wasn't coming back for a while. She preferred it that way.

The tour around Goldcrest Cove had been nothing short of a dream. She had never enjoyed her time with another man so much. They laughed and she mostly talked, but he was such an attentive listener. He didn't listen to respond, but listened to genuinely converse with her. He asked questions and showed so much interest in the town and the people that it hardly seemed real.

She had almost let herself believe that it was just the town he had been intrigued by. And then he asked her out. Just her. This trip had nothing to do with the town. Just the two of them. Alexa could hardly contain her excitement. It was a challenge to focus during the short ritual to help center herself before the appointed time.

She was dressed and perfumed, ready to go half an hour before six. Night had long since fallen over Johnson Avenue and the streetlamps illuminated the spot where Wesley would pull up to get her. Miss Macy had closed down the shop already, so she would have to hustle around the side of the building to meet him. But only once he showed up.

In between paces, Alexa checked the window that overlooked the snowy street and the time on her phone. The minutes ticked by like hours as she prayed to every god and goddess she knew for serenity and calm. Her heart, as hopeful as it was, refused to be at peace. All she could think of where the possibilities. More dates to follow this one. She thought of the seasons passing with Wesley in her life, a strong and compassionate warlock to guide her and love her.

The little demon of doubt continually pricked each vision of happiness with an illusion of its own. Those of betrayal, of abandonment, of rejection. *He won't even show. Why are you so excited? It's not going anywhere. He won't want a little half-breed like you when he finds out anyway. Just crawl back in bed where you belong.*

Each time, Alexa shook her head, tossing her carefully sculpted blonde curls around her shoulders to shake off the intrusion. She would enjoy this time with Wesley, even if it didn't end with a diamond ring and an altar. She'd take what she could get while she could get it.

The crunch of snow under tire wheels and the dull rumble of an engine sent her rushing to the window. Headlights gleamed ahead of a classic black Pontiac.

The grin hurt Alexa's cheeks as she saw Wesley slide out of the driver's seat and look straight up to her window.

In a flurry of delight, she raced across her room to gather her things.

"Okay, just stay calm. Don't run. Don't trip. Oh, got to feed Mr. Fish. Where's my purse? Damn, I forgot my lipstick. Ugh! Where are my keys?"

For a girl who had been waiting impatiently, she hadn't realized how truly unprepared she had been. After she checked and triple checked everything, including her hair and the way her bra settled, she left her apartment and out the back door as she always did.

The biting cold slipped its way beneath the long coat she had pulled on before stepping out and it hardly did anything to stop the spread of gooseflesh over her thighs. Just what she needed. Cold skin for a pair of warm hands.

Before coming into view of the Pontiac, Alexa did her best to not look as cold as she was as the snowflakes continued to swirl and melt in her hair. What she saw when she rounded the corner of the brick alley looked like a scene straight out of the romantic comedies she watched with her mom.

Wesley, clad in a soft leather jacket, leaning against his muscle car with his thumbs hooked on the belt loops of his jeans. The snow swirling around him, the growling of the engine, the smell of crisp ice and fuel exhaust. The way his eyes swept appreciatively from head to foot when she appeared. And then that smile, the kind that warmed her blood. She wanted to remember every detail of this night.

"You look great," he said as he opened the passenger door. The scent of leather and warmth of the heaters hit her just before the spicy aroma of his cologne.

"So do you," she replied, matching the onceover she had received and pairing it with a cattish smile.

In the six seconds it took for Wesley to get behind the wheel, Alexa had to keep herself from squealing like a child on Yule morning. She had gone on dates before, but never had she been picked up by her date.

She took this chance to adjust her dress one last time and prop up one knee to show an enticing expanse of inner thigh that could hardly be seen in the dim light of the dashboard controls anyway. Wesley noticed, though, and it showed in the way his eyes darted to the hem of her dress before putting the car in drive.

"You'll have to give me directions to get there."

Alexa agreed and when they drove past Perfect Books and Brews, she sunk against the leather just a bit in an effort to hide in case anyone was looking out the front window.

"You okay?" he asked.

So observant. "Yeah, I just... You heard Krystal say that if I had time, I needed to go back to work. But I didn't tell them I was going to dinner with you."

Wesley nodded in understanding. "And why wouldn't you tell them? Aren't they your best friends?"

Once they turned onto Reichman Street to head out of town, Alexa slid back up to watch the road. "They are, but..." She cringed. "It's not a big deal."

"Do you often keep secrets from them?"

Alexa blinked. "No. Never. I'll just tell them tomorrow."

Wesley smirked. "Damn. I was counting on being your secret for a little while."

She hoped he didn't hear the sigh of relief. "In all reality, I just... I just didn't want them to think things. You know?"

His eyebrow arch. "What would they think?"

This was far more personal than Alexa was willing to get on a first date. If they went any deeper, it would ruin everything. "They just might think I was being silly."

"Why?"

Alexa took a deep breath and plunged in, bracing for the hard lurch of the car brakes the moment she said it. "I just haven't always had the best luck with guys, so they probably wonder why I even bother anymore."

Still, the tires continued to roll right out of Goldcrest Cove.

"That doesn't sound terribly supportive."

"Oh, they're supportive," Alexa quickly recovered. "They've probably been the most supportive people in my life."

"And yet they wouldn't encourage you to have dinner with someone like me?"

He hit it right on the head. *Someone like him.* That was the key. He was way out of her league. A warlock. She had only ever dated non-magic men. Men who she would have more in common with. Men whom she could hide her nature from. She wouldn't be able to hide it from Wesley forever.

"It's complicated."

It sounded like a dismissal, but it was a good one. Most people would just leave the matter alone if they heard those words. But not Wesley.

"Nothing's that complicated," he said as he flipped on the blinker after she gave him the direction to get on the highway. "They either support you one-hundred percent or they don't. It's that simple."

No, it wasn't. It wasn't simple when Krystal decided to date a human cop. It wasn't simple when Valerie confessed that her Twin Flame was a werewolf. And it wouldn't be simple for her to tell them that she had the hots for a warlock that was better suited for a full-blooded witch who could match him in skill and craft. None of it was simple, but she wanted just one good night first before proving the demons right.

"Did your friends support your move to Goldcrest Cove?" Alexa asked, turning the tables on her date. It might have been unwarranted, but if he was going to get personal, then so was she.

Without hesitating, he replied, "Sure they did. They knew I needed a change of scenery and helped me pack my bags."

Alexa thought back to just a month ago when Valerie had almost left Goldcrest Cove for good in Caleb's truck. They would have never wanted her to leave, no matter the circumstances. They loved her too much. "Then I wouldn't say they were real friends. If they wouldn't fight to keep you, then did they ever really like you?"

That cued a stretch of awkward silence that Alexa wished she could have prevented.

To rectify the situation, she said, "This is a nice car. Pontiac Firebird... It's a '76, right?"

That earned her a look of utter astonishment. "You like cars?"

Alexa shrugged one of her slender shoulders, making the fabric slip just a half inch. "There's a classic car club that meets at the coffeeshop every week and I tend to listen in. They have a car show down Main Street every May. Maybe you should show this baby off."

Caleb grinned, his pearly whites sparkling in the moonlight that glowed off the snow. "I will, as long as you can be my girl sitting on the hood."

His girl. If Alexa's smile could've widened any further, the corners of her mouth would have touched her ears. "We'll see."

In reality, she wondered if they would even make it that far. If they lasted until May, it would be a miracle, or a sign from the universe that she was truly capable of holding a man for longer than a few weeks.

"Before we get to the restaurant, I want to ask you something."

Dread spiked in her gut. "Anything."

"Why do you keep so many crystals on you?" he asked, motioning to her lap. "You must be carrying around half a dozen at least."

Alexa felt the color drain from her face and her smile faded. How close could she come to ruin in one night before she ran out of ways to deflect? Any normal witch wouldn't need crystals or herbs or incense unless they wanted to amplify their powers for a massive spell. Alexa needed them just to execute a simple charm.

"Don't you carry any with you?"

"Sometimes, but not that many. You're really overdoing it."

Defenses that she hardly knew where there suddenly shot up. "How can you even tell if I'm overdoing it? None of the girls ever – "

"I've got a special sense for energies," he admitted. "I know you've got a Rhyolite, Chrysoprase, Labradorite, Peridot, and a clear Quartz to amplify all of it. That's a lot of light and happy energies you're trying to channel."

Alexa bit her lip, hardly knowing how to respond. Wesley had pegged her just right.

"As I see it, you don't need all of that," he continued. "You've got enough energy without it... Unless you're trying to block something."

Still, she didn't know how to answer. How could she explain that without these crystals, she nearly couldn't breathe? That if she put them down for too long, all those demons would rush in and consume her. That she'd remember how absolutely inadequate she was, about every failed spell, every charm gone awry, every time she wasn't good enough.

Then, she felt something solid and warm take hold of her hand. Alexa looked down to see that it was Wesley's grip that held her fast to the present. Could he have sensed the growing panic in her that easily?

"I'm sorry I pried. Whatever it is, I hope you can tell me someday, but... maybe we can work together, so you don't have to carry so many. Okay?"

Her breath caught in her throat and she couldn't decide if it was because of the way his fingers laced between hers or the promise he gave to help her. She hated to be the one that everyone wanted to help, to be the charity case who just couldn't quite get the simplest of charms. But he didn't make her sound like an idiot, like someone who should be pitied. Not yet anyway.

Alexa met his heartfelt gaze and wondered if she had ever woken up that morning. Maybe it was all a dream and Wesley wasn't even real.

Too choked with appreciation for everything he was, she could only nod in answer.

The feel of her hand in his was something he could get used to. The way she grimaced when she was hiding something wasn't. If they had more time in private, he would have pulled every trick in the book to find out why she felt she needed those crystals so desperately. The fact that she was a half-witch didn't seem enough.

But Emperor Jimmu's Sushi and Hibachi came into view of their headlights too quickly. This town was much bigger than Goldcrest Cove, but not nearly as expansive as Boston. Just large enough that every place was still open well after dark, unlike the shops on Johnson Avenue.

He helped Alexa from the car and escorted her up to the restaurant door. The place was fairly crowded, and as he usually did, he briefly scoped out their auras. Immediately, the volume of the restaurant rose to an unbearable level. Voices, both real and imaginary, were as loud as artillery fire in his ears. So much that he could barely make out the hostess's greeting or her question if they would prefer a table or a booth.

Wesley blinked away the auras and realized that as soon as the colors faded, the noise dimmed to a more manageable level. He could even hear the twang of the oriental music over the speakers.

"Are you okay with getting a booth?" Alexa asked next to him.

He forced a smile and nodded. "Sure. A booth sounds fine."

His date and their hostess saw nothing wrong, but Wesley's mind was in a whirlwind. What was happening? What exactly was he hearing when he slipped into his aura vision? Was this some new evolution of his skills or was it something completely opposite?

He was still deep in thought when they sat down in a quiet corner of the restaurant and were given their menus.

"It never occurred to me to ask, but do you like sushi?"

Alexa's voice, the only grounding force he could cling to, called him back from these troubling thoughts. "Yeah, I like sushi, but I don't get to have it much."

"Oh? Why's that?"

Unfamiliar with his options, Wesley unfolded the laminated menu and turned his eyes away from the more attractive dish in front of him. "They didn't have a place like this where I lived."

"I thought you said you were from Boston?"

Wesley gripped his menu a little harder, forgetting his cover story. In reality, the town he grew up in was no bigger than Goldcrest Cove, but she couldn't know that. "Sorry, I meant they didn't have one close to where I lived. There were plenty in Boston, but they were all out of the way."

Alexa nodded and seemed to accept that. Close one.

Before Wesley left the house, he had decided that he wasn't on duty tonight. He wouldn't try to find out more about the coffeeshop or the witches who ran it. Save for one. Alexa was his primary focus, his new mission. Winning her trust for the sake of his own enjoyment and possibly for the task at large. She had left out so much of herself from the tour earlier that afternoon that he was itching to know more.

Besides, it was hard to focus on business when she wore that dress that accentuated every inviting curve.

"What's good here then?" he asked. "Do they have any specialties?"

With renewed vigor, Alexa began to give him a crash course in the best sushi rolls the restaurant had to offer. She gushed just as much enthusiasm into her taste for oriental cuisine as she did for Goldcrest Cove and anything else that interested her. Passionate. That's what she was. She poured every ounce of her spirit into whatever she loved.

I want that to be me.

The errant thought struck him so hard that he missed half of the explanation she gave on the hibachi menu. Did he want to be that passionate about life, or to be the object of her passion? Things were shifting in him and the hot knot of feeling in his chest unsettled him more than it should have.

"Do you like chicken or beef better?"

Once more, Alexa saved him from venturing down a rabbit hole he couldn't turn around in to find his way out.

"Beef. Most of the time."

Her smile defused him and he let one of his legs slip further toward her side underneath the table. "Me too. If you want a little more substance with your sushi, I'd go with the teriyaki steak entrée then."

By then, the waitress with a heavy accent greeted them and asked for their drink order.

To his absolute amazement, Alexa began to give not only her drink order, but what must have been her dinner order as well, in perfect Japanese. The lady, who suddenly recognized his date because of her fluent talent, became excited and chattered back to her. Wesley, who usually prided himself on knowing the lay of the land before every engagement, found himself utterly lost.

Alexa gave him one look and masked her giggle behind her hand. "I'm so sorry! Did you have time to decide what you want?"

Too enchanted by her laughter to care if his man-card had just been confiscated, he rested his chin on his fist. "Would it be too American of me to get a cheeseburger off the kid's menu?"

It was meant as a joke, but the waitress didn't understand his sarcasm. He chuckled and waved his hand quickly to stop her from writing that down on her notepad. "No, no. I'll have the Black Dragon Roll and the teriyaki beef." He turned to Alexa. "Do I have to say it in Japanese?"

Pitying him, she shook her head and they straightened it all out before the waitress left them alone.

"You certainly are full of surprises," he mused as he marveled at the way her eyes sparkled in the pendant light above their table.

"I'm sure I couldn't hold a conversation outside of this restaurant," she said sheepishly.

"From the sounds of it, you could move to Japan and slip right in with the locals."

A blush complimented the rouge already on her cheeks.

"Now, if we were in a German pub, I could show off too."

Alexa beamed. "You speak German?"

"Fluently. My mother's family was from Germany, so I had to learn it. Otherwise, I would have been lost at every gathering and I wouldn't be able to read their grimoires."

For a second, it shocked him that he could speak of his mother so openly and honestly to someone he hadn't known for more than a day. He hardly spoke of his family to anyone within the Academy in all his years of training. Of course, if they had known the whole truth about his family, they would have banished him from the Force so fast his head would spin.

Taking firm hold of this bait, Alexa leaned forward and folded her arms over the lacquered tabletop. "That's fascinating. Did they descend from German magic folk too?"

The hostess had placed them in just the right spot that few would have heard her slipup. In a simple hand gesture that she would have disregarded altogether, he sealed off the table as he had done at McRae Morsels earlier. Non-magic folk didn't need to hear any of this.

"They did. My family line boasts some prominent witches and warlocks."

He would leave out that it was his family ties that ensured his true bloodline would remain confidential to everyone except elite members of the Council.

Alexa all but swooned. "You're so lucky. I don't even know who's all in my family tree."

"Your parents never told you? Surely there's a list of names in your family's grimoire."

He touched that raw nerve and it showed. That frown only fractionally diminished her beauty. "My... Okay, I'll just come out with it. I don't have one."

Wesley, who was well aware of her background, hadn't expected this. "Don't have one?"

"Well, I have one, but it's not my family's... It's just mine. I've been building it since I was old enough to start my studies."

He felt his brows involuntarily pinch together in puzzlement. "Your mom and dad didn't pass down theirs to you? That's usually how it works."

She cast her gaze to the open expanse of table between them. "I know it is. My mom doesn't have a grimoire and my dad... he just never got a chance to give it to me."

"Why's that?"

Wesley continued to dance on that nerve, testing his limits while hoping that she would tell him the truth. Once they can just get past this confession, maybe then she could finally relax. If what he had planned later would work, she had to get it all off her chest and let him in.

Come on. Just say it. I already know. Just speak it out, so it won't have power anymore.

The waitress returned before Alexa had the chance. The tension at the table broke the moment their drinks were set down in front of them, giving way for a change of subject.

"What about your grimoire?" she asked. "Did you take your mom's or your dad's, or both?"

That was an easy answer. "I took my mom's. It was larger." That wasn't a complete lie.

She nodded and dropped her straw into the glass of soda before taking a long sip. He wouldn't let her get off that easy.

"Is your dad... still with us?" he asked.

And there, he found her breaking point. She set her glass down with a heavy thud and squared her pretty shoulders. How he would have loved to leave trails of kisses across her collarbone and up her neck.

"My dad left my family when I was little. I don't know if he's alive or dead or whatever. I stopped caring a long time ago."

Wesley played sympathetic easily. He only had to replicate the face he made when he read her file for the first time. His case wasn't quite the same, but his empathetic nature still enabled him to feel her pain radiating from across the table. So fresh, so unresolved. She hadn't gotten over it. Hadn't moved on and accepted what happened. No matter what she said, she still cared.

"So your mom had to train you alone."

Alexa's voice hardened with the subject. "She raised me alone... But she didn't train me."

He waited, honoring the silence just before the truth fully emerged from its dark shadows.

She took a steeling breath and said, "My mom isn't a witch. She didn't know the first thing about it until after she married my dad. She stuck it out and made the best of it, because it looked like he was willing to give up his involvement in the magic community to be with her. It was different times then and it made a

huge stink. Then, I came along and my dad agreed to take on my training, but..."
Her gaze drifted again. This was the part he hadn't known. The part that none
of the reports could disclose. No one in the council kept track of Mr. Boyer the
moment he turned his back on everything.

"My dad met his Twin Flame," she finally said. "He went on a business trip and
met another witch by happenstance. It started as an affair, but my mom said that
she knew the moment he came home something wasn't right. He just wasn't the
same man. Two weeks later, he packed his bags and left."

Wesley's heart ached for Alexa. He wanted to see her aura, to see every sad
shade of black and gray storming around her. But after all his previous attempts,
he resisted. He settled for reading her expressions, for feeling her anguish and
bitterness. They were rusty skills, ones that he hadn't had to use since the days
when he'd had to take care of his own mother in her loss.

He reached out and impulsively placed his hand on her arm. "It's hard to lose
a parent."

Alexa's lips twitched into a mirthless smile. "Everyone says that. They all say
I've got a right to be mad at him, to hate him. He never visited. He called a few
times, but the conversations were always cut short. I stopped getting birthday
cards when I turned eleven. I haven't heard from the man in years and you know
what? It's okay."

"No, it's not okay," Wesley insisted. "I can feel how much it still hurts you."

Alexa slipped from his hold and that might have injured him more than her
words. "I'm fine. It's in the past. And after I've seen how Krystal and Valerie's
lives have changed because of meeting their Twin Flames, I get it. It does change
a person. The moment my dad met his Twin Flame, he wasn't my dad anymore.
Not really. We're all better off that he decided to go off with that witch than stay
with us. It would have been torture otherwise."

So many comebacks revolved in his head. So many words that would have fallen
on deaf ears if he spoke them now. He was far more upset that Alexa hadn't healed
from this than from the fact that she was a half-witch, just as he was half-warlock.

"If it's any consolation, I do know some degree of how you do feel." Now it was his turn to be honest, but not quite to the same degree. "My father died when I was barely a year old. My mom raised me on her own as well and it wasn't easy. Her family helped, but there was only so much they could do. My mom... she wasn't the same after my dad died. Just as I bet your mom wasn't the same."

"She was devastated," she said. "I remember days when she refused to get out of bed."

"Mine too," Wesley replied. "Sometimes, she'd sit at the dinner table and stare into space and I knew she was thinking of dad."

Alexa nodded. "There were times my mom would just start crying out of nowhere and there was nothing I could do." Despite the glistening of unshed tears that danced in her eyes, Alexa gave a soft laugh. "I remember when I was five years old and she was in one of those moods, I took one of my favorite blankets and put it around me like a cape and started dancing to some eighties song she loved just to make her smile."

She was too far out of his reach to stroke her cheek, but he could at least touch his foot to hers in some form of comfort. "I did something like that. But it wasn't nearly as amusing. I'd do things like make her favorite tea or put on one of her favorite movies. I indulged the moods rather than try to pull her out of them..." Wesley realized just how difficult it was to scratch at this scab of a wound without peeling it right open. "Maybe that's where I went wrong."

Alexa blinked. "Went wrong?"

And on continued the string of confessions. "My mom's not in the best health right now. She's being taken care of and looked after by someone else now. Someone else who can do the job better than I could."

Thankfully, Alexa seemed to accept that and nodded. "You did what you could."

"And you did what you could... There's no reason to be ashamed of what shaped you."

A ripple of some emotion between shock and indignation came over Alexa. "You did hear the part that my mom isn't a witch. She is completely human. Non-magic folk."

Wesley nodded. "I did."

"And that makes me a half-witch."

"It does."

Alexa evidently couldn't wrap her head around why he was so calm. "And... And you're okay with that?"

"Why wouldn't I be?"

The utter relief and bafflement she displayed pleased Wesley far more than it should have. "Just to preserve the moment, I won't answer that question. Just know I'm glad you're okay with it."

Wesley allowed himself an understanding smile. "Is that why you thought your friends wouldn't approve of this?" He motioned between them. "Just because you're a half-witch."

One shoulder lifted shyly. "It's always been a thing. They don't lord it over me, but they don't exactly let me forget either."

He understood that far more than she would ever know. And because of that, he knew that he would have to harden himself against Alexa Boyer. One wrong word, one wrong move, and the entire operation would unravel. They had too much in common. Too much to teach one another. Even though he believed wholeheartedly that he was the more experienced out of the two of them, Wesley also knew that there were things that grimoires could never reveal.

Chapter 4

With her stomach full – but not bloated, she had been careful of that – and warm inside Wesley's car, Alexa couldn't imagine a better ending to this first date. Save one. But in that scenario, it would never end.

They could never keep their conversation light. Never about anything shallow or mundane. Their talks drifted from family to magic to childhoods struggling with only one parent. They had so much in common that it seemed almost unreal.

What blew her mind more than their candid psychological and philosophical conversation was what had started it all. Wesley didn't mind that she was a half-witch. He didn't mind that she couldn't and would never be as powerful or as skilled as her friends. He didn't mind that she was damaged and inadequate. Nothing changed, except perhaps a stronger bond that defied logic. They had only known one another for a day and she felt as if she had known him for her whole life.

Their connection introduced an idea she hadn't permitted into her thoughts before this night. One that she had been wary of for months. Could Wesley be her Twin Flame? It was unlikely, given that there had been no strange fluxes in her powers to suggest that her dark magic ability had matured.

Then again, since she was a half-witch, would her dark magic even emerge? On that same note, did it emerge for Wesley?

Alexa looked his way as they passed the Goldcrest Cove welcome sign. He hadn't acted too off that evening. Did that mean they weren't Twin Flames?

Still, even if they weren't, she couldn't ignore this glow that spread through her like sunlight. Being with Wesley was like being in the presence of something sacred. She felt the deep need to possess him, to have him all for herself. Her own personal deity to worship and draw on for strength and love. Of course, she'd never abuse this gift. Alexa would cherish Wesley as long as she had him. To do anything less was blasphemy.

It took her a moment to realize they had missed Johnson Avenue completely. She glanced to the side mirror and watched the amber streetlamps shrink behind them.

"You missed the turn," she told him, thumbing back toward the intersection. Wesley smirked. "No, I didn't."

Alexa slid a skeptic, but pleased look his way. "Oh? And where are you taking me?"

"Back to my place."

A shot of cold countered the gush of warmth that came by the bidding of his words. His place? Courage left her at the thought. She could keep up her flirting all night, but Alexa knew better than any of her friends that it was like blowing smoke. Appreciating a man and handling him were completely different matters. One that Alexa's mother never bothered to teach her.

"You okay? You went white there for a second."

Alexa, eyes wide and a bit dry now that she hadn't blinked for a solid minute, looked to Wesley and put on a convincing smile. "I'm fine... Why are we going to your place?"

She suddenly felt like a dunce schoolgirl who couldn't take a hint. But Wesley was patient through it all.

"I told you I'd help you with the crystals."

Alexa hated the way her hand shook when she pointed back toward Johnson Avenue. "We could have done that at my place." Though, she wasn't sure which was worse, inviting a man into her apartment or stepping into his.

"No offense meant, but I don't think you have everything we need for this."

Alexa swallowed hard and tried to steady her breathing. Would he ask her to perform a ritual? She was so unprepared and he wouldn't understand that she couldn't pull on magic like he could. She needed time to center herself. Right now, she felt anything but centered.

It wasn't long before they pulled up to a rather new-looking house in a subdivision that Alexa hadn't visited before. She knew of it and plenty of people who lived inside of it, but the manicured lawns and home security signs in the front windows let her know that she was a fish out of water.

"You live here?" she asked, marveling at the beautiful modern architectural facades. Some brick, some stucco, but none dared come close to the historic charm of Johnson Avenue or the street Krystal and Sierra lived on.

"I do," he answered as if he were agreeing with the state of the weather.

"How can you afford it?"

"My dad left a trust fund for me and it had been accruing interest my whole life. I just decided to cash it in."

Alexa started. "And it was enough to buy you a house like this?"

"Not exactly. But enough to make me comfortable for a while. I'll have to get a job soon enough, though."

Shaking her head in disbelief, Alexa wondered what else she would discover about the warlock. Not only was he a fairytale prince, but he might as well have been living in a castle too. Or, at least something comparable. Her little apartment seemed so laughable now.

Wesley pulled up into the driveway of a house that was slightly smaller than the others, but no less stunning and contemporary with its featureless walls and white stone edifice. Alexa preferred homes with a little more character, a little more flavor than this bland exterior. She wouldn't dare say anything about it, though. Because while the house lacked style, it had what no other home in the world had. Wesley Griffith.

The starch had gone straight out of her legs and she wondered how she would ever walk inside. When Wesley came to help her out of the car, however, her strength returned somehow. Before she knew it, they were inside. The house smelled of dragon blood incense and cinnamon. The familiar aromas eased her fears.

He turned on the lights and illuminated the massive space that held the living room and dining room. A bar stretched between to divide the two and through an archway, she saw a barren dining table. In fact, most of the house was barren. A single, white-leather sofa faced a flat screen mounted to the wall. A coffee table separated them, but it too lacked any sign of settled living. Not an empty glass in the sink, not a magazine or unopened bill on the counter. A coffeemaker sat next to the stove range, but she would bet real money that if she looked in the fridge, she wouldn't see more than a few takeout boxes.

"Do you want some tea?" Wesley offered as he walked ahead of her toward the kitchen. "Or maybe coffee?"

Alexa gazed at the empty walls and spotless wood floor. "Tea would be fine... How long have you been here?"

"Just a few days."

And not a box in sight. "You're unpacked already?"

Wesley pulled down two white ceramic mugs from an upper cabinet. "I didn't have much to put away."

"I can see that," she remarked with a laugh. "No pictures, no accessories, nothing."

Next he brought up a kettle from a lower cabinet and filled it at the sink. "I'm pretty simple. I don't like a lot of decorations to get in the way of the flow of the room."

What flow? Alexa felt nothing here. Just like the exterior, the interior was plain and lifeless.

"Pretty Spartan living."

He shrugged. "It suits me."

Somehow, it did. With no distracting trinkets or paintings, the warlock stood out. He was the center of the room. Not a pot of plants or a hand-woven rug. He compensated for everything.

Alexa slowly strode toward the bar, watching Wesley pull down a glass container of dried herbs before preparing the teabags from scratch.

"This is my own special blend," he said. "I crafted it years ago when I found I needed a little extra help staying balanced."

Alexa bit back the laugh that would have been insulting. "You? Need help balancing?"

Wesley shot her a smoldering grin. "Everyone needs a little help once in a while."

The aroma of the tea leaves and herbs made her nose and sinuses tingle. "So, just a cup of this every day and I don't need to carry my crystals?"

He dropped the bags into their own mugs and held up a finger. "Not quite. Wait here."

With long, powerful strides, Wesley left the kitchen and disappeared down a hallway that she guessed led to the bedrooms of the house. What she wouldn't have given to take a peek in his room and see if it was as basic as the rest of the house. Did he sleep with a blanket? No pillow? Was he tidy by nature in all departments? Or did he leave just one garment hanging over his bedframe as she typically did?

More thoughts related to these crept in without much of her conscious effort. How did he sleep? On his back? His stomach? Did he wear flannel pajamas or did he sleep in the nude? Goddess, how she would have loved to see that warlock naked. The thrill of it burned low in her belly and she wriggled at the guilty pleasure of it.

"Have you ever done a ritual sky clad?" he called from the hall.

Shock flooded her. "What?"

"You know what sky clad is, right?"

Alexa refused to turn as his voice drew closer. For all she knew, he would be sky clad already and though she had just finished lusting after that very idea, she wasn't ready for it at all.

"I... I do know what it is. I've never practiced magic naked before."

The word felt so odd on her tongue when she wasn't speaking it in front of her friends. They could tease and talk nasty about strangers all day long if they wanted, but to talk of nudity to a man jarred her more than she expected.

Wesley, completely clothed, appeared in her peripheral and Alexa was at ease to watch him reenter the living room. Tucked under one arm was a box, its contents hidden from her as he slid it onto the counter near them.

"It's something you'll have to try someday," he said just as the water within the kettle began to roil and hiss.

Alexa hoped the heat in her cheeks would subside soon. "Maybe if I had better coverings for my windows in the apartment."

She might as well have given him permission to play the Peeping Tom. By the cunning look in his eye, he must have thought about it. Or maybe he was thinking about what she would look like, sky clad and in the middle of a ritual.

More heat rushed to her face and she was sure everything north of her off-shoulder collar had turned a blistering shade of red from embarrassment. Her eyes dropped to the gray and black speckled countertop, scolding herself for being such a ninny. She talked a big game for someone who blushed as often as she did.

With nothing but the simmering water on the stove as a backdrop to their next intimate conversation, Wesley leaned across the counter, his hands cupped around something as if it were precious but secret.

"What is it that you want more than anything else in the world?"

The question sent her mentally scrambling. What did anyone want? Love? Acceptance? Power? Money? Freedom?

"You hide a lot of your true self. I can see it, even when others can't. You put a smile on, but you're only smiling because the alternative is always tears. Isn't it?"

Alexa felt a lump form in her throat and she could only nod, because the truth was far more complex than she felt she could articulate to him or even herself.

"You carry around a great burden and if you ever expect to reach your full potential, you need to let it go."

His hands slowly unfolded to reveal to her a dazzling silver moonstone crystal. The sight of it confused her.

"Another crystal?"

Wesley held it up and rotated it so she could see the way the smooth surface reflected back the light. "Not just any crystal. Your last crystal."

Her eyes widened. "Last?"

"Last and only."

Alexa thought of her treasure chest of crystals back at her apartment, the ones she routinely cleansed and charged whenever she felt she had need of them in a ritual or in her daily life. To think that all of them, every last one, could be replaced by this singular, simple little moonstone left her breathless.

He placed the moonstone in front of her and proceeded to unpack the box he had brought with him. One purple candle he set beside the crystal, along with a small dish, and the dried petals of a rose. He placed them in the appropriate quadrants to honor the elements they represented.

Alexa, in reverence for the ritual about to take place, remained silent as Wesley filled the bowl with water and then took the kettle off to pour their teas.

"Take out your other crystals and put them in the box."

Though she wondered if she would ever see them again, she obeyed the warlock who knew better.

"Repeat after me and take the moonstone."

She held the stone between her fingers, but kept it within the center of the circle Wesley outlined with his finger. Already she could feel his magic inundate the space. His Latin was fluid and flawless as he called upon the elements and cardinal points to empower their ceremony. She heard the names of the deities he welcomed into the house and smiled as she recognized each of them. Wesley knew so much. How could he be any more perfect?

"I am beginning again," he stated, then gave a nod for Alexa to repeat.

"I am beginning again."

He reached out and took her hand in his, careful not to touch the moonstone himself as he guided her actions. He turned over her hand and edged the moonstone closer to her face. A simple cue, a puckering of the lips, told her what to do.

Alexa let out her breath upon the stone, doubtlessly catching some of Wesley's skin in the process.

"I breathe newness, energy, and light."

With his free hand, Wesley passed his fingers over the dry wick of the candle. It sputtered to life, the flame dancing upon his command. He drew her moonstone over the fire and she felt the heat of it at her fingertips.

"I have fire, passion, and glory at my side."

With another pass of his hand, the dark and wilted rose petals came to life again. Their silky texture soothed the rawness of her fingertips caused by the fire as she touched the moonstone to the petals.

"I am blooming, growing, achieving. I am beautiful, even in the worst storms."

Alexa's breath caught in her lungs. Beautiful. There was a word she didn't hear to describe her that often. Cute and pretty, sure. But never beautiful. Risking a fracture of the ritual's concentration, she met Wesley's gaze. Intense and consuming, she lost herself in his eyes that glimmered in the candlelight that continued to swirl and dance to nature's rhythm.

He brought her hand and the moonstone to the bowl of water and they dunked it together.

"I have healed. I have surpassed. I will never be broken."

Such promises seemed impossible before this night. Alexa wasn't just lost in his gaze, but in the magic of this moment. This ritual wasn't just to make her happy again. It was to make her whole. How could he have known that she needed that?

They lifted the dripping moonstone from its watery bath and Wesley let go for just a moment. He moved around the counter to stand next to her. He then resumed his hold over her hand and brought it to her chest.

The chill of the wet moonstone against her skin shocked her at first, but the feel of Wesley's palm on top of hers, directing this last action left her frozen. The magic they had drawn into the crystal seeped into her spirit, filling her with a thousand sparks that quickened her breath.

In her ear, Wesley whispered the final words of the spell.

"I have begun again and I will live my life as I wish, happy and free."

Her tongue sat between her teeth, the invocation sitting there like it needed some divine intervention to be spoken aloud. It was her wish. It was what she wanted more than anything. To be free from the shame of her birth, to live happy and not haunted by her failures. She wanted to walk tall and know that she was perfect and powerful in her own right.

But it had been nothing more than a wish up to now. Nothing more than a dream, something to work toward, but never achievable. How could she say it with the intent the incantation truly needed?

Wesley's mouth neared her ear, his breath sending shivers down her spine and dampening that sacred place between her legs that ached for something more than a wish. The warmth and firmness of his body pressed against hers, their curves flush together as if their nearness was part of the ritual too. Even if it wasn't, she savored the feel of him and wished it would last.

"Say it."

Alexa flattened her hand against her chest, trapping the moonstone against her heart. Wesley's did the same and she felt their combined powers meld into one cohesive burst to make it happen.

"I have begun again," she recited with her eyes closed, full of faith and trust in what she said. "And I will live my life as I wish, happy and free."

She couldn't see it, but the shift in her hair around her ear told her that Wesley was smiling. As light permeated their circle, Alexa found herself smiling too. She

believed the words, believed in its power, believed in herself to truly be liberated
from the past and the regrets that came with it.

Wesley couldn't sleep. How the hell could he? After he dropped Alexa off at Miss
Macy's Antiques, he had enough energy to run a marathon. Maybe two. That
ritual, as simple as it was, had done more for him than he had ever expected.

The remnants of the ritual were sitting on the counter when he came home,
a reminder of the moment they shared. What he would have given to have her
against him like that all night and breathe in the scent of her flowery perfume. The
buzz it all created, coupled with the magic of the renewal spell, sent him pacing
and searching for anything to do to occupy him.

The date was over. The game was through. But he couldn't shift gears again.
He couldn't get his mind back into business where it needed to stay until he found
out the truth about the coffeeshop. He had to plan his next move or find another
angle, but all he could think of was the curve of Alexa's neck and the way it crawled
with gooseflesh the moment he whispered in her ear. Or the way her breath tinged
his fingers when she blew on the moonstone. Or the way heat flashed across her
skin at each step of the spell to enchant the crystal. She could feel its power just as
keenly as he could. Wesley prayed to the gods that she would heed his advice and
cherish that crystal. She would need it in all the difficult times to come with the
coffeeshop, if his mission was a success.

His phone vibrated on the coffee table, and perhaps a little too desperate for a
distraction, he answered it without looking at the caller ID.

"Griffith, what have you got so far?"

Wesley hardened at the sound of Commander Henry Wise's voice coming over
the receiver. As if in the presence of his commanding officer, he straightened his
shoulders and stood at ease, his legs spread a comfortable distance and feet firmly
planted through the phone call.

"I've scoped out the town and investigated three of the witches."

"Anything?"

He hesitated, something he knew he should never do with any commanding officer within the Enforcers.

"Spit it out."

"I don't have any solid leads yet, sir. I still have three of the other witches to meet and I haven't met their partners yet. I believe, if I can earn their trust, they're more likely to let something slip than the witches."

Experience and training told him that, though they were all magic-folk, information could be harvested far easier with those of his own gender. However, they were harder eggs to crack than the girls.

"How much more time do you need?"

Wesley's eyes narrowed. "I was under the impression that there wasn't a deadline on this mission."

Wise's tone rose in annoyance. "There isn't, but the longer we allow the witches to continue violating our laws, the more endangered our secret becomes. You know that, Griffith. And the longer you're in town, the more awareness you'll raise to the true nature of your being there. Explore those avenues for intel and report back the minute you have something."

"Yes, sir."

The phone beeped, the call ended. Wesley lowered his phone and stared at the blank wall ahead of him. Why had he just lied to his commanding officer? He did have a lead. He had a few. He had more than enough reason to believe that the witches were practicing their magic on the townsfolk, but he hadn't said it. Why? It went against all his training at the academy.

Alexa's face burned hot in his mind. With it came emotions he had been trained to ignore. Lust, sympathy, compassion. All of these could easily ruin a mission, but he had allowed himself to get close, thinking he was above the cautionary tales of missions gone sour because of a pair of pretty eyes.

He took a deep breath and cleared his head. He couldn't let himself fall. Not now. This mission wasn't the most vital he had ever accepted, but it would be another glittering star upon his record. He had to succeed if he ever wanted the promotions he had been striving for all these years. Promotions meant pay raises. Pay raises meant that his mother would be more comfortable in the nursing home. That had been the plan. It always had been.

Alexa wouldn't destroy those plans, but she would set them back a few years if his heart gave into her. Because that would mean he'd have to give up the mission. That, he couldn't do.

Chapter 5

Alexa felt naked without her usual sachet of crystals. The single moonstone in her jeans pocket weighed far less, but its affects were keenly evident. She wasn't skipping, but her steps were light. She wasn't grinning like the Cheshire cat, but the soft curl of her lips betrayed her subtle happiness. She didn't put on near as much makeup and settled for a light covering of foundation, lip gloss, and mascara. Nothing flashy, nothing showy. She didn't feel she needed it to look pretty or impress anyone.

What she felt when she walked into Perfect Books and Brews that morning was freedom. Complete and total freedom from everything she thought she was supposed to be. Perfection wasn't her goal anymore. Peace was.

Krystal and Valerie may have noticed the difference, but they didn't point it out right away. After the Saturday morning rush, Alexa felt their eyes upon her as she poured a cappuccino for the last customer. She turned, cup in hand, and met their studying stares.

"What?" she asked with an oblivious smile, knowing that explanations were coming.

"You don't seem yourself," Valerie said with her arms crossed. "Did something happen yesterday?"

Alexa shrugged and slipped on the protective sleeve for the coffee. "Nothing bad."

"I tried to call you last night," Krystal began, "to see how the tour with Wesley went and you didn't answer."

She took the coffee to the waiting customer by the counter and faced her friends. "I left my phone at home."

They waited, but Valerie was far too impatient. "So, you weren't home? Where were you?"

Now, she allowed herself the giddy, toothy grin that her friends had come to recognize. "With Wesley."

"Still?" Krystal blinked, probably calculating the hours from when they left the coffeeshop to the time she tried to call that evening.

"Yep." Alexa twisted like a contented child, her light knitted sweater swaying with her. "We went to Emperor Jimmu's."

"What?" they barked in unison.

"And then back to his place for a little..." Alexa rolled her eyes, letting them infer what they would. The satisfaction in seeing their gaping mouths was well worth the little white lie. But the longer it took them to start swooning and giggling over her conquest, the less she felt like smiling. "What? We just did a little ritual, that's all... Nothing too... you know."

That clearly wasn't what they were concerned about.

"You took Wesley out on a date?" Valerie questioned in disbelief.

"He asked me," Alexa speedily defended.

"And you accepted after all that talk about trying to introduce him to Taylor?" Krystal chided.

Alexa's smile had completely disappeared now and her heart sank right into her boots. "Are you two serious right now? He asked me out. How else was I supposed to respond? Say, 'No, I'm sorry, but my friends were going to hook you up with this other witch?'"

Valerie stepped between them and held her hands out as if to hold back the tide of witchy furies that were about to collide. "Okay, okay! There's nothing we can do about it now."

Alexa bristled. "You make it sound like I did something wrong!"

Memories flooded back from Samhain and the second-hand charm fiasco. That had been her fault and similar words had been spoken when they discovered who was to blame. But this wasn't a charm. This wasn't some disaster that threatened the safety of the town. It was a damn date with a warlock. That was all. And they behaved like she had committed some atrocity.

All she wanted was for someone or something to stop this conversation. She didn't want to talk about it anymore and she didn't want to hear anything else they had to say. It hurt far too much to see that they didn't completely support her. Wesley's words floated back to her, but she didn't want to hear them either.

"You didn't," Valerie assured. "It's just..."

She didn't have the chance to finish when someone walked up to the counter. And not just anyone. Valerie's boyfriend, Caleb, leaned his elbows between the cash register and the half-full jar of tips.

"Something wrong?" the werewolf asked, his green eyes flitting from one witch to the other.

Caleb spent so much time in the coffeeshop that he might as well have been put on the payroll. He became as casual a fixture in the place as the books or the espresso machines that his presence often flew under their radar. It seemed a lifetime ago when they all nettled at the feel of the werewolf in the building and wanted him gone. Now, he was family.

Valerie was the first to fill him in while Krystal and Alexa refused to look at one another out of spite and embarrassment. It wasn't often that they let themselves get into tiffs like this. And if they ever did fight, they would forgive one another quickly and get on with business. Boys seemed to be the only conflict that stuck.

"Alexa went out with the new warlock in town when we thought we were all on the same page to let Taylor have a go at him."

Caleb cocked a dark brow. "Playing matchmaker? That never ends well."

"Clearly," Krystal grumbled.

"Did you have a good time?" the werewolf asked Alexa directly, his voice void of the resentment that met her from the other two witches.

Caleb might have had a soft spot for Alexa, though she wouldn't ask him to admit it. When he arrived to town, she had been far more welcoming of him than the others, though her fear of him prevented her from showing it. And when it was found that he and Valerie were Twin Flames, Alexa was the first to accept the union. She understood the sacred nature of Twin Flames and if Valerie was a perfect match with a werewolf – of all things – then she would honor it. Somehow, Caleb seemed to understand that and seemed more amiable to her than to Krystal, who had been opposed to the union from the start.

"I did," Alexa answered proudly. "We have a lot in common."

Krystal had opened her mouth and took a breath, but Valerie snapped her fingers together in a pinching fashion and threw a little magic behind it to shut her up quickly.

"She had a good time," Valerie repeated like a warning. "Let her enjoy that."

Krystal, unable to part her lips to answer, only let out a deep sigh and nodded. Valerie released her magic hold over her friend.

"I'm sorry for getting petty like that." Krystal's demure tone was just enough to sooth back Alexa's ruffled feathers. "I just had my heart set on seeing them together. But if Wesley really likes you..." She shrugged. "Then I'm happy for you."

It wasn't quite the truth. Alexa could tell that much. But she'd take it.

The tension between the witches eased enough that Caleb felt it appropriate to speak again. "Weren't you talking about doing something this evening?"

The question was addressed to Valerie, who brightened at the reminder. "Right! What are we doing about Imbolc? The usual?"

In all the excitement of Wesley arriving to town, Alexa completely forgot about the day. The first of February. Relieved for the change of subject, Krystal jumped on it.

"That's right! Are we still up for going out?"

"I pulled out my snowshoes from the attic last night," Valerie boasted, which amazed Alexa. She hadn't been one for going out to search for the first signs of spring since they began the tradition as children.

Back then, it had been a big affair. All the witches of Goldcrest Cove, young and old, would gather to rake aside the ice and snow, their eyes probing the ground and tree limbs for any green sprig that told them the harsh winter was finally at an end. It wasn't a major holiday upon their Wheel of Seasons, but Alexa wanted to take part in every little tradition she could. Anything to feel some connection to the half of her she so badly wanted to be the whole.

The moment she was ready to jump into plans, something inside her ordered her to wait. The Imbolc tradition was one of the many highlights of her late-winter season. Why should she hesitate?

Regardless of her silence, Krystal and Valerie went into the basics of the arrangement.

"So, we'll close up the shop a couple of hours early and meet at my house," Krystal said.

"Are you going to make those stuffed meatballs again? They were the shit last year."

Krystal preened under the compliment. "I can, but I was thinking about making some crab dip too."

"Oh, my goddess!" Valerie cried. "Do both! Stuff the crab in the meatballs!"

While Krystal mused over the makeshift recipe and Alexa tried to discern this apathy toward Imbolc all of the sudden, the coffeeshop door swung open. Alerted by the bell, Alexa spun, hoping to see Wesley. Instead, a shiny police badge and dark navy uniform greeted her.

Devin smiled to the witches as he made his way to the counter, but Krystal's smile was even bigger. Caleb moved aside so the human cop could join the party.

"You three look excited about something," he said after giving his fellow man a slap on the back.

Thankfully, Devin and Caleb had grown fond of one another over the last month as they all adjusted to the werewolf's existence in their lives. It was far easier for Devin, being that he could talk to Caleb about cars and boats and other manly things without having to think about what he really was.

"Tonight's Imbolc, honey," Krystal said. "Remember I told you about that a couple of weeks ago?"

The human's expression went blank and the witches giggled at his ignorance. While it was refreshing to share their atypical lifestyle with a non-magic folk for a change, it amused them whenever they shared it excessively and Devin gave them that look that told them as much.

A quick explanation into the tradition and their plans resolved the matter, but Devin seemed less than excited as he sighed.

"What?" Krystal asked, taken aback by his indifference.

"This is the second time you've cancelled something with me," he explained in mild aggravation. "First you cancel the cake tasting yesterday and now you forgot we were supposed to have dinner at my place. Every Saturday night. We agreed on that so we could get all this wedding shit figured out."

Alexa grimaced, knowing she was partially to blame for making a bad issue even worse.

"It's a tradition, Devin. Yesterday was a fluke, but we've never missed an Imbolc."

Devin shrugged. "Then this will be the first."

All three witches, even Caleb, started at such a statement. Even the werewolf understood the importance of these rituals and holidays for the girls.

Alexa could feel the storm coming and did exactly as Wesley said. She slipped her hand into the pocket with the moonstone and fisted it, drawing on its calming powers.

Her friend had grown into her passionate, fire zodiac and her temper had gotten that much shorter since the stress of planning the wedding. A little thing like this could set Krystal over the edge, and they all knew it. Devin could whisk her away from her friends for an impromptu date, but he didn't stand a chance against a witchy tradition like Imbolc.

Just be nice. Everyone just be nice to one another, please!

Caleb, as if hearing her thoughts, jabbed an elbow into Devin's ribs. "Hey, I've got an idea. Why don't we let the girls have their fun, but we wrangle all the guys together to talk about what exactly we'll do for the wedding. I'm one of the groomsmen, after all. I've been around for a while, but I've never been a groomsman."

Like air had been let out of a nearly bursting balloon, the hackles of the witches and the human lowered to a manageable level. Devin and Krystal exchanged looks, shifting between pleading and apologetic. Alexa bit her lip, mutedly imposing her will for peace even more as they seemed to be silently debating over the idea.

Finally, Devin nodded. "Fine. I think Aaron needs some help too. I don't think the man knows the difference between a tux and a suit."

Alexa passed a thankful look to Caleb, who once more saved the day from total disaster. Then, an idea slithered its way into her thoughts. Within seconds, it latched on and refused to let go.

"Can Wesley go along?" she asked the men.

They blinked, but for far different reasons.

"Who's Wesley?" Devin asked.

"Alexa's new boyfriend," Caleb answered, a note of insinuation in his voice that wasn't lost on the other witches.

"They just went out on one date," Krystal corrected. "I hardly think that means they're a couple."

Alexa waved her off. "It doesn't matter. He's new in town and doesn't have any friends yet. Why don't you take him out with you?"

Devin made a sign of indifference. "Don't see why not. If he's new in town, I think I better get to know him."

Valerie pointed a cautionary finger. "Don't interrogate him."

The cop held up his hands, well aware by now what it meant to be in the heat of the witch's glare. "No interrogation. Just a little friendly conversation so I can get a feel for him. That's all."

Alexa felt the wad of conflicting emotions begin to unravel. All was well again, and maybe when Devin found out what a great, upstanding guy Wesley was, he would try to convince Krystal of the same. Then she'd fully let go of that idea involving Taylor and admit that Alexa deserved a full-blooded warlock just as much as the rest of them.

"You're making a real impression on the girls."

Wesley never expected to get a call from Devin, Krystal's human fiancé. Nor did he expect to spend his Saturday night at the Torn Sails Bar by the harbor docks. And he certainly didn't expect to have a werewolf sitting next to him at the bar, talking to him over a couple of glasses of whiskey.

"I thought they were about to start slugging it out right there in the cof-feeshop," added Devin who sat on his other side. Shawn, Caleb's human room-mate, sat far opposite him and Aaron, Devin's partner, completed the party sitting on the outside of the group.

Wesley had been accustomed to the company of warlocks, witches, and even fae folk every once in a while, but this crowd was completely out of the norm. He would have forgotten how to act if it hadn't been for his Enforcer training.

He only made a look of befuddlement and tipped the glass to his lips for a good swig, as if being the focus of so many feminine minds was a difficult thing to bare. The men laughed at his expense. In all reality, he was right where he needed to be.

Far from Alexa and in the company of some of her closest friends. Perhaps now he could get that vital information he promised his commanding officer.

"What can I say?" he replied to them after swallowing the liquor. "Alexa's hard to resist."

Aaron raised his glass of brandy, the amber liquid rolling inside. "Almost!"

Wesley leaned over the counter to pin him with a challenging look. "Almost?"

The human cleared his throat and lowered his glass. "Well, Alexa's just a bit... Don't take any offense, but she can be a bit much, if you know what I mean. She wouldn't have been my first choice."

The two beside him who knew her better remained silent, but Wesley knew what the cop meant.

"Yeah, you had your eye on Valerie before Caleb snagged her up." Shawn, whom he was told was a teacher and coach at the high school. He bumped his shoulder against the werewolf. "Isn't that right?"

Aaron took a swig of his drink, but his refusal to respond said enough.

"You had a thing for Valerie?" Devin questioned. "You never mentioned it to me."

His partner looked down to the werewolf who held the heart of the witch and hastily tried to explain himself. "I was never going to act on it, I swear. She hates my guts. I knew nothing would happen, even if I wanted it to."

Wesley smirked at the sinister grin that split Caleb's face, the one he knew was intended to make the human squirm.

"Oh, no worries," he said, his tone far too cheerful for a man of his size and character. "I don't think you could have handled Valerie if she ever did set her eyes on you."

That, everyone could agree on and they said it with a laugh that trembled across the bar counter.

"And the best of us are about to marry the best one of the bunch!" called Shawn as he raised his beer bottle toward Devin. "To the lucky groom!"

They clinked the rims of their glasses together and threw back their drinks before calling for more. Devin was the only one who ordered soda, as he was the designated driver. Wesley licked his lips, mulling over the way he needed to pose his first question.

"How did they all become such good friends?" he asked. "They're all so different."

While Devin and Caleb could divulge more, they knew the girls for the least amount of time in comparison to the others.

Aaron only shrugged his shoulders. "They always have been. Ever since grade school, they've been inseparable. Always having sleepovers, trading notes in class, that sort of stuff."

"Their families are close too," joined Shawn. "Well, sort of."

"You mean Krystal's parents were close with Valerie's aunt and Alexa's mom." Aaron was probably too far in his boots to pay any mind to sensitivity. "Krystal's the only one with a nuclear family."

Wesley saw the way Caleb had to let go of his glass before he risked cracking it beneath his tightened grip.

"The world's made of all kinds," Devin wisely put it. "It's probably Valerie and Alexa's lack of family that made them all so tight-knit."

Caleb nodded. "I know how that is. You get a lot of people together from all walks of life, but give them one commonality, they'll make their own family."

Spoken by a true werewolf. Wesley recalled from his profile that he was without a pack. He had fled from his last one for unknown reasons, but it seemed that he had found a new one here among the witches.

Shawn lifted his dark brown bottle again. "And here's to families of all kinds."

Wesley marveled at the human's eagerness to become inebriated, but clinked his glass again and downed the firewater. That was his limit and he reached it far too quickly for his liking. He needed to stay focused. When the barkeep came around to refill his glass, he asked for water.

"What, Wes?" Aaron asked. "The liquor getting to you already?"

He understood these little jibes and waved it off. "Just got a big day tomorrow looking for a job."

"You're looking for a job?" Devin asked. "What kind of work do you do?"

Wesley paused to remember his previously rehearsed history. "I worked as a bouncer at a club for about five years." He knew that if he said anything remotely close to law enforcement – which was the truth – he'd be questioned about his time in Boston and their stories would never match up.

Shawn slapped Caleb on the arm. "Looks like you two have one of those commonalities you were just talking about."

Caleb looked him over and seemed to accept the idea that Wesley was cut out for being a bouncer. He, like Devin and Aaron, were built for tossing men around.

"There aren't any clubs close by," Devin said. "Only the bar, but Goldcrest Cove is pretty tame. We hardly get any calls for public drunkenness or anything like that."

"Makes our job boring!" Aaron added, his words beginning to slur.

"So, nothing weird or out of place happens here?"

Now Wesley knew he walked a fine line. He needed to pick his words far more carefully or the others would suspect something. Especially Caleb and Devin.

"There was that rash of murders last Halloween," Shawn answered. "But they caught that psycho. Turned out he had some sort of psychological break down over his wife leaving him or something."

Aaron pointed a finger. "And then there was the time in December when people were coming back from the dead."

The shock plainly written on Wesley's face was authentic. He knew about the murders, but not this. "Coming back from the dead?"

Caleb put a hand on his arm and shook his head, a sign that he shouldn't pry.

Aaron didn't see or didn't care to notice. "I swear for two days, we had nutjobs calling the department and saying their dogs were coming back to life, digging their way out of their graves. And the cemeteries were emptying like crazy. One lost half of its dearly interred!"

Devin smacked the back of his hand into his partner's chest. "We ruled that out as some sick prank. The bodies were back the next morning."

Wesley chewed on that for a bit. Had the witches performed resurrection spells? Or had it been a necromancer? Was there some link to the demon banishment that took place in Goldcrest Cove? And what was Caleb's behavior about? Why shouldn't he ask about the bodies?

"Funny enough," Shawn started, "the town has been really quiet here until the last few months. Now we're just waiting for the next fallout."

Wesley's brows crinkled together and he sipped at his water, wondering what kind of fallout he meant. His mind went to work, mentally tacking the items upon the board in his mind and calculating what needed to be tethered to what.

As the men all discussed their coming roles in the wedding that still didn't have a solid date yet, Wesley reviewed the profiles one more time and paid attention to the dates. The murders took place around Samhain. Aaron said the resurrection occurred in December, and the demon was banished about the same time near Yule. There was nothing within the girls' profiles for those dates, but there were for the men he sat with.

Devin arrived to town just a week or so before the murders. Caleb's registration for residency within a witch territory was approved after Yule, but back-dated for a week or so before as well. All of these events lined up. When these men came to town, strange things happened... And the witches found their Twin Flames.

That meant only one thing. Dark magic. But the murders had nothing to do with fire – Krystal's dark magic – and Valerie's abilities geared more toward energy transfer, which might have had something to do with the bodies rising, but not with the demon. The file for the demon's banishment had so much black tape that not even his commanding officer's level of clearance could disclose all the details.

Still, he had found a commonality amongst it all. Just how it could prove his theory that the girls were using magic on non-magic folk, he didn't know.

A pang of guilt spiked in Wesley's gut and it made him physically wince. Here he was, plotting the downfall of the witches these men had come to love and admire in the community, while toasting with them and letting them buy his drinks. It seemed unfair. Underhanded, almost.

"You all right?" Caleb asked under his breath so as not to rouse the others.

Wesley dropped his mask into place and nodded. "Yeah, just thinking about where to apply for a job and all that."

The werewolf thumbed toward the door behind them. "I think I saw a sign that said the bar was hiring. Why not give it a shot? Pun not intended."

He smirked at the joke, but let his eyes skim over the line of liquor bottles behind the tap handles. "I've never bartended before."

"It's just chemistry. And if I understand right, you and the girls can be pretty good at mixing a mean drink every once in a while."

Did he mean potions? Caleb had already turned away to talk to Shawn before he could get a better answer.

Maybe a bar wouldn't be such a bad place. He'd only work in the evenings and have the morning and afternoon to investigate the town. It also might give him a chance to see what the other townsfolk thought of the witches that ran Perfect Books and Brews.

He swiveled on his barstool and leaned back against the counter to survey the room. One could learn a lot of truths in a place where alcohol could loosen tongues. Guardedly, Wesley let his aura vision take over. The rainbow of auras barely had a chance to manifest before the voices assaulted him from every side, just as it had at the restaurant the night before. Only now, they seemed louder and more clearly defined.

It might have been the whiskey that told him he could work through it, to try and single out the voices that belonged to one person. He tried, focusing on one man and then the next, reading their lips from a distance and trying to find a pattern in their speech.

Wesley's temples began to throb and his stomach turned, ready to send his whiskey back up to burn his throat a second time. His breaths came more rapid, his nostrils flaring as if he were going right into a combat zone. To anyone else's eyes, nothing had happened. Nothing changed. Wesley fought a battle that was all in his head.

Caleb's voice rang loud next to him.

What's up with the warlock?

"You okay?" The shock of the audible voice following the murmured thought convinced Wesley that he had to give it up for now.

He let his vision relax and his muscles in his shoulders released their tension. Never had slipping into his aura vision drained so much of his energy. He barely had the strength to stay seated on the barstool.

He still couldn't come to one theory of why he could hear thoughts. That's what he had concluded the voices were. It made little sense, as magic-folk didn't possess the ability to read minds. They could read intent and auras, but never the audible thoughts of another being. However, that was the only explanation he could come up with. If he had time, he could have used it to his advantage. Instead, he could only wield it like a child with a claymore. Wildly and without success.

"Yeah, I'm good." Right about now he wanted something a little stronger than water. Limits be damned.

Chapter 6

"**F**or the love of the Goddess, light the fire!"

Krystal didn't have to be told twice. The moment all six witches bustled into the hallway of Hayden Mansion, her fingers reached toward the fireplace in the parlor. With practiced care, the logs burst into flames without hesitation, the bark crackling and spitting embers with the force of her magic.

Hats, mitts, scarves, and jackets were shucked in the hall, the wool and cotton lying in pools of fabric on the roughened wood floor. Giggles and sighs of relief echoed on the high ceilings of the warm foyer. This house was as much Alexa's home as it was Krystal and Sierra's, which was why no one was concerned about picking up their mess or kicking off the packed snow and soil from the bottoms of their boots.

Imbolc had been a success, much to their surprise. Shovels, rakes, and brooms were discarded on the porch, their duties complete. The honor of spotting the first sign of coming spring belonged to Amber, much to Alexa's chagrin. The innkeeper, much like Valerie, didn't always care for the tradition and wasn't even looking that closely when she pointed out a tiny sprig of leaf budding from an elm.

In their childhood days, the reward for finding new growth would have been a special slice of Mrs. Hayden's cinnamon bunt cake. Instead, Amber settled for a shot of Sierra's imported vodka, which was generously shared.

"You're letting her keep liquor in the house?" Alexa asked Krystal as she unwrapped the knitted scarf from her neck.

The witch threw up her hands in frustrated surrender. "I've been trying for years for her to keep that stuff out of my kitchen and I'm done!" She gestured toward Sierra, Valerie, and Amber who were all eagerly sloshing out their portions. "I can't win with her. I figured that out the minute she started using a cloaking charm on the bottles so I wouldn't find them."

"How else could I sneak this in?" Sierra called out.

The tallest of the bunch by a few inches, she often took on the role of mother, sister, and protector for them all. Smuggling in liquor for celebrations was just one of her many ways of "giving back" to the girls who meant so much to her.

Taylor stamped her feet to get some blood flowing as Krystal joined her sister in the kitchen to monitor their debauchery as best she could. Alexa found it hard to look at her green-thumbed friend during Imbolc. Whenever she did look to Taylor's brown braids or heard her meek voice over the group, she thought of Wesley and how everyone – except her – had believed they were the better match.

That, and the fact that she hadn't heard one peep from Wesley since the night before. They had shared such an intimate moment in his kitchen that she was sure he would call or text her. Nothing. Not a word. It made her wonder how much of the moment had been imagined. Had she been over-thinking it again? Did she put too much into his actions and sincerity? She had done it before with men who had done less that was for sure.

"You've been quiet tonight," Taylor said, startling her out of her thoughts.

Alexa turned to her friend, the witch who could grow just about anything anywhere she wanted, and blinked. "Have I?"

Taylor, her mouth ever touched with that charming little smile that made her so approachable, merely nodded and then looked across the hall to the other witches. "It's not like you to sit out from the fun. Is something bothering you?"

Shot glasses clinked together and Alexa wondered if she needed a shot of liquid courage right about then. "Can I ask you something?"

"Anything."

The two witches gravitated toward the sofa facing the fireplace. They were the only ones in the parlor and it was unlikely that the others would hear their conversation over the twittering and giggling in the kitchen.

"I met this guy and... we had a great date last night, but he hasn't called me back or anything."

"Is this guy the new warlock in town?"

Taylor's look of understanding threw her off more than she cared to express. "You know him?"

She nodded. "Amber told me he was coming. She saw it in one of her scrying visions."

The purple-haired innkeeper who liked her booze a little too much had a habit of keeping secrets from her little coven. Mostly for their own good, so Alexa couldn't be mad. If they knew Wesley was coming to town, they would have been all in a tizzy way in advance.

"His name's Wesley," Alexa confessed, suddenly feeling odd for even talking about him to the girl Krystal wanted him to hook up with. "He's so sweet and generous and..." She couldn't help but sigh dreamily at the memory of everything they shared the day before. "He's just perfect. Absolutely perfect." Alexa pulled out the moonstone from her pocket. "He helped me to charge this, so I wouldn't have to carry around so many crystals all the time."

Taylor observed the moonstone, aware that touching it would taint its magical properties for Alexa. "I'm glad. No one should have to carry around more than a couple."

That's when she remembered how acutely sensitive Taylor was to the flow and shift of energies within their world. She could see and sense things like no other witch in Goldcrest Cove. One more reason that she and Wesley might have made a great couple.

Alexa's excitement faltered. "It was his idea and his own crafted spell... But I haven't heard from him. We exchanged numbers when he dropped me off last night, but he hasn't called or texted or anything. I'm afraid I might have done something to scare him off."

Taylor's smile widened and she shook her head, the tips of her short braids dancing against her shoulders. "No, I don't think you did. Men are... they're dense. I can't put it any kinder than that. If he didn't text or call, then he must be busy. Or maybe he's waiting for you to make the first move. For all you know, he might have thought he scared you off by offering the spell. Charging a crystal is such a personal thing, maybe he's afraid that you'd think it was weird."

As if trying to convince the man himself instead of her friend, Alexa began to shake. "No way! It was so sweet of him to do this for me. I can't imagine why he would have felt weird about it."

Taylor placed a hand on her arm, light as the grazing of a feather. "Then make sure he knows it. It's a little late right now, but maybe tomorrow send him a text to thank him again for the moonstone." She wrinkled her nose playfully. "Just a little push to assure him that things are all right."

Alexa let out a long breath and tucked the moonstone away. "I'm just always afraid I'll come off as being too clingy if I text first, you know?"

"I can understand that... But from what Amber told me, Wesley isn't one who can be scared off."

Alexa leaned forward so she could catch every word. "What did Amber see in her vision?"

Taylor's eyes rolled. "Oh, she saw him working out. Training, I think. Maybe army? Her vision wasn't all too clear. He was doing things like running an obstacle course and practicing some sort of fighting." Her smile turned dreamy. "And then she saw him doing nice things like taking care of this older woman."

"That must have been his mom," Alexa said excitedly. "He said that she was... not so well off."

It almost felt wrong to tell Taylor all these personal things, but if Amber had already seen them in her vision, what was the harm of filling in a few extra details?

Taylor tilted her head inquisitively. "His mother? That's terrible. Amber said the woman looked so sick. But when Wesley came around, she smiled so big. It's no wonder they have a connection."

Just one more thing to add to Saint Wesley's already long list of virtues. And for a second, Alexa wondered if she should have let him and Taylor go out. They had so much in common. Sensitive, gentle, caring, beautiful, and wise beyond comprehension.

Guilt was the twisted knife in her stomach the longer she looked into Taylor's dark eyes. Maybe she shouldn't have been so selfish. Magic pulsed through their veins, more than it did for Alexa. They deserved one another.

But as the thought came to suggest a meeting for the two, her pocket thrummed with a new life she hadn't expected. The moonstone's frequency held her tongue and her heart in check. This was why Wesley charged the crystal the way he did. This was Alexa's new life, free of the shame of not being good enough. Free from the lies that she wasn't whole.

She would do what Taylor recommended. She'd text Wesley first, but not before tomorrow. She only wished it wasn't so late, so she could have that chance to talk to him tonight. If only he wasn't out with the guys and she wasn't here with the witches. She wanted their schedules to coincide somehow, so they could have the chance to talk sooner than tomorrow. She'd spend a sleepless night otherwise.

She closed her mouth and smiled to her friend seconds before the other witches piled into the parlor, laughter filling the warm, spicy air.

"You need to have red tulips!" shouted Amber, her wine glass far too full. "Red for passion!"

"I'm telling you," Sierra countered, "they need to be purple. Purple will match the bridesmaids dresses."

"I don't even want tulips!" Krystal screamed over them all. "I am perfectly content with my roses and white myrtles."

Sierra plopped down next to the flower expert. "Taylor, tell her that purple tulips are better than the roses."

All went quiet to hear the verdict. If they continued to shout over one another, Taylor would have never been heard.

"There's nothing wrong with roses," she laughed. "They're perfectly acceptable."

Krystal clasped her hands into a praying position around the stem of her wine glass. "Thank you! Someone has a sense of tradition!"

"Tulips are totally traditional!" Amber argued. "My mother had tulips at her wedding and I saw plenty in your mom's bouquet."

"Tulips are fine, but they're just boring and don't send the right message."

Sierra, still clearly in contest with her sister retorted with, "Tulips send just the right message! Undying love!" She leaned toward Taylor and even Alexa could smell a bit of the liquor on her breath. "It is undying love, right?"

Taylor only had time to nod before Krystal made her defense again. "We are Twin Flames!" she stressed. "We already represent undying love!"

On and on this went, jumping from the flowers to the cake tasting disaster to "how much lace was too much lace" controversy. Alexa's head swam with it all, dizzy and lost in the plans. For such a simple ceremony, there was so much left to decide.

"Have you even set a date yet?" Alexa asked.

Krystal rolled her eyes and leaned dramatically in her seat. "Oh, don't even get me started on the date."

"The summer solstice is perfect for a wedding," Sierra said. "Especially since you want all of this outside."

"I thought you said you wanted Beltane?" Valerie asked as she sipped on her tumbler of whiskey.

"Yes," Krystal answered. "I want Beltane. The first of May. You're all about meaning, Sierra, and you say I should totally bypass the day that represents fertility and joy?"

Sierra set her empty wine glass on the coffee table to further implore her sister. "It's so soon! You don't even have your dress yet! We'll have to order it and get it tailored and – "

"I've already found my dress."

Every jaw in the room dropped. Cries and questions flew at Krystal so fast that she couldn't answer them all.

Alexa scooted to the edge of her seat. "You went dress shopping without us?"

Krystal held up her hands to silence them all. "I found the dress, but I haven't bought it yet." Once they had all quieted, she continued. "When I was in Boston for that business woman's conference last week, I walked past an old thrift shop and I saw it in the window."

The minute she pulled out her phone, every witch was on her feet and rushing to Krystal's armchair. They pushed and shoved for room to see the picture of the exquisite vintage wedding gown with long sleeves and a lacey scalloped neckline that came off the shoulders.

They all swooned and mooned over the dress and all the fine embroidered details as Krystal zoomed in on the screen.

"It's perfect!" Taylor sighed, her chin resting on Alexa's shoulder as they both admired the gown.

"Why didn't you buy it?" Sierra demanded, slapping the bride's arm. "It could have been snatched up already!"

Krystal sneered up at her elder sister. "I put it on hold. I have another two weeks to go back and get it."

Alexa wrapped her arms around her friend's neck, her happiness bubbling over for Krystal and Devin and all the joy that awaited them. It was enough to distract her from her own troubles with Wesley. She could only hope that one day, she'd be the one everyone screamed at about flowers and cakes and guest lists. She wanted to be the one to wear the pretty white dress and walk down the aisle to her Twin Flame waiting at the altar.

One day, she promised herself. *One day.*

Wesley's fingers drummed against the back of his phone, still debating whether to do what he had been trying to avoid all night. Contact Alexa. Just before they left Torn Sails, he had the sudden and inexplicable urge to call her. Text her. Send a smoke signal. Anything to make her think of him in some way.

He couldn't account for it. He had missed her over the last twenty-four hours, but he had been able to fight off the need to reach out. What was it about this late hour that made him want her all of the sudden?

The one thing that kept him from unlocking his phone to do the deed was the fact that he was stuck between a drunken teacher and a werewolf in the back seat of Devin's Dodge Charger. Aaron was in the front seat, going on about someone on the police force who had done something ridiculous during their last business meeting, but Wesley wasn't paying attention. His heart continued to war against his better judgement. So far, his heart was winning.

"Just text her."

Caleb's sober words caught Wesley off guard. That had been happening far too frequently on this mission.

He looked to the werewolf, much of his scruffy face shadowed out by the street lamps they passed while on their way to the other side of Goldcrest Cove. "How do you know I want to text her?"

Caleb smirked and tapped his nail on the black screen. "I know that look. Just text her. She's probably waiting for you to do it."

Wesley's pale brows knitted together before he shoved his phone back in his pocket. "She's probably asleep."

"If I know those girls," Devin added from the driver seat, clearly listening, "they're nowhere near asleep."

"Trust me," Shawn said, his rancid breath spilling unwarrantedly over Wesley's face. "Those girls won't disperse until morning."

"Maybe not even then." It was a miracle that Aaron could even keep up with the conversation. Drunker than a sailor on shore leave, he turned in his seat and strained against his seatbelt to face the three in the back. "What do you see in that chick anyway? She's always so damn happy."

"No one's that happy all the fucking time." Shawn slapped a hand over his mouth. "Shit, I really need to stop cussing."

The car exploded with laughter again, but Wesley could only smile. Their indirect insult to Alexa had him too agitated. Caleb was the first to come to his defense, which wasn't expected out of a werewolf.

"There's nothing wrong with being positive."

Aaron snorted rather obnoxiously, still bracing himself to fill the space between the two front seats. "That girl's a walking rainbow. I've never seen her get really upset or cry or anything! That's just not natural for a woman."

"I've seen her upset," Devin added, once more coming to Wesley's aid when he didn't ask for or deserve it.

"When?" demanded Shawn, himself grabbing for the back of the driver seat to pull himself closer. "When did you see her upset?"

"I saw her cry a bit last year," he answered. "The details aren't important, but I promise you that Alexa has some other emotion besides bright sunshine."

Wesley's jaw tightened. What instance was he talking about? It had to be in the last few months of the year. What kind of trauma would have brought that out of Alexa while she was still charged on her crystals?

"I'll admit I'm a little curious about what drew you to her as well."

He felt Caleb's stare upon him as it had been for most of the night. Intense, penetrating. Like the stare of a stalking predator. If Caleb hadn't been trained to combat werewolves, especially alphas, then he might have been intimidated.

"She's... I don't know, really." He had the chance to lie or to tell them all the truth about these budding feelings. He could stick to the mission and say he wasn't attached in the least. Or, he could earn their trust by displaying some level of honesty. "Alexa's... She's not like most of the girls I've dated before. She just stands out."

Aaron let go of the console and gave Wesley the "jazz hands" motion. "Big fucking ray of sunshine!"

Again, there was laughter, but it wasn't shared by the three men who knew Alexa far better than the others. They knew that all three girls were more complex than anything they could have imagined.

"Holy shit!"

Devin braked hard and swerved the wheel. The force of the deceleration threw Aaron back to sit right in his seat, nearly hitting the dash. Wesley, whose seatbelt only restrained his lap, felt a hard rod of flesh slam into his chest. Caleb had held both him and Shawn back from being launched into the front seat as he braced himself at the same time.

Loose items like empty water bottles and takeout trash flew around them as the Dodge fishtailed into the opposite lane. Wesley smelled burning rubber as the tires squealed in protest. They hadn't been going fast, but the effects of the near sudden stop was all the same to them.

When the car finally jerked to a halt, every man turned to see what Devin had narrowly missed.

A woman, standing in the middle of the road. The moonlight gleamed off her long, straight black hair and fair skin. She was watching them too, just as startled as if she hadn't expected them to miss her either. More peculiar than her sudden appearance in the road were her clothes. She wore no coat and the white skin of her legs were exposed to the frosty night air as her skirt fluttered with the wind. No shoes, either. Just clad in a sleeveless, off-white gown. Besides her dark hair, she nearly blended in with the snowy ground.

"What the hell?" Aaron quickly went to unfasten his seatbelt, but Devin grabbed for his hand to stop him.

Wesley watched the way the cop's face hardened as he examined the girl from his place behind the wheel. He didn't trust this either. The woman simply manifested in the middle of the road, completely out of nowhere. Devin had been watching where he was going the whole time. There was no way he wouldn't have seen her sooner if she had been standing there the whole time.

His mind whirled through the catalog of demons and fae that matched her description, coming up with a few options, but no conclusive answers.

Not a soul moved in the car and the girl didn't budge. It was as if the whole world had stopped and waited for someone to make a move.

Shawn was the first to unbuckle and open the car door.

"Get your ass back in here!" Devin ordered. Perhaps the cop realized this wasn't normal either and erred on the side of caution.

Shawn poked his head back in, completely sobered by the near accident and the frigid air that blew into the cab of the car. "It's freezing out here and she's barely wearing anything." His tone was condemning as he shed off his own heavy canvas jacket. "Why don't you get your ass out here and help her?"

Before the teacher could slam the door shut, Wesley acted. He held out his foot to catch the door and slid out. If the human was going to try and tangle with a spirit, he wasn't about to sit by and watch. Secrecy be damned.

"Are you okay?" Shawn called out as he heedlessly crossed the icy street toward the girl.

She shuffled back a few steps, eyes wide and darting between him and Wesley. If only he could have used his aura vision to see exactly what she was. All witches and mortals had an aura. Fae and spirits did not. They appeared as great balls of light to him, nothing more. But after the headache he had incurred at the bar, Wesley wasn't ready to shift just yet.

Instead, he kept his distance from the scene, placing himself between the two and the car in case things got ugly. He could, however, reach out with his senses and tell that there was something unnatural about her. She wasn't quite a magic folk, but neither was she fae or human. This closer look allowed him to narrow down his list of what she could be.

Despite her timidity, the woman permitted Shawn to come closer and wrap his coat about her shoulders. It nearly swallowed her, covering her thin and shivering frame. She couldn't have been more than five years into her twenties. Body fully woman, but face flawless with youth.

"Is she in shock?" Shawn asked Wesley, as if he would know.

"Maybe," he answered, searching her over for any obvious injuries. "We did almost run her over."

Behind him, more car doors opened and shut. The girl nearly slipped as she made some move to retreat, but Shawn held her firmly in place.

"We're trying to help you," Shawn assured in a slow, calming voice. "Are you hurt?"

Once more, the girl was mute and hesitant. Her frightened stare lingered on Wesley more than anything else. She must have sensed his magic. To quell her fears, he lifted his hands to show her that he meant her no harm. None of them did.

Then, Caleb stepped out of the car. The air along the road shook so dramatically that Wesley thought the girl was about to unleash something. Electricity shot through the atmosphere, making the hairs on the back of his neck stand at attention, regardless of the cold. He braced, but she did nothing more than gape at the werewolf and shrink right into Shawn's arms. She knew exactly what Caleb was and wasn't afraid to show it.

The human seemed amused by it and enveloped her, as if by request. "Oh, don't be scared of him," he laughed, rubbing her back as if to help warm her. "He's big and rough looking, but he means well... What's your name?"

This swing in behavior had Wesley signaling the rest of them to stay back. Bombarding her with more attention would only make it worse. Thankfully, they obeyed. Even the drunk Aaron.

It took a few minutes and a little more coaching from Shawn before the girl spoke in the tiniest of voices. "Kit... My name is Kit."

Wesley picked up her heavy accent and pinned her as oriental, which fit her facial features. Most likely Japanese, but he couldn't be sure until she talked a little more.

"Nice to meet you, Kit." Shawn spoke as if he were addressing a child. "I'm Shawn and that's Wesley. Are you hurt?"

Kit's throat worked and she shook her head in response.

"Well, that's good. What are you doing out here all by yourself?"

Wesley glanced over his shoulder to the guys by the car. Caleb, seeing how she had reacted to him, sat in the backseat with his feet on the slick pavement, door opened so he could still keep an eye on things. Devin had drawn much closer, assessing the situation just as Wesley was but with an utter lack of expertise in this department. Aaron only watched, phone in hand and ready to call for more help. They wouldn't need it.

"I... I was running away." The softly spoken words were almost lost in the wind.

"Running away? From what?"

Thick, dark lashes fluttered and her pretty face soon scrunched at some painful memory that brought on tears. She buried herself further into Shawn's chest and he gratefully obliged to be her shoulder to cry on.

He tried to sooth her, but something didn't seem right. It was all too dramatic for Wesley. Standing in the middle of the road, scared half out of her mind, and now these crocodile tears? It was fishy, but he couldn't put his finger on what it was that made it so. The only one who seemed to pick up on that was Devin, but he wouldn't have a clue.

They needed time to question her, to find out what she was running from and why. But they weren't going to get anywhere with Kit tonight. Not while she seemed to be in a fragile state of mind and in need of some clothes.

Wesley turned to look at Devin and they seemed to share the exact same thought. They needed the witches.

Chapter 7

Half of them were good and tipsy by now, still pouring into their glasses as the time ticked away. The conversation flowed from the wedding to the honeymoon and on to future matters. One question dominated the hour.

"What if you and Devin have kids?"

The answer should have been a simple one. They would be half-blooded, just like Alexa. Alcohol numbed their sense of tact as each witch added their own opinion.

"I don't see how it matters," said Valerie and Taylor, the two who never seemed overly bothered by the idea of pure blood magic folk. "As long as they're raised right, who cares?"

Sierra and Amber, the two who had been steeped in tradition, had plenty to say about that.

"But who would raise them? Mother or father? What do you focus on more?"

Krystal, who had clearly put some thought into it, answered them all. "We will cross that bridge when we get there."

"Yeah, but you have to at least know the options on the other side of that bridge!" protested Amber as she dished out another helping of Krystal's crab dip onto her plate. They had all gathered in the kitchen, now that the warmth of the parlor had spread through the rest of the downstairs.

"You know how mom and dad will feel about it if you choose not to teach them about magic." Sierra shot her sister a look, but the bride didn't crumble beneath her censure.

"It'd be impossible for them to grow up not knowing about magic," Krystal replied, the one who had drank the least of them all.

"But you can't push it on them," Valerie said, her scolding finger getting a good workout in the discussion. "If you push it on them, they'll hate you for it."

Krystal held up her hands. "No one is going to push anything on my future children."

"What about Devin?" Taylor asked shyly. "Have you asked him how he feels?"

"Devin refuses to look beyond the wedding day right now. He's the sort of man that can only deal with one thing at a time."

Amber might have been the only one to notice that Alexa hadn't spoken. "What do you think? You're the only half-blood witch I know. What would you want Krystal to do if you were her daughter?"

Alexa began to shake under the pressure of their gazes. Somehow, it seemed that her opinion would hold more weight than anyone else's, save for Krystal. She was in the perfect position to give a viewpoint, but she wanted nothing more than to just stay quiet. She didn't want to say something that would hurt either half of her friends.

"I think," she began slowly, "it should be their choice. When they come of age to use magic, give them the choice to choose their path."

"Did someone give you a choice?" Taylor asked beside her.

Alexa's throat went dry. She couldn't remember a time when anyone had taken her aside and gave her that ultimatum. Walk down the path of magic, or live as mortal as her mother. She had a choice. She still had that choice. It wasn't as if magic came all that easy to her in the first place.

"I know I didn't," Amber snorted. "My mom had me casting spells the minute I could talk. It would have been nice to choose."

"Or at least go at my own pace," added Sierra. "You know how dad had his heart set on me becoming an apprentice in the Council."

Krystal nodded. "Exactly. I think giving them a choice is the perfect way." Her friend passed Alexa an appreciative smile, as if she had a hand in bringing this awkward and stressful conversation to a close.

She returned the smile, though she hardly felt at ease about the hard questions she had to grapple with now. When had she decided? Why had she picked this route that had caused her so much grief? And could she really turn her back on it in favor of the peace she needed? Could she turn her back on her friends? If she chose the easier route, she would have to give up their companionship.

Her thoughts were blessedly interrupted by the sound of car doors slamming, the deep voices of men, and the sharp rap of a pair of knuckles on the door. Every witch exchanged questioning looks before Krystal went to answer. They followed her into the foyer.

On her doorstep was Devin, Wesley, and a young woman dwarfed in a canvas coat that dropped well to her thighs.

"Devin?"

"I know you're having your Imbolc thing right now, but we've got an emergency."

Clearly.

But Alexa's attention barely touched on the girl who stood barefoot at Krystal's doorstep, and rested solely upon Wesley. In turn, his eyes were on her, unreadable and yet full of some nameless emotion that scared her.

This had been what she wanted all night, for their paths to cross one more time, but not like this.

A few of the other witches fled to Krystal's side to get a good look at the girl, while Alexa and Taylor hung back at the kitchen entryway.

"Is that Wesley?" she asked.

Horror streaked through her. Now they would have to meet and a bit of territorial aggression rose up in Alexa. She smacked it down before it had a chance to rear its ugly head.

"Yeah, that's Wesley."

"You forgot to mention how hot he was."

Alexa would have never expected those words to come out of Taylor's mouth and it left her speechless. Just enough time for the guys to escort the strange woman into the parlor, accompanied by the light crowd of witches who were intensely interested.

"She was in the middle of the road," Devin began. "She just showed up out of nowhere."

"Out of nowhere?" Sierra asked of her future brother-in-law. All the witches knew that if someone simply manifested out of thin air, it was no coincidence. And Devin knew better than to use a turn of phrase rather than speaking plainly like that.

"Where's the rest of your bunch?" Amber asked.

"Caleb took them home," Wesley replied. "He's just as sober as Devin. And Kit didn't..."

He stopped himself, and Alexa wondered why.

"Is that her name?" Valerie questioned as she snatched up a throw blanket from the back of one of the armchairs.

"That's what she says it is." Devin took the blanket from the witch and used it to replace the jacket. Kit was lowered to the sofa, her wide eyes set upon the flames. Alexa, now in the parlor with the rest of them, noticed a slight flicker of fear in the way she regarded the crackling embers.

"Give her some space," Taylor ordered, slipping her way into their midst. Not a witch or warlock could disobey her and they all took a few steps back to allow Kit some room to breathe.

"I'll make some tea." Valerie left them to do as she offered.

Taylor, examining Kit's pale and shaken countenance, advised, "Make some chamomile. Her nerves look shot."

"I'll get some from the herb garden so its fresh." Krystal, after giving a quick kiss to Devin, left the parlor and walked out the back door to their tiny greenhouse.

"Wesley said she's... something," Devin told the witches who were left. "But she hasn't said what."

Kit's gaze snapped to the magic folk in the room, mute and observant.

"She's not a witch," Wesley explained. "I can tell that much."

Sierra nodded in agreement. "No, she's not... But she's something."

"Fae?" Amber suggested.

"I've met plenty of fae and she doesn't fit the profile."

Amber put her hands on her hips and shot Wesley a defiant look. "Have you now?"

It was then that Wesley must have realized he hadn't met half of the witches in the parlor. "Oh, sorry. I'm Wesley Griffith. I just came to town – "

"We know," Amber snapped. "But you've been around fae? That's not something many warlocks can say."

He blinked and fell silent.

"Not fae," Kit stuttered out, shocking them all. Instantly, she was the center of attention again. "Kami."

By their blank looks, Kit must have assumed they didn't understand her. So, she looked to Alexa and repeated herself.

When they all turned to her for the translation, Alexa was too stunned to say it right away. "A... I... How do you know I know what a kami is?"

Kit, still shivering from the cold replied, "You see."

Not a soul in the room knew what she was talking about. But Wesley ended the confusion. "A kami is a Japanese spirit. Something like a deity or a spiritual representation of an idea or aspect of nature."

Alexa's chest swelled with unsolicited pride for Wesley's vast wealth of knowledge.

"A spirit?" Taylor repeated, her voice breathless with wonder. She, more than any of the other witches, devoted her magical studies to the idea of animism.

"A spirit of what?" Sierra asked. "What are you a kami for?"

"There are over three hundred different types of kami in Japanese mythology," Wesley added. "She could be anything."

"But why are you here?" Amber asked gently, coming to Kit's side. "Why were you out in the road?"

Kit, her big dark eyes still honed in on Alexa, didn't answer them. For now, it seemed all they would get out of her was that she was a kami.

"She said she was running away from something," Devin said, his arms folded as he was witness to something few humans could scarcely imagine. He had done well to simply roll with their strange ways and beliefs by now.

"Or someone," Wesley added. "She said she wasn't hurt, but she's really jumpy."

"What would a kami have to run from?" Valerie asked as she reentered the parlor, the water in the kettle already on the stove.

"Nothing that I can think of. They're like deities, but they're not omnipotent and they really only have power over what they represent. The believers in Shinto worshipped the kami so they would bless them. They have no enemies that I can think of."

"Then she'll have none here," Sierra assured, giving Kit a warm and comforting smile. "She's welcome to stay in our home. We have plenty of room."

Something in Alexa balked at that. It was a spirit. A spirit that could bless and curse. All spirits needed to be appeased in one way or another and they had done a fine job of it so far. But Alexa wanted to play her part. She wanted to understand what Kit meant and what she was there for. It seemed unfair that Krystal and Sierra should play the hostess, just because they had the room. It would have been an honor to help a kami, if what Wesley said was true. And once more, Alexa wanted to be selfish and demand that honor.

"I think Alexa should take care of Kit."

Devin's sudden input alarmed all of them. Most of all, Alexa.

Amber sputtered. "She hardly has any room in her little apartment for herself."

"The girls have their hands full with planning the wedding," Devin clarified. "And she has some aversion to Caleb, which I guess might have to do with him being a werewolf. And you were saying a while ago that all your rooms are booked, right?"

"I have room," Taylor offered.

Alexa panicked, seeing her friend's offer as far more valid than her own, but her tongue wouldn't budge to oppose her. Taylor would know how to make a kami like Kit perfectly comfortable.

But she didn't have to say anything. Kit herself finally spoke up. "I stay with Alexa."

Though they were all puzzled by this inexplicable favoring of the half-witch that seemed to settle the matter. Alexa got what she wanted. Again. Then why did her guts turn like she had just signed up for something she couldn't handle?

Alexa's hand slipped into her pocket and she fingered the moonstone again, willing it to give her the confidence she needed to take on this task. She didn't have a second bed – barely had room for one – and she didn't know what a kami needed to be contented in her little apartment. She knew how underqualified she was to take this on, but after Amber's one dissenting comment, no one else offered a better idea. Kit's final decision on the matter silenced them all. If the kami thought she would be happy recuperating with Alexa, then she'd have to trust that.

Her gaze floated up and landed on Wesley. A burst of confidence rushed through her at the sight of him. More than Kit, more than herself, he appeared the most agreeable out of the bunch.

His blue eyes, soft, entrancing in the fire's glow, and full of trust, Alexa found the strength to smile through the anxiety of the situation. Then, he gave the faintest of cues that he wanted to speak with her in private. Her heart rose in her throat and a bit of sweat from her palm transferred to the moonstone nestled in her grasp. This had also been what she wanted. Another chance to see Wesley and talk with him. But once more, she felt unprepared. Everything was happening so fast.

Wesley strode out of the room as Krystal came to present Kit with her cup of chamomile tea. Alexa, once convinced that no one would notice, slipped out and followed him into the kitchen. Maybe he would have some tips for her. Or maybe they could talk about something other than their new arrival.

It's said that absence makes the heart grow fonder. Whenever Wesley thought of that adage, he imagined an absence of months or years was necessary to make someone ache for another's presence. It had been barely a full day, but when he laid eyes on Alexa for the first time since he dropped her off, he felt as if they had been apart for a decade or more. He hadn't realized how much he missed her vitality until he could experience it first-hand one more time.

His blood hummed with the need to charge across the room and take her into his arms, but he couldn't understand why. He was drawn to her unlike anything he had ever felt, just like he confessed to the guys. Those words did so little to fully express his need, his desire. Only action could prove it, but this neither the time nor the place. It never would be.

As he went to the kitchen, Alexa following not far behind, he tried to push it all out of his head. He needed to stay focused. Stay alert. That kami, if that's what she really was, couldn't catch him with his defenses down. If he had to protect these witches, as well as try to incriminate them, then so be it.

"Everything okay?" Alexa asked as they slipped out of sight from the others across the hall in the parlor.

He turned to face her, watching the sparkle of devotion dance in her blue eyes and regretting ever agreeing to this mission. She was slowly ruining him and bringing him to life at the same time.

Wesley cleared his throat and decided to approach this slowly and formally. That was the only way. "If Kit is going to be staying with you, I need you to do me a very important favor."

Alexa straightened. "Anything."

Perhaps their attachment would prove useful for more than one purpose.

"I need you to keep a close watch on her. I don't think she's telling us the whole truth. She's in shock right now, but she'll come around by morning." His gaze roamed over her, taking in the way she stood so rigidly at attention. She would have made an excellent Enforcer, if witches were allowed in the program. "I'm actually glad she's going to stay with you. I wouldn't trust anyone else to keep an eye on her."

"You want me to... what? Interrogate her or something?"

He made a face as if he didn't like the idea. "More or less. Just find out why she's here and where she came from. Then tell me what you find. Can you do that?"

Alexa lifted her chin. "Absolutely. I don't understand why though. Do you think she's evil?"

"Japanese spirits, like the kami, are neither good nor evil. They embody certain virtues, but they also have flaws. I just don't know which kami she is and if she's here for... malicious intent."

She smiled. "You know so much... I mean it when I say having a warlock like you in Goldcrest Cove will be a relief. We've been in a lot of situations that really threw us off our game." She took a brave step closer and he failed to move back. "But with you, I think we'll be just fine."

Gods, how he wanted to catch her up and kiss her right there in the kitchen and jeopardize everything. But he could only return her smile. "I'm glad I can be of some help. Promise me you'll be safe around Kit and tell me what you find out? Any little bit of information can help us avoid a disaster, if it should come to that."

Alexa, like a little schoolgirl who had just received a gold star for excellent behavior, nodded eagerly. "I definitely will... How have you been?"

Wesley slipped his hands into his jean pockets, allowing himself to relax just a hair so she wouldn't see how strongly he fought his baser instincts. "I'm all right. I think I'll apply for a job at Torn Sails. They're hiring for a bartender."

"Really?" she asked, clearly impressed. "You've bartended before?"

"No, but how hard can be it."

"About as hard as being a barista at a coffeeshop," she quipped. "Maybe even harder. I've heard mixing cocktails can be a real chore."

"I'm a fast learner."

Once more, she took a step closer. The flowery aroma of her perfume made his mouth water. His body responded to her nearness and warmth. "I bet you are," she said softly, gaze taking on a cattish quality that stirred him.

Alarms sounded inside Wesley's head. Too close. Too much.

He finally stepped back from her charms, but the aftereffects of Alexa might never fade. "How's the moonstone working for you?" If he couldn't run away, he could at least change the subject.

Undeterred by his withdraw, she pulled out the moonstone to show him. "It's working great. I've had to use it a few times, but I feel so much better."

"That's great."

"Did I say thank you for doing all of that for me? Because I am thankful." She slid the crystal back into her pocket and Wesley couldn't help but follow her motions and linger over the way her jeans hugged her hips. "It's been so liberating to carry just one crystal instead of five or six."

He snapped his eyes back to hers. "I'm glad it's working for you."

Silence stretched between them, but Wesley found it anything but awkward. Simply being next to Alexa made him feel at peace. Like he was at home. Like their halves made a whole and separation seemed unbearable. Still, it had to happen. Not just now, but when his mission was complete. His very soul ached with the knowledge that he would have to see her arrested soon enough.

Unless he found a way to exonerate her guilt in the proceedings. If he could prove that she wasn't involved in whatever mischief the coffeeshop was brewing, then she could be spared. Wesley clenched his teeth. He couldn't do that. It went against every bit of his training. Guilty was guilty. Innocent was innocent. No exceptions could be made. Not even for a sweet half-witch who didn't deserve imprisonment.

Wesley inwardly groaned at the mess he had gotten himself into. Never had he accidentally placed himself between a rock and a hard place. Nothing in his training could have prepared him for this.

"Well, I better go," he said, masking as much of his regret as he could. "You have my number. Text me anything you find out."

A goodbye kiss, a hug, a pat on the shoulder. He would have taken anything if he thought it was appropriate. Instead, he only nodded and didn't wait for her to respond before dodging out of the kitchen and into the hall. He called out a goodbye to Devin and the other witches and then snuck out the front door before anyone could ask him to stay longer, even though he wished he could have stayed all night with Alexa. The long walk home in the cold would have to clear his head if he expected to get any sleep that night.

Chapter 8

Alexa didn't realize how in over her head she was until she and Kit were back at her apartment looking for a spare blanket. The kami stood in the open doorway, her eyes clear and hands steady after two cups of chamomile tea. Right about now, Alexa wished she had accepted a cup from Krystal when it was offered to her. Her nerves were wrecked well before they left Hayden Mansion.

As she fluttered about the room, preparing it for her guest, Alexa played over the conversation between her and Wesley for the hundredth time. He wanted her to spy on Kit? What reason did she have to do that? Why did Wesley want to know so much? And why did he feel different tonight?

His manners weren't the same as they had been. Aloof, evasive, distant. He barely wanted to talk to her at all and their talk was far too casual for her liking. She thought they had shared something the night before that would forever change the face of their relationship, if that's what she could call it. Now, they seemed little more than acquaintances. He hardly seemed to be the same guy.

Alexa made up a bedroll for herself on the rug, a plush dog toy serving as a pillow since she wanted Kit to have only the best. The kami would take the bed and as many comforts as she pleased.

"The bathroom's not the cleanest," she apologized. "If you want to wait a little while, I can wipe it down for you."

She met Kit's amused expression and tried not to let the fluttering butterflies in her stomach get the better of her.

"It is fine," Kit laughed. "I am just thankful to have a place to sleep." She stepped over the threshold and set down her pack of clothes on the ground.

Krystal let her borrow some of her jeans and shirts, but they promised to take her shopping for more clothes whenever she felt up to the trip. She still wore the white gown they had found her in and hugged Shawn's canvas jacket to her middle. Alexa saw the way she prized that thing and wished she could have been there to see the moment when Shawn gave it to her.

"I know the Japanese really value cleanliness, though."

"We do," she replied, her smile still serene and unoffended. "But I have learned not to let it get in the way of enjoying myself."

Alexa let the muscles in her shoulder slack a bit with the relief. Maybe having a kami in her apartment wouldn't be so stressful after all. At least she wasn't a demanding spirit. If she were, they would all be in trouble.

"So, how long have you... like, been in this state? Or is this always your state?"

"I have not been in Massachusetts long."

Alexa gave a nervous giggle. "No, I mean, the form you're in right now. Is that normal for you or...?"

Kit's smile widened. "Oh, this." She pinched at her dress. "It is always my form, unless I do not want it to be." When her eyes settled on Mr. Fish, she strode closer to examine.

"So, you have a physical form pretty much the majority of the time?"

"Yes." Kit tapped on the glass bowl and though Alexa wanted to rebuke her for it, she bit her lips together. "How long have you been here?"

Alexa crossed her arms. "My whole life. Well, not here exactly. I've always been in Goldcrest Cove. I've been living in this place for a few years now."

"By yourself?"

She nodded, though the kami couldn't see her. "Uh, yeah. By myself. My mom moved out of town after I graduated, so I had her before that, but I'm alone now."

"Must get lonely. Is that why you willed them to let me stay here instead?"

Alexa's eyes went wide. "What? I didn't – "

Kit turned to cut her off with a grin. "Yes, you did. I am not mad. I am flattered."

While Alexa's mouth tried to form the words for the proper question, Kit continued.

"I have never met a witch who could manipulate so seamlessly. You must have an incredibly strong mind..." Her dark eyes took her in one more time and she shook her head. "Though you do not quite seem like the other witches. You are lighter. Your magic is not as... potent."

Alexa swallowed hard and though she was confused how the kami could possibly know any of that, she replied, "I'm a half witch. My mom is human, but my dad's a warlock."

Kit inclined her head in understanding. "Of course. Which means... Well, I suppose it does not matter. But it is remarkable that at half your potential, you can still do something many seasoned witches cannot fully grasp."

Finally, Alexa centered herself in the moment and held up her hands. "Hold on. Can you tell me what it is that I'm doing?"

She tilted her head, black silky hair dangling. "You have a strong will. I always heard it called the Gift of Influence. You can sway those around you to do what you want them to do... You have not noticed?"

Alexa snorted. "Nope. Hardly anyone pays attention to what I want." But upon second thought, she was nearly compelled to retract that statement.

Kit came closer, studying the subtle change in her face. "Yes, I think you do notice. But you do not even realize you are doing it? Extraordinary!"

She hardly thought that word would ever apply to her. Alexa was anything but extraordinary. Her magic would be nearly nothing if she didn't perform her daily rituals to enhance her powers. Was she doing something different to bring about this gift that Kit mentioned?

"But... How am I doing it?" Alexa asked, bemused and dazed by this sudden revelation. She might not have been so plain after all.

"It is very simple," she said. "You wish for something so strongly until it manifests. I could tell you did it when they talked about where I would stay. You wanted me to stay with you instead of with the other witches."

Alexa pointed a finger. "Yeah, but you said you wanted to and that's what made them decide it was okay. That didn't have anything to do with me."

"Then why did the human suggest it in the first place? He must have felt your will and responded to it."

She shook her head. "Devin's the most level-headed guy I know. He wouldn't have been influenced by a little magic. And if I was using magic, then why didn't the others feel it?"

"It is a subtle magic. It can barely be detected except by those who know its secrets." Kit took a step closer, her bare feet barely making a noise upon the roughened wood planks. "And I do. I also have the Gift of Influence. It took me years to master it and I am still not as skilled in the art as some I know."

A kami like Kit couldn't do something that Alexa could do without even trying? It seemed impossible. Unthinkable. Unless...

Alexa gasped. "Dark magic!"

Kit's brows furrowed. "Dark magic?"

Her thoughts tumbled out in a confused, muddled mess as she paced and put the pieces together. "It's like Krystal's ability to harness fire. Or Valerie's ability to change energy. It's their dark magic. It's stuff that seasoned witches can't always do perfectly, but they can. And it's because of their Twin Flames! Devin and Caleb! If I have the Gift of Influence and can use it so easily, maybe that's my dark magic! And if that's my dark magic, that means I've met my Twin Flame! I think it might have started yesterday. Krystal let me go take Wesley on that tour, even though it cost her the cake tasting appointment. I thought it was weird that she would just let that slide. Then there was the thing with you and... Oh! I wanted to see Wesley so badly and he showed up with you and Devin and... Oh my goddess!" Alexa turned to Kit and nearly squealed, "Wesley is my Twin Flame!"

The witch, like a giddy teenager who had just been asked to go to the home-coming dance with her crush, began to prance and dance around her apartment, giggling and shrieking with delight. Kit only watched and her joy became infectious as she began to laugh and rejoice with her, though she couldn't have understood why. Alexa had wanted nothing more than to meet her Twin Flame for the last few months, since she realized they weren't just a fairytale. Now, she had met the other part of her soul. It was almost too good to be true.

After a few moments, Alexa planted her feet and took Kit's hands, ignoring any formalities that might have been necessary. "I'm sorry, but I'm just so happy! I've always wanted to meet my soul mate, but I never thought it was possible! But it is! It's possible I could have my happily ever after!"

She wasn't sure if the Japanese had such fairytales like the Western cultures did, but some bit of understanding flooded Kit's eyes. "You found love?"

Brimming with unbridled delight, Alexa nodded. "I think I have!"

"Then I am glad for you," she replied. "Tell me all about him."

Together, they sat on the floor and Alexa let her tongue run on and on about Wesley and how they met and how absolutely perfect he was. Most of all, how she hardly deserved him. He was a powerful warlock, hardly the ideal match for Alexa. And yet, they were Twin Flames. The universe certainly had a sense of humor.

"I wonder what his dark magic is," she mused as she reached the end of her lengthy trail of gossip and girlish delight.

"Warlocks have dark magic too?"

"They should," Alexa replied thoughtfully. "I know Mrs. Hayden's dark magic is scrying, but I don't know what Mr. Hayden's is. But, they're definitely Twin Flames. No mistake there."

"And your friends have their dark magics too?"

Alexa nodded. "Yep. All except for Sierra and Taylor. Amber has her dark magic, but she's never told us about her Twin Flame. I wonder if he was killed or something, but we never pry."

"It is truly exciting to meet another with the Gift of Influence. You will have to teach me."

Alexa's jaw dropped. "Me? Teach you? More like the other way around. Dark magic is great and powerful, but I've never known it to come easy. Everyone's had to have some level of training. Valerie wears an amethyst all the time to help her control her dark magic. Otherwise, the whole town would probably rot."

Kit's eyes widened in horror. "Rot?"

She quickly reached out to pat her knee. "No, no. It's not that bad. She just has too much negative energy and it spills out from time to time. But that's what I mean. She needs help to control it. I probably will too. Who knows what trouble I've caused with just wanting something bad enough."

Plenty of scenarios ran through her head of all the ways her dark magic could go wrong. If she had one ill wish for someone who annoyed her, they might wind up dead the next day. Memories of last October came back to mind and she cringed. She didn't want to be the cause of another string of murders in Goldcrest Cove. When she put her dark magic under that light, it no longer seemed so harmless.

"If you want me to teach you," Kit said, "I can try."

Alexa placed her hand on top of the kami's and beamed. "You're amazing."

Kit adopted a sly, foxy look. "Besides, I have to repay you for your hospitality somehow. Consider it one of my blessings to you."

Again, Alexa was overwhelmed with gratitude. "And please let me know when I use my dark magic. I don't want to be caught off guard and cause a problem... Would you consider coming with me to the coffeeshop in the morning? Just to keep an eye on me."

She nodded, not a hint of hesitance or reluctance in her. "I can do that."

Alexa couldn't believe her luck and thought to hug the kami, but refrained out of respect for her space. This night, which started out not so glamorous, ended like a miracle. She had come into her dark magic, identified it quickly, had acquired a mentor, and found out who her Twin Flame was. Nothing could have been better.

Wesley tried in vain to convince himself that he set out for the coffeeshop with only two intents. One, to spy on the witches and watch for any illegal magic use. Two, to check on the kami and see if Alexa had been able to find out anything the night before. Still, his heart hammered excitedly in his chest for a completely different reason.

He'd get to see Alexa again. He caught himself rehearsing what he'd say to her, forming a script in his mind that he could refer to if things got out of hand. He wouldn't deviate from it or his objectives. Not this time.

He parked along the curb a block away from Perfect Books and Brews, expecting there to be a rush of customers getting out from church service before noon. As he neared the door, he found it once more without a line spilling out into the sidewalk. Perhaps it was better that business wasn't as it should be, or it would make it that much harder on the community to see the place close down once he had his evidence.

He stepped into the spicy warm air of the coffeeshop and went rigid at the feel of it. The kami, Kit, was there, sitting in a chair near the counter. She wore a fresh change of clothes, jeans and a simple white shirt that fit her just right, and her long hair was pulled back into a high ponytail. She was smiling with the witches and he had walked in on the tail end of an entertaining conversation, as all four were laughing about something.

The werewolf was present too, sitting against the brick wall and typing away on his laptop. Caleb paid him little more than a glance and a nod of greeting and went back to his keyboard. Wesley couldn't help but wonder what it was the werewolf worked on. His newest book? He hadn't divulged as much at the bar last night, but Caleb's profile leaked the fact that he was a bestselling author under a pseudonym.

It was a wonder that Kit was as calm as she was with Caleb in the same room. She had been so fearful of him last night, but perhaps that was more attributed to her state of mind than any preference. In his research, he couldn't find many examples of the powerful and magical kami being so afraid of a werewolf, or dogs for that matter.

Only a few customers sat at the tables around the lobby and apart from the girls' laughter and the soft jazz music that played over the speakers, the place was far too quiet.

His first objective almost seemed ruined. With the werewolf and kami close by, the atmosphere of the coffeeshop seemed electrified. The place was infused with magic just by the pure concentration of their essences. If the witches were doing anything illegal, he wasn't going to find out easily.

Not until he passed one of the tables where a mother sat with her preteen daughter. The girl was doing homework of some sort, but the woman was just as engrossed in her own studies of bills with a leather checkbook open. He glimpsed far too many red marks and negatives in the register, but that's not what drew his attention.

He slowed his stride and focused on the feeling. A tinge of something magical surrounded the two like a bubble. Vibrating and humming as the woman took a sip of her coffee. Risking an attack of thoughts, Wesley slipped into his aura vision.

Sure enough, magic radiated from the cup of coffee like a lighthouse beacon. Charmed. And there were only three possible suspects.

So, that's what they're doing, he thought to himself. *They're charming the coffee.*

Oh, my god. How am I going to get these paid? My next check doesn't come in for another week and these two are due tomorrow. Becky's out of lunch money too. When was the last time we went grocery shopping? Can I make something out of what we have at home? How am I going to get through this?

Wesley blinked back the woman's worries. The rest of the thoughts around the coffeeshop were nothing but white noise, but hers came in crystal clear. Likely due to proximity.

Mom's so worried. I wonder if I could shovel some snow to help out. I know she'd be pissed, but I can't stand to see her like this. I can skip school a couple of days to do some odd jobs. She'll never know.

He glanced to the girl, whose eyes cut to her mother and the piles of overdue bills. His heart ached for them. Did they not have a man at home to help? How long had they lived from paycheck to paycheck?

Their auras spoke their moods just as plainly as their thoughts, but the woman's aura began to shift the more she drank the coffee she probably couldn't afford. He wondered if Krystal had given it to her on the house. Gradually, the dull shades around them took on a new feel rather than a new color. They pulsed stronger as the magic enveloped them in a cocoon. What was the purpose of the charm? Why would the girls cast it on this woman who had enough to fret over?

Her phone on the table buzzed and Wesley, now invested in their story, watched and continued to listen, though their thoughts grew fainter as he continued to walk away from the table.

Yes! He finally deposited the child support check! I thought it would never clear. Now we can at least keep the lights on. Another night of Ramen, but this bought us some time.

The mother let herself smile and gave her daughter's arm a fortifying squeeze. They shared in the moment, and Wesley had the feeling that they were going to be all right. At least for a little while.

Why is he just standing there?

Why's he watching Marsha?

Oh, my Goddess! It's Wesley!

Oh, no. It is the warlock.

He immediately shut down his aura vision and looked to see all three witches and their guest looking up to him with pleasant grins.

"Coming in for coffee or a chat?" Krystal asked, the one who had been concerned over his focus of the mother and daughter.

It was then he realized that he hadn't moved in a while, frozen in place by the scene he had been privileged to. No other human or magic folk in the place would have known what he now knew.

The girls had charmed that woman's coffee with a fortune spell. The coincidence of a check clearing on a Sunday, a day when the banks were all closed, made it clear. There was no natural way that woman's luck could have turned around so quickly. Magic had been used on a non-magic folk. He had his hard evidence.

And yet, he didn't feel that rush as he had on previous missions. He looked to the faces of each of the witches, his gaze steadying upon Alexa, and could only feel an ominous dread settle in his gut. Like he had just done something morally wrong or invasive.

But he showed none of it and returned their grin with one that was carefully crafted. "Maybe a little of both."

His second objective, to talk with Alexa about Kit, might have also been spoiled by the kami's presence in the shop. It would look strange for him to pull her aside in private and it would only make his pressing need that much harder to ignore.

"An Americano?" Valerie asked.

"Good memory."

Over the last two days, it seemed that the witches had warmed up to him. That had been the goal, but now he wasn't so sure how to feel about their hospitality. Was he their friend or a traitor?

"Did you get enough sleep last night after all the excitement?" Krystal asked as she rang up the order.

"I did," he lied as he fished out his wallet. "I probably don't even need the coffee, but I've never had a better Americano."

"We're glad to hear it."

Alexa, unable to hold back her excitement, rushed to the counter. "Good morning!"

She was back to being the peppy fairy he had met the other day, but this was genuine. She didn't need any crystals. He imagined if he let his aura vision return, she would have blinded him. Was that the work of the moonstone or something else?

Whatever it was, Wesley didn't have to fake his smile for her. "Good morning, Alexa. Did you get Kit all settled last night?"

Alexa glanced to her new friend. "We did. She insisted on sleeping on the floor, though."

The kami stood and joined them at the counter. She certainly seemed refreshed. "As I told Alexa, I am used to it. I would not have had it any other way."

The look they exchanged gave Wesley pause. Something was up between them, though he couldn't begin to guess what it was. They had only spent one night together and they were already close, if that look indicated anything.

"Then, I guess it was a good thing you decided to stay with Alexa instead of Krystal."

Something in what he said prompted more furtive looks and smiles. A dark thought entered his mind that this might have gone beyond friendship and perhaps something more. They were getting along much better than what seemed natural. Somehow, he was wounded by their instantaneous connection and it sent him through a tumble of emotions he hadn't been prepared for. It felt as if a tourniquet had been put around his heart and squeezed tight. Was Alexa not truly interested in him? Lesbian witches wasn't an uncommon concept and if the kami was one who embodied seduction or deception, then it would make sense.

And if that were a true conjecture, he had been fooled. His longing for Alexa had to be put down before someone got hurt. Namely himself. Even if this sudden suspicion was utterly false, it would have been for the best. If only his pride was as tough as he believed he was.

Valerie arrived and set his Americano in front of him, bringing him back to the present. Like a horse with blinders, he ignored the ache in his chest and paid for the coffee.

"Do you have your own special blend?" he asked after he made a point of focusing solely on Krystal. "I'm just trying to figure out why it's so good."

Krystal brightened, completely unaware of what Wesley intended. "We import our beans, but we mix in a little something special we get from Taylor and roast them before grinding. You met her last night. She supplies us with most of our herbal teas too."

Perfect.

"Do you sell bags of the grounds?" he asked, motioning to the hefty dispenser at the coffee bar.

"Sure do. Would you like a bag?"

"How much?"

Krystal waved him off. "It's on the house. Call it a thanks for what you did for Kit last night. I don't think Devin would have had enough sense to send her our way." She reached under the counter and brought up a monogrammed bag, sealed and ready for sale.

He took it and his Americano to-go cup. "I'm just glad we were able to help." He gave one last look to Alexa. "I'll call you later."

Calls and texts might have been the safest thing for him right now. To face her and his embarrassment for thinking he had a chance was far too painful at the present.

He turned and made his way toward the front door, letting little stop him.

"Wait!" Alexa came bounding across the lobby and tugged at his sleeve. He turned, forcing himself to appear neutral and uninjured, though his chest still felt as if he had been shot with a rifle.

She, however, looked as if she'd never see him again if he walked out the door that morning.

"Why don't we talk over dinner?" She slid a look toward Kit, who was well out of earshot. "If this is about what I think it is."

Wesley made a face. "I've got some stuff to do around town and I need to brush up for that interview tonight for the bartender job."

Hardly dissuaded, Alexa beamed. "So, you're going for it then? Despite it being a little complicated?"

He shrugged. "Hardly complicated. But yeah, I'm going for it." All he wanted right then was to be going for the door.

"Let's meet at the bar, then," she offered. "If you get the job, we're in a great place to celebrate. If you don't, then at least you'll have someone to be down with."

One side of Wesley's mouth tilted up in a half-smile. How could he resist her? Deep down, he did want her by his side, more than she would ever know. "Sure. Why not. The interview's at six."

"Meet you just before six, then?" Alexa bit on her bottom lip and grinned eagerly.

He nodded, though he wondered if this would upset any plans with Kit. But if Alexa wanted to be with him, far be it from him to push her away. Not yet. Not until this mission was near completion and he would have to leave for good. Whenever that would be.

First-hand testimony of the charmed coffee was good, but if he could find out more about the coffee itself and have hard, material evidence for the case against Perfect Books and Brews, that would be even better. If potion work was involved, then that would be just one more nail in their coffins.

Again, his gut churned uneasily as he made his afternoon plans. He didn't intend to stay home and learn how to fix the perfect martini.

Chapter 9

"Did I do it that time?" Alexa hurriedly asked of Kit. "It looked like he was forced. Did I force it? Could you tell?"

Kit smiled and placed a gentle hand on Alexa's trembling shoulder. "You did not do it that time. Not forced at all."

Then why did Wesley look like his arm had been twisted into spending time with her? Didn't he feel their connection? Didn't he have some clue that they were Twin Flames?

Alexa tried to steady her breaths as excitement and anxiety merged into one big glob of gut-roiling energy. She made another date with Wesley, but something didn't feel right. First, last night, and now, they barely said more than a few sentences to one another.

"Did you see the way he was looking at Marsha?" Krystal asked Valerie not too far off near the register. "I wonder if there's something there."

Alexa thought her heart would stop as she spun to listen more.

"He's like ten years younger than her," Valerie said with a hint of disgust.

Krystal only shrugged. "You never know. Maybe Marsha wouldn't mind someone younger?"

"Imagine how awkward that would be for Lucy."

She finally summoned up her courage to speak. "Guys, I'm right here."

The two witches turned to look at her, but they didn't seem to understand. "Yeah, we see you."

Alexa, too wound up with her fears, had to keep herself from crying out at the injustice of it. "You both know I'm into Wesley." That was putting it mildly. After discovering that he was her Twin Flame, she was ready to confess love and plan the wedding. But that might have been too forward, especially now when he acted like he would rather swim with hungry sharks than have drinks with her.

The pained looks on their faces had nothing to do with the guilt and shame they should have felt for trying to pawn off Alexa's Twin Flame on someone else. Instead, it was pity.

"He doesn't seem that into you," Valerie admitted. "I know you really like him, but maybe you're coming on a little too strong again?"

Alexa flexed her fingers, forcing them not to curl into fists. She knew she could be too much for some guys. She knew she could be pushy and maybe a little clingy, but Wesley was different. He had to be.

"It's not like that," she defended. "He's just... He probably just has a lot on his mind or something. He's going to a job interview tonight, so maybe he's really wrapped up with that. I'm telling you, he wasn't like this the other night."

"But he was like this last night," Krystal said. "You two didn't talk long in the kitchen and he didn't seem all that eager to stay."

Alexa knew that all too well. But two cold encounters couldn't erase the facts. She took a deep breath and decided to cross that line. "I think he's just scared, but it's not because I'm coming on too strong... He's my Twin Flame."

Neither were impressed. Not the way that she had been when Krystal and Valerie had confessed the same. They exchanged looks that told enough. They didn't believe her.

"He must be coming into his dark magic and it's making him nervous," Alexa continued. "You both know how you were with your guys when you learned the truth."

Valerie took a step forward and reached out with compassionate intent. "Alexa, you've said this before."

"Over the last three months, you've claimed more than a few times that some new guy that came into the shop was your Twin Flame, but he never was. Nothing happened and nothing's happening with Wesley."

Alexa slipped out of Valerie's hold, indignation driving her words more urgently. "But it is! You just can't see it, because you don't want to see it."

Valerie folded her arms. "Okay. If he's your Twin Flame, then what's your dark magic? Have you figured it out yet or do you need a few more weeks?"

Clearly, she was referencing to the numerous false alarms in the past. Those times, her dark magic hadn't been clear either and she told them just to wait a little while. The dark magic never came, but this time it had. Alexa felt like the boy who cried wolf and now, no one was taking her seriously.

"Kit calls it the Gift of Influence," she said, motioning to the kami who was a spectator to all of this. "It's like mind control. I can manipulate people into wanting or doing something. It's already happened a few times."

With the backing of their new guest, Alexa's claims seemed more legitimate and the girls edged closer, lowering their voices to secrecy. "When?"

Excitement rose in her voice as she thought her case might actually be heard now. "On Friday when Wesley came in. Remember how you cancelled your cake testing so I could go give him a tour of the town?"

Krystal seemed thoughtful, but not wholly convinced.

"And then last night when I really wanted to see Wesley again and he came over with Kit."

"That's just a coincidence," Valerie said. "That kind of stuff can happen all the time."

Kit finally spoke up. "No, not completely. Alexa wanted those things strongly enough and they happened. That is part of the Gift. And I knew it when she used her Gift again last night. She wanted me to stay with her more than anything, and Devin suggested it."

"He had good points to back up his argument, though," Krystal countered. "It's not like he just mindlessly suggested it."

"Did you mindlessly give up your cake appointment?" Alexa asked. "You're normally way too rational for that sort of thing and you just passed me off like it was nothing, when you two had been talking about introducing him to Taylor."

Valerie's brows lowered. "So, you used your dark magic to manipulate us so you can hook up with Wesley?"

"Not intentionally!" Alexa replied quickly. "I didn't even mean to do it. I don't quite know how I'm doing it."

"Then how do you know you're even doing it?" Krystal asked, still the skeptic. "If you don't know how you do it, then who's to say that you're doing it at all."

"I can sense when she uses her Gift," Kit replied. "She used it last night."

That quieted them both, but enraged Alexa. While she could be thankful for Kit's intercession, she wondered why her friends would more readily believe the kami they just met over a friend they had known since childhood. What made her word any less credible than Kit's? Why should they be convinced by her and not Alexa?

"I found my Twin Flame," she announced slowly, letting each word roll off her tongue. They didn't taste as sweet as before when she had said it to herself getting ready for work. This was all she had ever wanted and they didn't care. "Why can't you guys just be happy for me and quit questioning it?"

Now the guilt set in. Krystal came forward and wrapped her friend in a hug. "We are happy for you. We just..." She pulled back and stared with an undeniably torn expression. "We don't want you to get all excited and hopeful if something isn't right about this."

"What could possibly be wrong?"

"The fact that Wesley's been giving you the cold shoulder for the past two days."

Alexa pinned Valerie with the most hateful stare of the century. "You just haven't seen him in any other situation. He's always been sweet to me."

"This wouldn't be the first time that you've read a guy wrong. You see sweet, but he's just being polite."

Krystal put her hands firmly on Alexa's shoulders to keep the petite blonde from charging at her friend. "How about we focus on the more important issue. Alexa has her dark magic. How do we deal with it?"

Alexa's nostrils flared, too agitated to think straight. After all the support she had given Valerie in the past, all the time she let those biting comments slide in favor of maintaining the peace, she had the gall to be so negative. She took deep, calming breaths and tried to smother the multitude of vicious thoughts that circled in her mind.

Caleb, who must have intuitively sensed that his mate was in danger of the witch, came up to casually lean his hip against the counter. Like Kit, he remained a spectator, but Alexa wondered if he was there to break up a fight if one should ensue. Secretly, Alexa wished Valerie would give it a try. It was more likely that he had been eavesdropping on the conversation from across the lobby and couldn't focus on his book any longer.

"Should we call your parents?" Valerie asked. "We never called for either of our dark magic problems, but in hindsight, we probably should have."

Alexa shook her head. "No need. Kit said she would help me."

All eyes went to the kami again and she gave them a confident smile in return. "I also have the Gift of Influence and can help Alexa harness the skill."

"I'll admit, I've never even heard of this Gift," Krystal said with a note of disbelief.

"You had never heard of Val's dark magic before either, but it still exists." The witches no longer minded Caleb's input in magical matters. Sometimes an outside perspective helped more than they realized. "My vote is that you call the Haydens."

The air around Kit spiked and the witches jerked at the sudden hostility.

"You doubt me, wolf?"

Caleb glared. "I don't doubt you, but you haven't been here for that long. These girls went through hell trying to get a handle on their dark magic before they had some intervention. I'm saying they shouldn't make it a repeat performance." He looked straight at Alexa. "Call Catherine. You'd be doing yourself and everyone a favor."

"How would mind control even be harmful?" Valerie asked. "I'm not saying we shouldn't call Catherine, but could it be all that dangerous?"

"Second charms aren't supposed to be that dangerous, but look what happened."

Alexa was usually the first to throw herself under the bus for what happened last October, but to have Krystal dig up buried business was unlike her. More daggers pierced Alexa's heart and she wanted nothing more than for this conversation to be over. She didn't want to call Catherine, didn't want to believe that Wesley had eyes for anyone else, and didn't want her friends to hate her for all of it. She just wanted to be happy. That was all.

The door to the coffeeshop opened, the bell cheerfully jingling to announce a new customer had arrived. It was hardly anyone new, but certainly someone unexpected. With the arrival of Shawn, not one mouth would dare utter a word about magic or Twin Flames.

Caleb greeted him first, moving to intercede and give the witches time to properly close the conversation.

"Just promise us you won't do something by yourself, okay?" Krystal whispered to Alexa. "We don't want you to get hurt."

She knew they were talking about more than just her dark magic training. They meant about Wesley too. Don't do something reckless that would make her look like an idiot. Alexa couldn't make any promises. Not when it didn't seem to make a difference to them anyway.

Shawn joined them at the counter, Caleb's arm around his shoulders and looking like death.

"That hangover hitting you hard?" Valerie teased, clearly glorying in her room-mate's misfortunes. His squinting eyes rimmed in red and dark blonde hair a mess, he still found the will to smile at her ribbing.

"It's been a long time since I drank that much," he said, then pointed to Caleb. "You had just as much as I did. Why aren't you hurting?"

Caleb grinned, his sharp canines flashing. "Just lucky, I guess."

"You want your usual coffee?" Krystal asked, taking down his mug from the shelf. She passed off the white ceramic mug with the words "World's Best Teacher" on the side to Valerie.

"Yes, the usual," he replied. "But I think you should come up with some miracle cure for a hangover. It'd sell, I promise."

Alexa caught the sly look and she knew what Valerie would do. She'd charm the coffee with something to help Shawn make it through the morning without puking his brains out.

The teacher nodded and then looked to Kit, who perked up considerably when the man walked in. "Are the girls taking good care of you?"

Kit's face split with a grin and she nodded. "Yes, they are. Thank you. I don't have your coat with me, but I am sure you want it back."

He waved her off. "No. You can keep it. I've got plenty at home."

Kit's pale cheeks colored. "In that case, thank you again."

"Anytime."

Alexa was sure she was imagining it, but Shawn didn't look like such a wreck now that he was talking to Kit. His eyes brightened a bit, his posture straightened, and his smile didn't look so haggard and grim. All for Kit.

She had wondered about Kit's many questions regarding the non-magic teacher. The kami knew far more about him than he did about her, because Alexa picked up on that interest and didn't hold back one bit. Of course, there was so much more to discover.

"Weren't you saying last night you wanted to ask Kit something?" Caleb mused, the tilt of his question insinuating. Evidently, Shawn wasn't the only one who felt the pull.

He shoved the laughing werewolf out of the way and gave his full attention back to Kit. "Ignore him. He's just fooling around."

Krystal tapped her nail on the cash register to draw the two love birds back into reality.

"And Krystal isn't," he replied sheepishly before pulling out his credit card from his back pocket.

"Sure you wanted to ask her something!" Valerie added as she came up to the counter to hand off his mug. "I heard you going on and on about it after I got home last night."

Shawn shot her a scathing look, but Valerie didn't care. She looked right to Kit and said, "Alexa can't cook in her apartment, so you're welcome to come over to our place for dinner."

Mortified, Shawn wouldn't even look at the kami who appeared to be debating over the soundness of that plan in her head. Kit finally shook her head after glancing to Caleb. "I'm not so sure..."

Alexa, realizing that the rejection had nothing to do with Shawn or the idea of having dinner with him, snuck in to save the day. "I told her that you two had Thor and she said she's allergic to dogs."

"Oh, in that case, maybe we could go out instead?" Valerie offered.

Caleb leaned over the counter, coming as close as he could to his mate. "Remember we were going to go see that movie after you get off."

Valerie snapped her fingers. "You're right."

"Maybe Kit and Shawn can go have dinner somewhere together?"

Suddenly, it was as if the whole world were bending over backwards to get these two together. If only they had put that much dedication into Alexa's love life, she might have had more success with Wesley.

She did wonder, however, why Krystal would have been complacent to the idea of a kami, a Japanese spirit creature, dating a human. It wasn't quite the same as a witch dating a human, but very close to a witch dating a werewolf. There was longevity to consider in the distant future if the stars aligned just right, and they weren't even close to being the same race. Yet, she remained silent and smiling the whole time. Krystal could accept this, but not the fact that Alexa, a half-witch, found love in a warlock?

Finally, they locked eyes and everyone knew they won. Both Kit and Shawn agreed to the plan, which was fine with Alexa. She had a date of her own. Valerie had Caleb, Krystal had Devin, Alexa had Wesley, and now Kit had Shawn. It seemed that half of Goldcrest Cove would be matched up before Valentine's Day.

When Wesley stepped inside The Green Man Nursery, it was as if he had stepped into another world. More specifically, one ruled by the fae and other fairy folk. If he didn't already know beyond a shadow of a doubt that Taylor was a witch, he might have suspected that she was one of them and looking to merge the two worlds somehow.

Flora and fauna of countless species festooned the walls and long tables that stretched down the length of the greenhouse. The sign on the shop door said that she could be found somewhere back here, but the place was the nearest thing to a jungle that Wesley had ever experienced. It'd take days to find her.

The greenhouse wasn't just one spacious, hermetically sealed tent, but an expanding network that he could have easily gotten lost in. The maze of colorful flowers and heady aromas that infused the air had him dazed for a solid minute while he tried to look for her in the wilderness.

"Hello?" he called out over the light droning of bugs and whirl of the irrigation system.

"I'm back here!" Her voice was nearly drowned out by the buffer of flowerpots and hanging plant baskets.

"Where's here?" he asked, taking cautious steps away from the door, his only exit.

Taylor giggled, a sound even more muffled than her voice. "Take your first left and then a right."

He did as instructed, his boots shuffling over spilled fertilizer on the concrete floor. He found Taylor, a light sheen of sweat on her forehead and gloved hands occupied with watering a delicate looking orchid of some kind.

"I'll admit that I never thought I'd see you in my nursery," she began in a soft, lighthearted voice. "But, I'm glad either way. What can I do for you?"

The witch looked every inch a florist. Dirt smeared on her knees, the tail of her plaid button-down shirt damp from spattered water, and eyes bright with wonder at everything she had grown in this nursery. He had known some witches to possess a naturally green thumb when it came to growing gardens and cultivating, but this was something else.

His Enforcer training tried to convince him this wasn't natural, but what was the harm? As long as she didn't use magic on humans, she wasn't violating any rules. That thought brought him back to the task at hand.

"I just had a few questions about your role in the coffee roasting process for Perfect Books and Brews."

Now he sounded like a cop, but Taylor didn't seem bothered by his question at all. She spritzed the leaves of the orchid a few times, then moved on to its neighbor. "I help them. I give them a few herbs for the coffee beans. It gives the coffee a unique flavor."

"Which herbs?"

Taylor turned her head and gave him a sassy look. "You're not planning on stealing their secret recipe now, are you?"

Wesley realized he needed to ease up and smirked. "Not at all. I like their coffee and I was curious about the process. That's all."

Under her scrutinizing gaze, he stood firm and unyielding. Finally, she turned back to her orchids and nodded. "In that case, it's just a bit of nutmeg and something else, but I won't tell you what it is. That's more of a secret than the nutmeg."

Wesley ground his teeth, debating whether now was the time to pull his Enforcer card to get an answer. He didn't get the chance, even if he decided to.

"I've got a sunflower just around the corner here, if you'd be interested in it."

He blinked at the randomness of the offer. "Sunflower?"

"It's Alexa's favorite. Her favorite color is yellow too. But I guess you would already know that if you saw her Volkswagen."

The emotions in his gut knotted again, after he had managed to force Alexa out of his mind. He didn't want to think about her or feel for her. That included thinking about her favorite flower.

"I'm not here for a sunflower," he replied, words hard and feathered with bitterness that Taylor picked up on instantly.

She turned, one hand still supporting a drooping leaf. "I promise she'll love the gesture."

Wesley jammed his hands into his coat pockets. "I'm sure she would, but I'm still not here for a sunflower."

Taylor leveled a look at him. "You wouldn't want to make a girl's day by gifting her with a pretty flower?"

He chafed under the question. "When you put it that way, it makes me sound like an asshole."

"You are an asshole if you intend to lead on my friend and make her think you feel something for her when you really don't."

Never would he have expected the tiny, meek package in front of him to pack such a punch. The light dusting of freckles across her nose were deceiving.

He was too stunned by the accusation to articulate any kind of defense.

"Alexa likes you," she said. "*Really* likes you. I haven't seen her so giddy over anyone the whole time I've known her. You've made a real impression and I think you have to own up to it."

Wesley straightened his shoulders. "I don't have to own up to anything, especially something that's only in her head." The less she suspected, the better. It would make the fallout easier if they all thought he never had feelings for Alexa, even when he did.

Taylor let go of her leaf and set the water bottle on the table between the pots. "Are you saying that you don't like her? After what you did for her with the moonstone?"

Shame tugged at his heart and balled his hands into fists inside his pockets. "I'm... I'm not saying that."

"Then what is it? Alexa seems to think you two have a connection. Is it one-sided?"

Wesley was almost ready to answer her when he realized the absurdity of this back-and-forth. "Why am I even talking to you about this? I barely know you."

Taylor put a hand on her hip. "You're deflecting. We're having this conversation, because I don't want my friend to get hurt."

"If she gets hurt, it's not my damn fault."

The witch made a visible effort to stay calm with him. "Listen. Alexa is... not exactly gullible, but for as long as I've known her, she's been a romantic. You can't just take her out to dinner and then cozy up to her for a crystal charging and expect her not to take it seriously. She honestly feels there's something between you two. If you don't own up to the truth, you're only dragging her heart around like a toy and she'll be devastated. She's so childlike, it's easy to hurt her feelings sometimes."

She used that term again. "Owning up". He had made a life out of owning up. Owning up to his responsibilities and forcing others to own up to their crimes. Coming clean and living a respectable life had been his foundations and his weakness.

"I can't say there's nothing between us."

The hard lines of Taylor's face softened. "Well, that's a relief. Then why not get her the sunflower?"

The truth proved harder to contain, now that he had let a little leak out. "Because I... I don't want to lead her on. You've got me all wrong. The dinner and the ritual were... they were great, but I don't know how much more I could do without it getting messy." In a bold move, he continued, "It looks like she's got something else in the works anyway, so – "

Taylor held up her hand to stop him. "Excuse me? You honestly think Alexa's got more than one iron in the fire?"

He shrugged. "It sure looked like she was getting really close with Kit when I stopped by the coffeeshop."

The explosion of laughter from the witch nettled him. When she caught her breath, Taylor said, "Alexa doesn't lean that way. I promise you. She's only ever made eyes at boys. She wants a knight in shining armor, not a damsel in distress."

A knight. Wesley quirked a brow at the thought. He would never consider himself a knight or anything noble. A mercenary, assassin, and Enforcer, but never a knight with lofty morals. He intended to betray the witches, after all.

"It still doesn't change the fact that getting her a sunflower or taking this... thing any further would be a bad idea."

"Why would it? You like her, she likes you. What's bad about that?"

Wesley grimaced. "It's complicated."

"Just getting over a breakup?"

"You know, I would have never pegged you for the gossip type."

Taylor smiled under the half-way compliment. "I'm usually not. But when it comes to my friends, no subject interests me more. Answer me this..." She came closer, lowering her voice as if they weren't alone in the nursery. "Does she know what you are?"

A rush of heat traced down his back, but he wouldn't let his face betray him. "She definitely knows I'm a warlock."

"That's not all you are." Taylor stopped just a couple of feet from him. "I know you're a half-blood, just like her. I have a sense for these things and I knew you were different the minute you walked into the Hayden's place. I think that's why you and Alexa would be a great match. Your halves would make a whole. It's always been a really sensitive issue for her and if she knew that you knew what she was going through, you'd have her in the palm of your hand forever."

His nostrils flared and a bit of his shield cracked. Not even his fellow cadets at the Academy had ever suspected the truth of his lineage. Few outside of his more intimate friends knew the truth. And this little witch had sniffed him out.

He considered her words carefully. Their two halves would make a whole. They were weak apart, but strong together. He had spent his life training to make it appear as if he had all the usual powers of a full-blooded warlock. What would happen if they joined forces? Would they balance each other out somehow? Was that what he felt during the ritual the other night?

Even if they could somehow lean upon one another, it wasn't meant to be. Not with how much he knew already about the coffeeshop and their operations.

"I don't need her in the palm of my hand," he said to a disappointed Taylor. "Like I said, things are complicated and... hurting her is the last thing I would ever want to do."

In the end, he had to. He had to turn in the witches. He had to report back to the Council who were still waiting for his word. There was no way this could end with Alexa and Wesley standing side by side, two half-blooded misfits finally finding a home in one another. She might have been a romantic, but he wasn't. He couldn't afford it. If there was a way to save them all, Wesley would have taken it. As it was, he couldn't see a clear path out of this mess. That broke his heart more than any of the witches could have possibly understood.

Chapter 10

Not many in Goldcrest Cove could be found at Torn Sails Bar and Grill at this time of the day. Only those who had an unhealthy respect for work on Monday would come to drink this early. Alexa let her gaze wander around the room, trying hard not to stare at Wesley behind the bar with the owner. She looked at the two guys playing poker in the far corner, the couple on a date near the center of the room, and at the few out of work fishermen and blue-collar types sitting in the barstools.

From what she could tell, based on the smiles and pleasant gestures, the interview was going well. Preemptively, and possibly jinxing Wesley's big chance, Alexa dug out her black cocktail dress from the very back of her closet. She wore it only once for a class reunion a couple of years back and was thankful to find that she could still squeeze herself into it. The fabric clung to every inch of her, showing off curves that she hoped Wesley would take notice of.

She let her grip on the wine glass loosen, remembering Kit's warning before they parted ways for their respective dates. Don't want anything too much. Don't make a conscious wish for anything. Don't let the need for control blind her to reality.

Right about now, she wasn't sure what reality was between her and Wesley. They were Twin Flames. She would bet what little magic she had on it. But there was one part of the Twin Flames physics that she feared. In every relationship, there was the runner and the chaser.

From where Alexa sat, she looked like she was the chaser and Wesley was running, but she couldn't understand why. She was the one begging for attention. She was the one to want this with every ounce of her being. Wesley acted like it didn't matter if she was there or not. He hadn't even looked at her since he went to talk to the owner.

Something was holding Wesley back. That much, she could see. But what was it? What complication kept them from falling headlong into this whirlwind of feeling that Krystal and Valerie had both attested to? Devin and Caleb had, in the manliest way possible, confessed they had gotten lost in their Twin Flames from the very start. All four found the instant attraction startling, but not enough for them to resist it so completely like Wesley did – save for Valerie, who had always been reserved anyway.

With a little luck and a little flirting, maybe the last of Wesley's barricades would break. Then they could finally be together as the universe intended.

Alexa allowed herself to watch the final stage of Wesley's interview where he had to mix a series of drinks for the owner. If he got just one wrong or one tasted a little off, that was the end. Nervously, she twisted the stem of her wine glass, studying the expression on the owner's face with every drink he tested. So far, it looked good. But the man was probably putting on a front, so Wesley wouldn't know his progress either.

A thought entered her mind. Maybe she wouldn't use her dark magic against Wesley, but she could use it on the owner. If Wesley had a job in Goldcrest Cove, it would ensure he stayed. Taking a deep inhale, she concentrated on that feeling. She let it overtake her, becoming her one and only desire. She wanted Wesley to get this job and ace this interview. She needed him to.

Alexa held onto that need for a solid few minutes before the owner finally nodded and shook Wesley's hand. She couldn't read their lips, but the smiles told her enough. She grinned, completely believing that she had a hand in landing him that job.

When Wesley turned and strode toward her table, she had to keep herself under control and act as if she weren't ridiculously happy about the news he would share.

"I got the job," he said as he took the seat next to her. "I have some paperwork to fill out tomorrow, but he wants me to start as soon as it's all taken care of."

Alexa nearly squirmed in her seat. "That's awesome! Congratulations!"

Breaking the cardinal rule of the magic world – not to use magic on non-magic folk – was well worth the happiness written on Wesley's face.

"I'll admit I was a little unsure of myself on the last few drinks, but he said every one of them was perfect. Hard to believe."

Alexa wouldn't let a bit of her composure slip. "Well, believe it! Are you sure you weren't a bartender in a past life or something?"

Wesley eased back in his chair. "I wouldn't go that far."

"Whatever it was, I'm glad of it. Now you can afford to stay in that nice house."

He nodded, but there was a glint of something in his eyes that made her wonder if he wasn't so sure of it.

"So, how should we celebrate?" she asked, sweeping her blonde hair over her shoulder and leaning forward so the open back of her dress was clearly visible to him. "A round of drinks?"

Wesley's eyes trailed down the expanse of smooth skin and his mouth twitched with some devious plan. "I have another idea."

Alexa took a subtle breath to clear her mind. Was she still using her influence? She admitted that's precisely what she would have wanted him to say. She didn't want to waste their time together in a bar. But she wanted it to be his decision. His move. Not hers.

Don't ruin this. Don't move too fast. Don't force this.

His brows contracted to the smallest degree, but she saw it and tried to smile it away. "Oh? And what's that?" she asked, hoping he didn't notice the way she anxiously continued to twist her wine glass.

Wesley sat up and propped his folded arms over the table, angling his head so their conversation would be private. "I was wondering if you'd like to go back to my place and do a little... magic."

By the smoldering look and secretive tone, Alexa couldn't tell if he meant true magic, or magic of another kind. Both of which she tried to convince herself would be fantastic.

She dipped her chin and cast her eyes to the knot of wood in the table. "What kind of magic?"

"Something I think you'd like."

His whisper in her ear made her flesh tingle. Alexa bit back the smile and tried not to let herself get lost in this. She still had to watch her dark magic. Wanting this, wanting him too much, would only render this fake. That's the last thing she would ever want. *Stay calm. Be cool. Don't force it.*

"Only if you'd want to, that is."

Alexa slid a glance his way, drowning in the rich blue of his eyes. "Only if you want to."

Wesley's dazzling smile could turn her into jelly. "I'd always want to."

It had been hours since he met with Taylor, and yet those words kept echoing in his head. Two halves making a whole. The concept latched into Wesley's brain with such tenacity that he hadn't expected. It made him wonder, drove him to scheme.

If he could get her back to his place, if they could just merge their powers somehow, then they might both know what it was like to be a full witch and warlock. If the two could become one, just for a split second, he could forgive himself for invading her privacy and manipulating her into coming home with him.

He had read her thoughts at the bar. While he couldn't understand them, he understood the sentiment. Alexa cared enough about their relationship that she didn't want to be the reason they fell apart. It was just as Taylor had warned him.

Wesley knew he would have to break her heart, but he would let them share this one thing before dealing the final blow to her and her coven.

To his knowledge, no one had ever done magic like this before. There was no ritual, no roadmap for joining their powers. Half-magic blood was so hard to come by after all the cautionary tales witches and warlocks were told since childhood. Never get tangled up with a mortal unless they wanted it to end badly.

Sometimes, love doesn't listen to those cautionary tales. Wesley thought of Alexa's parents, and his own. They hadn't listened and thought love would be enough to keep them together, despite the challenges. But love was what drove her parents apart in the end. Love and the invincible forces of Twin Flames.

He found it astonishing that Alexa could still be so open to love after what happened to her. She saw what true love could do to a couple who had taken their vows. Twin Flames didn't listen to reason or morals. They just happened, and still she believed in fairytale endings. Just one more thing that he wanted to understand.

Wesley shook off that need when he opened the door for her. Even if he wanted to know, he wouldn't have the chance. He wouldn't be in Goldcrest Cove much longer. He made it clear to the owner of Torn Sails that this was a temporary gig, and he seemed fine with that. If only Wesley was.

"Have you thought about buying some art for the walls?" Alexa asked as they made their way to the kitchen as they had done before.

"Not really."

"It would mess with your flow?"

He grimaced as he pulled out the kettle from the cabinet. "Something like that." In reality, he knew buying more furniture or anything else to make this house homier would be a waste of time and money. He'd have to leave it all in a couple of weeks. "Tea?"

Alexa's heels tapped on the tile as she came up to the kitchen bar. "Yes, please! I really like that blend."

Wesley glanced and saw the way she leaned over the counter, the plunging neckline of her dress showing off the soft flesh beneath. Gods, how he wanted to do so much more than magic with her. Tearing his eyes away, he filled the kettle and set it on the heating eye of the stove.

"So, did you find anything out about Kit?" he asked, hoping to avoid all the feelings he couldn't afford in the moment.

Alexa hesitated, but then shook her head. "No, not really. She won't talk about why she came here or what she's running from."

Wesley stayed focused on her eyes, denying him the scope of her breasts as he stood with the bar counter separating them. "Anything about her past? Any names she's dropped?"

She blinked, her mascaraed lashes batting in confusion. "No, she hasn't said anything... Why don't you trust her?"

Wesley sighed and looked past Alexa, trying to find an easy way to explain everything. "Something's just off about her. She showed up out of nowhere with some story about running away, but she won't tell us from what. Kami can be unpredictable and I'd rather know her motives before it becomes too late."

Alexa laced her fingers together in front of her. "She doesn't seem malicious. She's been very nice to all of us, except maybe Caleb. But we weren't nice to Caleb in the beginning either. Shawn really likes her. They're out on a date right now."

His attention snapped back to her and his Enforcer training kicked in. "Where did they go?"

The dramatic shift in his attitude finally got her attention and she stood up. "How should I know?"

He saw his error and grounded himself again. Shawn, a human, was going on a date with a Japanese spirit of gods only knew what. It was dangerous. Potentially life threatening. But there wasn't anything he could do without blowing his cover.

Wesley held up his hands in surrender and bowed his head. "I'm sorry. You don't deserve the first-degree."

"I honestly don't think Kit is capable of doing anything bad or evil," she replied. "In fact, she's offered to help me."

He wanted to demand more answers from her, to know what it was that Kit offered to help with. But he knew he would get nowhere tonight and that's not why he invited her over. Behind him, the kettle simmered and it would soon be time to pour. He decided to busy himself with taking down a pair of mugs and promised himself that he wouldn't ask any more questions.

"Can... Can you explain something to me?"

Wesley turned to see the distress that had come over Alexa. "Anything." He hoped he wouldn't come to regret it.

"What's going on with this?" She motioned between their two bodies. "I mean... I'm always the first person to misread something, but I thought for once that I understood... Well, I just want us to be on the same page. I know where I stand... I know what I feel... But what do you feel?"

Here was the moment of truth. He could lie and say he felt nothing, that she was nothing to him. It would be easy to lie and break her heart. It'd be easier than admitting his heart and going on with the mission.

Wesley, all through his training, chose the hardest tasks. He pushed himself to complete every course in record time. He studied night and day to complete his guise of a warlock who could do it all. He had never taken the easy way out. He had never let himself surrender when it was too much. Now was no different.

Except, when he opened his mouth to tell her, the words caught in his throat. This was different. It wasn't a matter of pulling off a master level spell for his finals or coming back from a suicide mission. That was all physical. All of that he could do, because he wouldn't let his heart and mind interfere.

This was completely heart. All mind. All spirit and soul in one confession that shaped their future. Not just for the next few weeks, but for a lifetime. He would never forget the way he betrayed her and the other witches to the Council. And she would never trust another warlock as long as she lived, because they would all look like him.

Wesley walked around the counter, his eyes trained upon Alexa's waiting, hopeful expression. "That's why I wanted you to come here... I want to show you what we can do together. What we're capable of."

She didn't have a clue what he was talking about and it showed.

"I want to try something with you," he continued, drawing closer until he could feel her spiking energies.

"What?" she asked, her words breathy.

"I believe I can make you feel like a full-blooded witch. Not for long, but just long enough."

Excitement and doubt mingled in those candid eyes that he poured himself into. "How does that answer my question?"

"It's not easy magic," he admitted. "It involves bringing the two of us together on a spiritual level that few can pull off." Wesley took her hand and gloried in the soft feel of it in his palm, supple and trusting. "But I think we can. I'm willing to give it a shot for you, because I know being whole is the one thing you've always wanted."

Taylor had said she was a romantic. And they said that actions always spoke louder than words. Let Alexa read into his offer. Let her see what she wanted to see from it and that would be something she could hold onto when her world fell apart. Because, no matter what would become of them, Wesley did care for her. Let this show it.

The seconds ticked by as he waited for her reaction. Reticence was supplanted and she finally nodded her consent. That's all he needed.

He had everything they needed. The candles, the crystals, the incense. All of it originating from that mysterious back room she had yet to see. Wesley was there now, saying he had one more thing to do to get ready.

Alexa waited, her core exploding with fireworks at the idea of what was about to happen. A full-blooded witch? She couldn't even begin to imagine. Perhaps it was like just after she finished a power amplification ritual. It was like electricity arching across her skin and through her bloodstream. But she hoped that it was more than that. More than anything she could have ever dreamed of.

She wouldn't waste this opportunity. Wesley, no matter if he realized they were Twin Flames or not, wanted to do her this one kindness. At another time, in another situation where she didn't know so much, that might have been enough. Now, it wasn't. She wanted to hear the words from his lips that he loved her, wanted her, needed her. That was the only response she expected earlier. But this would have to do. After all, they had time. Wesley wasn't going anywhere.

Alexa had her back to the hall when she heard the soft slap of bare feet on hardwood floor. She turned and went as rigid as stone, as if she had just been caught in Medusa's stare.

Wesley walked into the living room wearing nothing but a dark green towel about his waist and a gentle smile that told her he meant to present himself that way. Muscles rippled across his body, the product of working out – she assumed. She would have never guessed that's what had been hiding under his shirts this whole time.

He wasn't a warlock. Not by a long shot. He was like a god. Powerful, masculine, and undeniably sexy from his toes to his blonde tousled hair. The broad expanse of smooth-muscled chest made her mouth go dry, but the sculpted ridges of his abs made it water again. What she would have given to let her fingertips flow across the chiseled triceps and feel the magic pulsate through them. It made her head giddy just thinking about all the things she wanted to do, but couldn't.

Before her lusty gaze could wander to the regions concealed by the towel, Alexa turned. It was horribly delayed if her attempt was to respect his privacy.

"I didn't hear the water running for the shower," she said apologetically, though she knew no part of him was a bit wet.

"I didn't take a shower," he answered, his words accompanied by more footsteps drawing closer to her. "I want to do this sky clad."

Alexa's hand impulsively rushed to her lips to keep her excited laugh from escaping. That must have been why he closed the blinds on the front window before leaving to undress. Never had she performed a ritual sky clad, or ever seen someone else do the same. Would he at least keep the towel on?

By the soft thud of fabric hitting the ground, she realized he wouldn't. Heat crept up her neck as her legs fought for the strength to keep her standing.

"Is... Is sky clad supposed to help?" she asked, prolonging the inevitable. If she turned and beheld Wesley in all his naked glory, she wasn't sure she could keep her composure.

"Ideally. It's returning to how nature intended us." He was just behind her now, so close she thought she would burst. "No restrictions. Nothing to hold us back from true potential."

He spoke like a real naturalist. Like clothing was some social construct and nakedness nothing to be ashamed of.

It wouldn't take much for her to do the same. The open back of her dress and the low nature of her neckline would make it so easy to just pull down the shoulder straps and be as vulnerable as he was. But her fingers were shaking so violently, she wasn't sure she could do it without broadcasting to him how nervous she was to be standing in a room with him, her naked Twin Flame, without any assurance that he loved her as she did him.

Alexa didn't have to worry about it much longer. Fingertips touched her shoulder and with aching slowness, pulled down the straps of her dress. She let out a shuddering breath, realizing that Wesley was stripping her with all the tenderness of a lover who had been given permission. She hadn't. Not verbally. Yet, somehow, she didn't mind.

Cold air hit her chest and chills washed over her breasts. Her nipples hardened and peaked. Her arms reflectively came up to shield them as Wesley worked the black velvet down her sides and to her hips. The occasional brushing of his skin on hers made her shiver uncontrollably.

"You're shaking."

She could only nod, her teeth clamped tight.

"There's no need to be afraid." He pulled aside her hair and whispered in her ear. "If you tell me to stop, then I will."

Curls of her blonde hair tickled her exposed back as he gathered it over one of her shoulders. She wanted to believe him. That there was nothing to be scared of. She was with her Twin Flame. She was the safest she would ever be.

She squeezed her eyes shut and took deep, relaxing breaths when his fingers hooked the hem of her dress and tugged it the rest of the way off. The cocktail dress pooled about her feet and she stood in nothing but her heels and black, lacy underwear.

Alexa could have sworn she heard a low, satisfied groan from Wesley as he stood back up. Her eyes rolled when his hands cupped her hips, thumbs working to snag at her panties, so he could pull them down with just as much ease and casualness as he had with her dress.

It took only seconds for them to both stand, sky clad and bare both body and soul to one another.

"Take off your shoes," he ordered, tone still smooth and melodic in her ears.

His hands fell to her hips again to steady her as she brought up one foot and then the next to undo the buckles on her heels. They fell to the wood floor with a clatter that startled her more than it should have. It was the most noise that echoed through the nearly empty house for the last few minutes.

Heat gathered between her legs as she continued to dwell on the reality of what she was doing. She had nearly forgotten what they were about to do as her mind roamed to all the things that they could do instead. The feel of silky sheets on her legs, the delicious sensation of her breasts pressed against him, his powerful hands cradling her in the final moments of a climax that existed in her own mind.

"Face me."

With unsure, shaking steps, Alexa turned in place to obey him. *Don't look at it. Don't look at it. Don't look at it.*

An unexpected chuckle rose in Wesley's throat. "You can look. I don't mind."

Alexa swallowed hard and let herself have one peek southward. No more. But, oh, what a sight it was. She didn't feel so cold anymore. Not under his stare. She looked to the burning candles across the room to keep herself from focusing on him again and realized all of the lights were still on.

"The lights..."

Wesley lifted his hand and with the precision of a conductor, ordered the lights to dim and shut off completely. The amber glow of the flames danced across their skin, bathing them in shadows and light that made this experience even more erotic.

The hand that had commanded the lights reached up to intertwine with hers. Her arms were still pressed to her breast, protecting them.

"I'll need your hands for this."

That's what she had been afraid of. If she lowered her arms, she'd be completely defenseless. But why was she afraid? Why not give herself completely to Wesley the way she wanted to? What annoying sense of self-preservation kept her from dropping her arms in the first place? It was just her body, but it felt like so much more than that. No man had ever seen her naked. She didn't even like undressing in the locker room during high school. Wesley would be her first for a lot of things and that newness, that novelty, was what terrified her.

Because in the back of her mind, she wondered if this was all genuine. If this was real and if she had been delusional this whole time. What if she was really imagining her dark magic? What if it wasn't Wesley who was her Twin Flame? What if she got this all wrong and she was about to give everything to a man who wouldn't respect her?

He must have seen her fear. Wesley tipped up her chin with the gentlest of touches so their eyes would meet.

"I promise," he began in a low, husky voice, "I'm not going to hurt you. I don't think I ever could. Trust me."

Breaths ragged and heart slamming against her ribcage, Alexa gave in. They joined hands and together, they made her arms fall away from her breasts. Her nipples, betraying her arousal, ached and stiffened, begging to be touched like the rest of her body.

His gaze didn't once deviate from her eyes in a move that showed respect. With a simple tug, he guided them toward the nexus of the candles behind the sofa. In an effort to ignore their state, Alexa never broke eye contact.

"I want you to focus all your magic into our hands," he explained. "Imagine it flowing from your chest, through your arms, and into mine. Visualize our magic mixing and merging together... Can you do that?"

Alexa nodded, but she wasn't sure if she could. There was so much else distracting her from the ritual. But for him, she would try.

Taking his cue, she closed her eyes as he did and tried to imagine all of her energies, every last drop of ineffectual magic she possessed, coursing through her nerves and bloodstream. Her skin and scalp tingled as it traveled, slow and sluggish through her body. When it reached her chest, it was like she had swallowed a chunk of meat without chewing it. The magic stuck there and burned, hardly allowing her to breathe.

"You're doing fine. Just push a little harder."

Wesley's hands gripped hers tighter and his voice revealed his own struggle in the task. Bursts of shaking breaths spilled from her nostrils as she summoned her magic up further into her chest. Firecrackers skittered around her heart and lungs. Finally, it reached her shoulders and dumped into her arms.

When their powers converged at their hands, a backflow of magic surged through them. Sparks danced behind her eyes. Shocks like popping electricity filtered across her body in the reverse direction she had sent her own magic.

But it wasn't her power that flooded back to her. It felt different. It didn't feel the same. Warm, emboldening, and tinged with a familiar essence that she could only associate with one other person. This was Wesley's magic integrating with hers. Together, they shared this flow of magic. For a moment, anything was possible.

She opened her eyes and found their sky clad bodies encircled in a pink and teal aura. Like fairy dust, it swirled around them in a windless eddy of magic. He was looking at her too, chest heaving with each breath.

Was this it? Was this what it felt like to be at full strength? Was this what it meant to be a full witch?

"Do you feel that?" she whispered, voice quivering under the magnitude of it all.

"Yeah... Yeah, I feel it."

Tears pricked at the corners of her eyes. She had never felt so invigorated, so alive. How could she walk around from day to day, knowing that this was her full potential? Visions of discontent and dissatisfaction swam before her. How could she continue to live as she was when she could be so much more?

Wesley had done her a disservice. Now she knew what it was like to be a full witch, but also how imperfect she had always been. There was no going back. She had to have this forever. Not just for a moment in a ritual.

With the excess magic circling them, Alexa held onto Wesley's hands, refusing to let go like a child who was afraid of losing a friend.

In a move so sudden and unexpected, Wesley closed the distance between them. His lips connected with hers, their bodies collided as arms wrapped possessively around one another. Her fingertips dug into his strong back, a silent need for them never to separate.

As mouths slid and savored, hands roamed and memorized the shape of their partner. Tiny moans and gasps slipped out as curves and edges were explored with hungry vigor. Alexa could feel his cock harden and rise against her, pressing into her belly.

"Is this part of the ritual?" she asked, breathless and so rapt with need for him that she couldn't see straight.

"No. It's just us. You and me." Wesley kissed his way across her quivering jaw, down her neck and to her shoulder. His hands cupped her ass and pulled her closer like a ravenous animal who hadn't eaten for days.

Her hands found their way into his hair, combing and tangling as he continued to travel south with his kisses and nips and her back arched in response to him. When his mouth enveloped one of her taut nipples, Alexa tossed back her head and let herself cry out at the jolt of pleasure that made her knees buckle. If he weren't holding her up, she might have crumbled to the floor.

The magic between them hummed and throbbed, amplifying it all. His tongue flicked and rolled in delectable patterns that made her tight and aching. Her legs spread, one coming up to hook over his waist so he would know how much she wanted him.

Wesley took the hint and hoisted her up, her legs circling his waist and the tip of his pulsing cock just at the gates. She opened her eyes for only a moment. He met her stare with his own, ready and full of that same need. But he wouldn't take her. She wiggled against him, wordlessly demanding it of him. He had brought her this far and it was only fair.

Instead, he carried her out of the circle of candles and down the hall, plunging them into darkness as they entered his bedroom. Wesley lowered her to the bed, laying her out before him so his eyes could feast upon her nakedness. All the while, their magic continued to glow in effervescent swirls of mist around them, colors raging and illuminating their skin.

Wesley sat back and Alexa stretched like a sunbathing cat beneath him, arms raised to the metal headboard behind her. Her fingers gripped the rails, inviting him to do whatever he wanted. Hands came down upon her body, stroking and tracing paths from her breasts to her hips and everywhere in between. All the while, Alexa could only gasp and shiver, a willing prisoner.

When his finger slipped between her folds, a wicked grin split his face. "You feel that?"

Alexa arched and let out a groan, unable to answer as the tidal wave of ecstasy swallowed her. She moaned again when his mouth seized her nipple once more.

Her whole body rocked in time with his, rolling and surging in a rhythm that was as old and sacred as time itself. She never wanted it to end, while still longing for more.

She whimpered when his fingers slid out of her and traced cool, wet outlines along the sensitive expanse of her thighs.

"Don't stop," she begged, tilting her pelvis up in hopes to come into contact with something a little silkier. The pressure was too much to bear and he was the only one who could relieve her suffering.

Wesley wouldn't listen to her. His hands pinned down her hips, his mouth leaving her breasts to follow the ridge of her ribs and down to the hollow of her stomach. Alexa gasped with each kiss and grazing of lips as they neared the center of her need. Tongue did what fingers had done earlier and she resisted the urge to buck against him.

She squirmed and sighed, drawing closer to the brink of that release she desired. She wanted him more than anything. Needed him inside her to receive that burst of pure magic.

Her ankles dug into the mattress, his hands having a firm hold of her knees and spreading them wide for him.

"Please!" she grieved. "Please, take me!"

Wesley let his tongue flick against her nub one last time before reversing his previous course up her body. The metal of the headboard rails bit into her palms as she held on tighter, willing herself to stay submissive while knowing full well that she was at risk of using her dark magic.

The tip of his need met hers and slid inside. Her mouth gaped at the surprising and utterly delicious feel of it all. He filled her in every aspect. Spirit, soul, and body. Twin Flames became one again and together, they soared with the magic they created.

With every slow, pulsating movement between them, Alexa could feel her powers intensifying. She let go of the headboard and clung to him, her only lifeline as she lost herself totally in the writhing, primal sensuality. Wesley was so gentle in his lovemaking, never rushing it, never forcing it.

Between fluttering eyelids, she could see their magic thickening, building until it filled the room with a kaleidoscope of color splashing against the walls and ceiling.

The release crept up on her, so suddenly and violently that Alexa nearly screamed. Wesley seized and moaned with her, coming at the same time.

For what felt like an eternity, their magic melded into one. Two auras spiraling and blending into a hue she had never seen before. It fit nowhere on a color spectrum, just like this rush of orgasmic bliss could never compare to anything she had ever felt. No ritual, no spell, no charm could ever duplicate what they just did.

Then, the magic began to fade, but not completely. The crescendo in this symphony of color waned to how it was before they ever kissed for the first time. Still brilliant and wondrous in their slow, ambling flight around their joined bodies.

Alexa, her blonde hair matted and damp around her temples with sweat, reached up to kiss Wesley's quivering lips. He supported himself upon his elbows and knees, but she could tell that he was losing the strength to stay suspended over her.

With just a slight push, he was on his back and she on top of him. She let herself sink into him, his pulsing cock still hard and filling her.

"Is that good?" she whispered, flipping her hair to one side so none of it would be in his face.

Wesley, eyes closed and gasping for breath, only nodded. There was an odd satisfaction in seeing him so sedated after sex. Maybe because, for one of the few times in her life, she felt as if she had done something right.

She wanted to feel it again and again and again until the sun breached through the darkness of their night. She wanted them to always be like this. Joined, connected, whole. She kissed down his bold jaw and to his neck, mimicking the same paths he had taken on her own body earlier. She would return the gift he had given her and together they'd feel the storm of magic one more time.

Chapter 11

Wesley was so fucked. In the literal and figurative sense. It had been a couple of hours since Alexa had to leave to go back to her apartment and he hadn't left his bedroom. The candles in the living room were most likely all burned down to cold wax puddles on the hardwood floor. He'd have to clean that up and pour out their stale, bitter tea that they never got the chance to drink.

The sex wasn't planned. It wasn't anywhere on his radar. But when he saw Alexa standing in front of him, their magic essence spinning in colorful auras around her, he couldn't help it. He had never wanted a woman so badly in his life. He wanted to taste her, to feel her warmth, to penetrate through the complex layers of her soul and find the true Alexa beneath. He had. And she was anything but the skipping ray of sunshine he had first met. She was perfect. Half-witch or not.

Round after round of sex, he had gotten used to seeing their magic outside of their bodies. To lay beneath the comforter without her made the world look dull and gray.

He knew he had crossed a line that could never be uncrossed. There was no way they could go back to the way they were, and it would be impossible for him to pretend they didn't spend an entire night, magic flowing between them to make them both whole and complete. It was addictive.

Suddenly, everything seemed perfectly clear. He couldn't finish his mission. He couldn't turn in the witches. Not even if he said that Alexa had nothing to do with the crime. He knew what would happen when he gave his report to the Council. The coffeeshop would be forcibly shut down, and all three would be placed under arrest. The other three witches of the town would be interrogated and if they were found to be accomplices, or failed to notify the Council of the crime, they would be punished too. Even if he could spare Alexa that fate, she would never forgive him.

If he were to lie and say that there was nothing going on in Goldcrest Cove, the Council might have taken his word for it, but then he would have to explain away all the strange phenomena. And that wouldn't ensure that they wouldn't send another Enforcer to investigate. If he gave up the mission and told the truth that he had been compromised, they would definitely send someone else to take his place. Someone who wouldn't understand what he now knew.

The witches weren't harming anyone. The purpose of the rule was to protect the non-magic folk from malicious witches and warlocks who wanted to harm them, as well as ensure their secret was kept safe from the public. Krystal and the others were careful and were actually helping the community, not hurting it.

The Council wouldn't see it that way. Rules were rules. Black and white. No shades of grey or fuzzy lines. But what could he do? How could he soften the truth or avoid it completely to spare them?

Forcing himself out of bed, Wesley shuffled to the kitchen, half of his nakedness covered in a pair of flannel pajama bottoms. Perhaps an option would show itself after a cup of bracing tea.

While the kettle was warming up and he began to clean the mess of exhausted candles, he heard his phone ring from the bedroom. The generic ringtone could have never warned him of who was calling until he checked the ID.

Taking a fortifying breath, he answered his commanding officer.

"It's been a few days," Wise began. "What have you found out?"

Wesley ran his hands through his hair, searching for the right words that wouldn't give him away. "I'm still exploring some avenues of information. I've talked with a few of the townspeople and haven't found much. I've gotten a job at the local bar and hope that I'll hear something there."

"What about the coffeeshop? Have you staked it out?"

"Yes, sir. I've seen nothing out of the ordinary."

He had lied again, but nothing in his voice would have betrayed him. He had hard witness evidence that they had used magic on non-magic folk.

"Hang out there for a few more days. Have you earned their trust?"

"I believe I have."

"See if they'll slip up. Once they're comfortable around you, they'll start to act different."

He knew that already. It was basic Enforcer training. Wesley didn't need to be told that, but his commanding officer clearly believed he needed a refresher. He gritted his teeth and hoped Wise wouldn't hear it on the other end of the line.

"We don't have much time and I need you on another case."

"What case?"

Wise let out a tight breath. "The Council was attacked last week. One of the elite warlocks was nearly assassinated. We didn't have a positive ID at first because the assassin escaped, but we managed to find them on surveillance."

Something in his gut tickled in the way it usually did when he was onto something. "Can you send me the debriefing?"

"You have enough to worry about with this case."

"I just want to be prepared when this is over." That much was the truth. If he couldn't be on this mission for much longer, then he needed to be distracted with something else. It'd help ease the pain of separation.

"Fine. But don't try to juggle two jobs at once. We're not even totally sure where the assassin disappeared to or what their motives were. We have all the covens on the lookout and Enforcers are combing every district."

Wesley's brows knitted together. "Sounds serious."

"It is. You'll see why when I send you the files."

They ended the phone call and Wesley soon heard the ping notification that he received the confidential email. Still, he waited until he could sit down on the couch with a clean floor and steeping cup of tea before opening the files on his laptop.

What he found both impressed and troubled him. The summarized debriefing said that the assassin managed to sneak in under the guise of a security warlock. They went completely undetected until they arrived to the Council chamber lobby where the warlocks and witches congregated before every meeting. The assassin wove their way through the crowd to Council member Harrison from Ohio and almost stabbed him. An apprentice of Harrison saw the assassin and tried to cast a binding spell. It failed, there was a chase through the Council facility, and then the culprit vanished.

He closed that file and opened the surveillance footage attached with the debriefing. The assassin was of light build and never showed his face to the cameras. Down hallways and corridors, the surveillance feed followed his progress. He had gotten so far into the compound. Wesley shook his head. He had been telling the Council for years that they needed to up their security, and this was a perfect example of why.

On the video player showed the Council lobby, packed with the elite of magic users from across North America and their attendants. Wesley spotted the intruder and tracked him through the crowd until he reached Council member Harrison. Just as the report said, he was bound by a trapping spell, broke it, and then ran.

Wesley propped his elbows on his knees and watched the ensuing fight. He didn't know what the Council expected the Enforcers to do. The video didn't even show a face. Not until the very last minute before the assassin vanished.

He turned, his face visible to the one camera. What struck Wesley was how he had looked so fixedly at the camera, as if he didn't even see it there. Or maybe he saw it there and was just too stupid to look away. It was for only a few seconds before the assassin vaporized into thin air.

Wesley backed up the video to the few frames of the assassin's face and squinted. He zoomed and cleared up the pixelated image until he realized the truth. The assassin wasn't a man, but a woman. And not just any woman. Long, dark hair spilled out from the hat at the last minute during the fight and her unique features pinned her for an oriental.

Wesley blew up the picture to consume his screen. He didn't want to believe it, but here was the evidence right in front of him. He had been right all along. There was something off about the kami and now he knew why. The assassin in the video footage was Kit, and she was running from the law.

He sat back from his laptop, mind swimming with too many thoughts to pin down. Kit had attempted an assassination on a warlock Council member and she had fallen right into their hands. He didn't know why she thought she was safe here, or perhaps she had some other plan. But he was getting ahead of himself.

His first objective had to be to ensure the safety of the witches. Kit was staying with Alexa. An assassin slept on the floor of her studio apartment.

He snatched up his phone and tapped out a hasty message, but paused before sending. It was a simple message. "Did you get home okay?" It's nothing that would have roused her suspicion, but still he hesitated. If he showed too much concern or asked too many questions about Kit, Alexa might have become defensive as she had last night. The kami had earned the unwarranted trust of the witches and if he was the one person against her, they might turn on him too. Then where would he be?

He deleted the message and rubbed at the pale stubble on his chin. He had to find a way to expose Kit, detain her, and turn her over to the council. But as his commander said, he wasn't to switch missions. Not yet. Not until he had more damning evidence for the witches. One mission would condemn them. The other would save them. How could he do both?

The answer was simple. He couldn't. And still, he had to try.

Alexa didn't have much time. Krystal only gave her an extra hour to get her ass down to the coffeeshop and that hardly seemed enough, but she'd take what she could get. If she had just gone home after the third or fourth round of sex with Wesley, she wouldn't be so late.

Yet, the big grin on her face when she thought of those extra few hours spent with her Twin Flame were well worth it.

She had given Kit a spare key the night before, so she wasn't worried about the kami getting locked out. She did, however, worry if she would wake her. Sneaking into the apartment was harder than she imagined it would be. The door squealed as it gradually swung open and the floorboards refused to let her arrival remain quiet.

With each step into the dim room, she cringed and scowled at the noise she made.

"Alexa?"

Kit's mumbled, sleepy voice broke the false hope that she could get in and out with a change of clothes without waking her.

"Yeah, it's me," she sighed. "I'm sorry for being so loud."

Little light shone through the curtained window, but she could see the shadow on the floor move.

"It is all right. You were gone for a long time."

Alexa closed her door, unafraid of letting it squeak anymore. "I was with Wesley," she replied, hardly keeping the enthusiasm from her words.

The shadow moved closer to the coming dawn, illuminating part of Kit's face. "Really? So, you had a good time at the bar?"

She bit her lip as she slipped off her heels and let them clatter to the floor. "More than just at the bar. He took me back to his place and we... you know."

Kit, like a friend who was truly invested in Alexa's love life, became instilled with fresh energy and crawled up to sit on her heels. "Tell me everything!"

She really didn't have the time. Krystal and Valerie would be waiting on her to help with the morning rush. But the chance to gossip and swoon over the amazing time she had with Wesley might have been too much to pass up. After a moment of thought, Alexa fell to her knees and told Kit everything. Absolutely everything.

It was so easy to talk to Kit. She didn't care or even realize how detrimental it was to be a half-witch. She didn't judge, didn't stigmatize. She was genuine and Alexa wanted more of that.

When she was finished and the dawn washed through the apartment, absorbing the shadows around her furniture, Kit was grinning just as broadly as she was.

"That is wonderful!" the kami exclaimed. "I am so happy for you!"

Alexa beamed, feeling for the first time that someone finally got it. All she wanted was to be loved and accepted. Wesley and Kit did that for her, and suddenly she didn't care if she showed up to work. Fuck them all. They wouldn't have been this supportive if she went on and on about how amazing Wesley had been in bed. They would only try to shut her up and tell her to calm down, that it wouldn't last. But it would. It had to. Everything they said to each other, everything they felt, it all pointed to something lasting and real. He was her Twin Flame, no matter how much everyone didn't want to think it was true.

Alexa, still clad in her black cocktail dress, replied with, "Oh, look at me talking about my night. What about yours? Did you and Shawn hit it off?"

A blush rose to Kit's cheeks and she nodded shyly. "I think we did. He was so sweet during dinner. We talked about many things and found that he knows some of my language as well. He learned it from... Manga? Is that what it is called?"

Alexa smiled and nodded. "Yeah, I think that's it. Shawn loves videogames. That's not too surprising."

"He said he liked games too." Kit's hands twisted nervously in her lap. "I only feel bad, because I could not be completely honest with him. I wish he knew more about magic. That would make things easier."

Compassion swelled in Alexa's chest and she reached for Kit's hand. "Maybe you could tell him when the time is right. We have this saying we use when we want to tell someone what we are. It's 'coming out of the broom closet'."

By the blank look on Kit's face, she realized that she didn't understand the cultural reference. After she explained it, the kami giggled at their subtle jab at humor and nodded. "Yes, perhaps one day I will come out of the broom closet too."

Alexa wagged her brows. "Did you two… have a special goodbye last night?"

If Kit could flush a deeper red, she would have been shocked. She didn't have to say anything for Alexa to know the answer to that.

When was the last time she and her witch friends laughed about boys this much? It had to be before last October. Relationships and dating were never serious before then. A few dates here and there, but nothing lasting. Nothing permanent. Now, everyone was finding their soulmate and the matter of a kiss wasn't so innocent anymore.

This is what she missed. The laughs, the smiles, and the candid talk. Why couldn't they go back to the way things were?

Alexa's phone buzzed in her purse that she had tossed aside by the door. It took some effort to stand back up without tearing or stretching her dress. It was a text from Wesley and she was glad she wasn't in heels, or the giddy jumping might have put her flat on her ass again.

"Is it Wesley?"

She nodded and opened the text. She half expected a sweet "Good morning, sweetheart" sort of message. That wasn't quite the case. It was an offer to go out that night. But not just with her, with everyone else.

Her shock drove her to read aloud, "I don't have their numbers. Can you forward the invitation?"

She looked to Kit, who wore the same puzzled look.

"He wants all of us to meet at the bar tonight. I guess to celebrate him getting the job."

Kit tilted her head. "Why not invite you only?"

Alexa set the phone down and realized it probably needed to recharge. "I don't know. I guess he wants everyone there too."

"Maybe you two will do something together afterward."

Her emotions were too tangled to think straight, but she had to put herself in Wesley's shoes. She had wanted him to have friends, to get along with the other guys and be on good terms with the witches of Goldcrest Cove. This was what she wanted and the streak of selfishness wasn't warranted.

Alexa forced a smile and nodded. "Yeah, maybe we will."

"I will go with you, but only if Shawn can come too."

The smile no longer became forced and she nodded. "I'm sure Wesley wouldn't mind hanging out with Shawn again. They hit it off well the other night."

Kit nodded in appreciation, then rose from her bedroll on the floor and straightened out her twisted pajama pants before making her way toward the bathroom. "I will only be a moment and then I am sure you need to get ready for work."

She didn't have a chance to agree before the bathroom door closed behind the shuffling kami. Alexa knew she wouldn't have time to shower, so she slipped out of her dress and pulled a pair of jeans and blouse from her drawers.

Just as she was hopping into the first leg, something flashed on the floor near Kit's bed. She looked and saw something like a jewel poking out from beneath her pillow. It was uncovered just enough to catch the sunlight from one particular angle.

The water began to run in the bathroom and Alexa took this chance to get a closer look. More than anything, she wanted to know if it was a crystal and if so, what type. Without touching it, Alexa examined it. It was about the size of a die or board game piece. The surface was smooth and glossy, but the cut was unlike anything Alexa could identify.

It wasn't a crystal, but she couldn't tell what sort of gem it was either. Its shade was iridescent, shifting colors depending on the angle and how much light passed through its prisms. Whatever it was, it was beautiful, and it held a certain measure of magic. That much she could tell.

Alexa stood and tugged on her shirt before grabbing a jacket and sliding on a pair of socks before her boots.

"I'm going to go ahead and go down!" she called to Kit.

She heard some mumbled word of affirmation before Alexa was out of the apartment and on her way downstairs into the antique store. Part of her didn't want to tell the others about Wesley's invitation, but she knew that would be wrong. If he wanted everyone to be there for his big debut as a bartender, then she'd make sure everyone knew it was their duty to come and support him. They might not have supported her, but they better support him or they would have one angry half-witch to contend with.

Chapter 12

They were all here. All but one. They came trickling in by the pairs. Krystal and Devin first, then Valerie and Caleb. The most recent, Kit and Shawn, piqued his interest more. The kami was getting cozy with the human. Was it part of her scheme to blend in or something else?

Behind the counter, Wesley could watch them all. He poured their drinks and socialized as was protocol for his job – and his mission. While he should have been focusing on the witches sitting on the barstools, he continued to check the door for the last of the party. Where was Alexa?

"How do you like Goldcrest Cove, Wesley?"

The question came from Krystal with Valerie settled in on one side and Devin on the other.

Wesley pulled a tap for a beer order at a far table and smiled as kindly as he could while ignoring the tickle of anxiety in his gut. "It's a friendly place."

"I'm guessing you'll stay for a while?" Devin asked, tipping his beer bottle to his lips.

Concentrating on the angle of the glass and making sure the suds didn't spill, Wesley shrugged. "Possibly. The future's never certain."

He passed off the glass to the waitress when he was through and looked down the line of people he wished he could call friends. He had been on plenty of missions before where he had to keep a low profile but still mingle with the suspects. Never had he become so attached to any group – or individual – in all of his missions. He had been able to stay aloof and disconnected before. Why was this place any different?

"Don't tell Alexa that," Valerie warned teasingly. "If you're not planning on staying, that is."

From the witches, he received a particularly assessing stare. One mixed with suspicion and borderline coolness that made him wonder how transparent he had allowed himself to be.

"I didn't say I wasn't planning on staying. I'm just saying that the future is uncertain."

"Man makes plans and God laughs." Shawn lifted his beer to Wesley as if that alone would help defend his case.

Wesley pointed at the one human of the group who had no clue what they all were. "Exactly."

The man didn't know how right he was. Falling for Alexa hadn't been the plan. Falling for this town or these people wasn't his plan. And now he was fucked six ways to Sunday with no route of escape that wouldn't hurt everyone involved.

"Is Alexa enough to make you want to stay?" Krystal questioned. He could hear the subtle threat in her tone and he knew that an unfavorable answer would get him in hot water with the witches.

"She might be," he replied honestly. "But, we'll see where it goes."

That, clearly, wasn't the right answer. After a pause, Valerie and Krystal bent their heads together and began talking, their backs turned from the bar. Devin seemed to notice, but minded his own business. Caleb, who had been nursing a whiskey since he came in, looked Wesley up and down with that same severe eye that came to be his trademark.

More than any of this, the sour look on Kit's face inspired feelings of unfounded guilt. What had he said wrong? It wasn't as if he and Alexa were engaged or anything more serious than that. They had made love all night and he felt an undeniable pull to be with her every waking minute of the day, but that wasn't enough for him to promise a lifetime commitment. Or was it?

That thought almost made him drop the glass he was pulling down from the shelf. He wanted Alexa. His need for her was deep and visceral, something he had never felt before. The thought of leaving her or this town almost made him physically sick. Was this love?

I can't believe he may not stay. Alexa will be crushed.

I swear to the Goddess that I will fuck his ass up if he hurts her.

What's wrong with him? Doesn't he see that Alexa's head over heels for him?

Wesley can't be this dense. Doesn't he know?

Alexa is so in love. I can't see her hurt like this.

All at once, the thoughts and feelings of Alexa's defenders came crashing through. He wasn't even utilizing his aura vision. Still, their voices rang through his mind as clearly as if they were speaking aloud. He turned his back to pour the gin and tonic for a customer, his hands shaking and temples throbbing. As soon as he could, he squeezed his eyes shut and willed away the voices. He had to focus. He had to remember the mission and the fact that a wanted assassin was sitting at his bar. This was to watch her, not to get caught up in emotions.

I almost wish he hadn't come here.

What's Alexa going to do if he leaves?

They're Twin Flames, but he's acting like this is nothing. That's not right.

Wesley turned and met Caleb's stare. Twin Flames? How could he even know? Why would he know?

I wonder if this was all in Alexa's head. He should be nuts for her too.

Should I tell her that he doesn't feel the same? Will she even listen?

How do Twin Flames even survive being separated?

He could answer Devin's question with two simple words. They don't. Twin Flames can't survive long without one another. His mother was a perfect example. His father died and she fell to pieces. The idea of Twin Flames had been one surrounded by misery and heartache. Nothing good could come of it.

Wesley glanced back to Caleb, whose brows furrowed at the sudden attention.

"You okay?" the werewolf asked. The only way he could tell this was a verbal question and not a thought was because his mouth had moved.

He smiled and pushed back the wave of anxiety. "Yeah, I'm good. Just a little loud in here."

He passed off the drink he had made and the voices finally began to fade. His power was growing, but not quite for the better. He thought if he could stay out of his aura vision, he was safe. Now it seemed that his mindreading capabilities would rear its ugly head whenever it wanted.

Not if he could help it.

The woman of the hour appeared in the doorway and with her came a rush of cold air and feelings that Wesley wasn't ready for. This was the first time he had seen her since this morning, and he didn't realize how much he missed her until now. Having her near, every bit of fear and worry melted away. He didn't hide the smile on his lips when their eyes locked onto one another.

Alexa wasn't dressed in a sexy cocktail dress, but she could still make jeans and a sweater look hot. What made her beautiful was her smile and the spirit of peace and life she carried with her. They had all turned and greeted her, but Wesley didn't hear a word. Just as it had been too loud a moment ago, now he could hear nothing but the pounding of his own heart.

She approached the counter and without any prompting or instruction, he leaned over and kissed her lips. Sweet and soft. Just like her. This was their first show of intimacy in front of her friends. Whoops echoed from Shawn at the other end of the bar and a whistle sounded from a table nearby.

"Glad you came," he said, head dizzy from her perfume and some other emotion he didn't care to name.

"Thanks for inviting me."

The touch of sarcasm worried him, but he let it slide. "What can I get you?"

"I'll just have a soda. I drove here." Alexa took a seat beside Devin at the counter, closest to where Wesley prepared the drinks.

"I could always take you home, you know."

That elicited a few more whoops of approval from the party at the counter, but Alexa only blushed as he poured her drink.

"How was your day?" he asked when he set the glass on a napkin in front of her. He hadn't asked anyone that. He often didn't care. But for Alexa, he did care. For Alexa, he forgot the world even existed. He almost forgot about his mission entirely.

A new spark glimmered in her eye under the attention. Wesley found himself transfixed as she excitedly prattled on and on about her day at the coffeeshop, the various customers who came in, and how much she had been looking forward to meeting with him that evening.

All the while, the rest looked on and whispered amongst themselves, but Wesley didn't pay them any mind. Not until the waitress handed over a drink order he had to fill. That was the only reminder that he couldn't submerge himself in Alexa's light for much longer. He was here to do a job. A couple of jobs.

He looked toward Kit and saw her talking with Shawn. Their smiles, their calm demeanor, all of it conjured that worry that Alexa had somehow willed away when she came in.

"Are you going to make that?" Alexa asked, gesturing to the order in his hand.

Wesley, as if snapped out of a dream, replied, "Oh... Yeah. Give me just a minute, okay?"

She nodded and grinned in her usual jovial way before he walked to the other end of the counter. Implementing his training, Wesley forced himself to forget Alexa, forget the Twin Flames panic, and focus solely on Kit and the mission. He had been lax for the last hour, but he couldn't put it off any longer. They might have been ready to leave.

He fixed the drink order, then approached Kit. "Do you want me to refill that?" he asked, pointed to her wine glass.

Unaware that she was in the midst of the one who would have to arrest her, she nodded and pushed it forward.

While he poured, Wesley made an effort to flip on his new ability. If he could just get a confirmation, he'd have probable cause to arrest her.

Looking at Shawn, listening to him go on about a student in his class, she thought, *This man might be my only defender if things go wrong. How long can I stay here? Am I willing to put him in danger? I care about him so much. He's incredible. I hope this lasts.*

That was enough. Wesley tuned her out and took care of the nearly empty glasses along the counter. What danger was she thinking of? What did Shawn have to defend her from? And why in the hell was a kami falling for a human? It didn't make sense. Then again, why would a human and a witch fall in love?

He needed more answers, none of which he was going to get here. He needed to get Kit alone, bind her, and put her under a truth spell, if that was even possible for a kami. It was a last resort for most missions, especially ones where he was only ordered to gather information, like with the witches. This was different. This was an attempted murder case.

The tricky part was getting her alone and keeping his intentions from the rest. They had cocooned around her so tightly, rallying to her protection that it'd be hard to do.

Then, it occurred to him. If he couldn't get her alone naturally, he'd need to do it with magic. But who would notice if he charmed her drink? Would she notice? And what exactly would he do? One to make her sick or one to make her bend to his will?

And most importantly, how could he do it without alerting Alexa? If he ran out with Kit in tow, she'd be sure to follow. She was closer to Kit than any of them.

Would he have to charm her drink too? This became messier and messier by the minute.

Her head was still spinning from that kiss. Such a simple act of affection, but it resonated almost as loud as the orgasms from the night before. Wesley kissed her in front of her friends. That was proof enough. They had to honor what she continued to harp on for days. She and Wesley were Twin Flames. They had to see that now.

And still, something else was going on. He had been so attentive to her when she first arrived, but business had picked up in the bar. Now the place was packed, much to her dissatisfaction. It seemed odd for the place to be this busy on a Monday night, but Alexa wasn't qualified to judge when a bar should be busy or not. Before yesterday, she had hardly ever stepped foot in the place.

Wesley was given drink orders left and right, refilling as needed and up to his eyeballs in work apart from fixing beverages. She hoped two things. One, that he was getting paid well for being a bartender and a waiter. Two, that this neglect of her and sudden fixation on Kit at the other end of the bar was all in her head.

She saw the way he looked at her, studying her. Jealousy wasn't a new sensation. She felt it when the other girls talked about fixing Wesley up with Taylor. But this rise of anger and sickness in her stomach at seeing how he seemed to be watching her more closely than the others was ready to make her burst.

Keep your cool. He's just distracted and doing his job.

Her foot restlessly jumped on the barstool stretcher, breaths coming deep and slow so she wouldn't lose her mind over the slight. She didn't want to be proven wrong or discover that Wesley had a wandering eye, especially for Kit.

If she let her thoughts and impulses roam, she could have her way. She could make Wesley stop looking at Kit. She could make him want her right here and now and they could slip away somewhere quiet to fulfill that need. No one would know except for her and maybe Kit, that Alexa had forced her will upon her own Twin Flame.

But she held back and bit her lips together, as if that would help hold in the dark magic. Making someone do what she wanted wasn't the way to go through life. It wasn't like her to need control over everything and everyone. So she had to hold back that need, restrain that urgent wish for Wesley to be the romantic and compassionate man she was in love with. And she knew she was in love. Every last ounce of her being proclaimed it loud and obnoxiously to the universe. Only, he couldn't see it. If he did, he wouldn't be staring at Kit while she laughed and smiled at Shawn.

A new distraction came through the Torn Sails front door and approached the bar beside her. They all turned and greeted Aaron, who still wore his cop uniform.

"Did you just get off shift?" Krystal asked, leaning to inspect his clothes.

Aaron let out a long sigh and dropped onto his stool. "I did. You won't believe the flood of calls we just got in."

Devin now craned his neck to watch Aaron run his hand through his disheveled hair. "What kinds of calls?"

"Domestic disputes. All over town."

Everyone strained their ears to hear what the cop had to say. Devin set his second beer down and it looked as if he wasn't prepared to pick it up again. "Like?"

"Any and all. You name it. Screaming and property damage mostly, but there were a few violent cases. Pete's going to get a lot of business down at his car shop. There's at least three cases of tires slashed and quite a few broken windows."

Mouths fell open in disbelief.

"Is it a full moon or something?"

Shawn's question might have warranted a sneer from Caleb, but none were exchanged. He only answered, "No, it's not." Then he let Aaron finish his story.

"We've got several locked up for the night to help them cool off. We could talk some of them down, but people are just fucking crazy tonight."

"Sorry I wasn't there to help you out," Devin lamented.

Aaron only waved him off and took the beer Wesley offered him. "It's fine. I'm just sorry I missed half the party."

The witches looked to one another, all sober enough to see that something like this wasn't natural. Something like this in Goldcrest Cove wasn't common. They might have had the occasional drunk husband or vindictive wife, but nothing like broken windows and slashed tires.

"Who did you have to lock up?" Krystal asked, probably thinking the same thing as everyone else. If they could go check out the people, they might be able to find out if this was some sort of magic problem and if it was linked with them.

Aaron gave the names, but none of them rang any bells.

None of them came in the coffeeshop, so it couldn't have been one of our charms. What could be causing this?

Alexa felt Wesley's stare hot upon her and she boldly met his gaze. What she saw nearly terrified her. Hurt and indignation seethed beneath that calm exterior. Why was he looking at her like that? Did he know something? She gave him a questioning look, but he wouldn't respond. Instead, his stare shot to Kit.

The kami, more so than the witches, appeared particularly upset. Her face was ghost-white, eyes fixed and unblinking, pointed at some random spot on the wall across from her.

A few seconds passed before she snapped herself out of the daze. Then, in a flurry of movement, she muttered something to Shawn and slid off her barstool.

"Are you leaving?" Valerie swiveled in her chair, but had to be halfway supported by Caleb, as she had more to drink so far than anyone.

Kit didn't even reply. She was too far across the bar to hear.

"She just said she had to go," Shawn told them. "Said she wasn't feeling well."

"Doesn't she need a ride home?" Devin looked over his shoulder to see her sweep out the door.

"She said she's walking." Shawn wouldn't even pay them a glance, but stared after Kit's fleeing image as long as he could.

"In this cold?" Caleb retorted before slamming down his empty whiskey glass. "No way."

The werewolf stood to chase after her, but Wesley darted out from behind the bar. "No. You stay."

Alexa made to grab for his arm as he passed, but missed by a few inches.

"Don't you have a bar to take care of?" Aaron gestured to the unmanned taps.

"It'll only be a minute."

Wesley disappeared out the door before anyone could stop him, coworkers or boss included. That wasn't good enough for her.

"Where are you going?" Krystal pleaded as Alexa slid out of her seat.

"I'll be back," she promised before halfway jogging out the door to catch up with them.

But the moment she stepped out into the wintery night air and looked out over the parking lot, she realized how silly this was. It wasn't worry for her friend that drove her to give chase. It was the green monster of jealousy whispering in her ear, lying to her that the looks and the way Wesley raced after her meant something more. It didn't. It couldn't. They were Twin Flames.

A short distance into the parking lot and she tried to push back her shame. This wasn't her. Alexa turned back with the intent to march to her seat and maybe charm her own drink with something to calm her down.

But as she neared the front door, a crash and flash of blue from the alleyway behind the dumpster caused her to freeze. A second later, sounds of some struggle reached her. She knew the right thing to do would have been to go back inside and get Devin or Aaron to check it out. But the radiation of magic from the alley told her they couldn't handle this.

Her feet moved before her mind could convince her to stay put. The moon shone its silvery rays upon a scene she never thought she would see.

From Wesley's hands slithered blue trapping magic around someone. Not just anyone, but Kit. The kami stood erect like a proud statue, chin lifted and eyes burning with a rage Alexa never thought she was capable of. Neither of them had noticed her arrival into the alleyway.

"I demand you tell me your real name and purpose here," Wesley began, his voice deep and grave with authority.

Kit only glared and refused to say anything.

"By order of the Magic Council, I demand you speak!"

A new thread of green weaved in with the blue and touched Kit's mouth. Her lips finally opened in a gasp and the words came out. "My name is Kita Saika."

"What are you doing in Goldcrest Cove?"

The battle to keep her tongue still was obvious, but Kit was powerless against the warlocks' magic. "Hiding."

Wesley let out a tight breath from his flared nostrils and pulled something from his pocket. Alexa had never seen them in person, but she knew what it was. A binding amulet. Using his magic so he wouldn't have to come into contact with her, the amulet floated from his hands and dropped around Kit's neck. The blue binding magic fell away like dispersed smoke, but the kami couldn't make a move to run, though she still tried.

"Kita Saika, you're under arrest for the attempted murder of a warlock council member."

Alexa's eyes went wide. Under arrest?

"You're... You're an Enforcer?"

Wesley spun to face Alexa, shock etched into the shadows of his face. No one spoke for a solid minute as her addled brain tried to make sense of it all. If Wesley was an Enforcer and he was on a mission, was this why he was in Goldcrest Cove? What was true from his stories and what had she foolishly believed?

Her throat closed up with tears that sprung from a wounded heart. "You've been lying to me this whole time?"

He took a step closer, boots crunching on the old snow and ice on the cement. Alexa countered by taking a step back and shook her head.

"It's not what you think," he said, bringing his hands up in surrender. His voice was so calm now, so gentle and unlike the one he had just used on Kit. What was the real Wesley?

"It looks like you just arrested my friend! What else could this be?"

"She's wanted for murder, Alexa. I can't just walk away from this."

"But you lied to me!" The tears came hot and stinging to her eyes. "You've been an Enforcer this whole time and never told me! Is she why you're even here?" The truth of the matter came like a sledgehammer. "No... You were here days before she showed up... Why did you come here?"

Wesley's throat worked, but no words came.

Alexa stamped her foot and summoned every bit of her dark magic, heedless if it was a good idea. "Tell me right now, damn it! Why are you here?"

It worked. The truth spilled out, whether Wesley wanted it to or not.

"The Council grew suspicious of the activity around Goldcrest Cove. They sent me to investigate if it had anything to do with the witches using their powers illegally. I was to find out what I could and report back to my commanding officer so action could be taken."

The very breath in Alexa's lungs choked her. He had come to spy on them. That's why he was here. That's why he asked her out and was so nice to her. It had nothing to do with her or any matter of the heart. He just needed information and she gave it all willingly.

Alexa's face twisted with rage and pain at the injustice done to her. "I trusted you!" she screamed. "I thought we... I can't believe I thought you actually liked me."

Wesley took two bounding steps to close the distance between them, but Alexa was quick to jump away from his grasp. "Just let me explain!"

"Don't touch me!" Wesley staggered back out of reach, just as she wanted. "I don't want to hear it! Fuck you and fuck the Council!"

There weren't enough words to ever describe this new level of agony. Betrayed was the only thing that came close, and yet it didn't seem to do the feeling justice. This felt worse than betrayal. Alexa turned and ran as fast as she safely could down the frozen alley and into the parking lot, sobs wreaking havoc on her body as she climbed into her Volkswagen.

She almost couldn't see the road through her watery tears as she sped away from Torn Sails Bar and Grill. She didn't know where she was going, but she knew she didn't want to be anywhere near Wesley, Kit, or her friends. All they would say is,

"We told you so" and then she'd hate them all the more for it. She didn't want to hate. She just wanted to be alone and grieve through the flood of emotions until she could think straight.

Chapter 13

"Hi, you've reached Alexa's phone! Sorry I didn't answer, but I'll call you back as soon as I can! Leave me a message!"

The phone beeped, cueing Wesley to leave that message, but he hung up before it could save. He had already left six voicemails. All begging her to call him back, to give him a chance to explain. What had come over him in the alleyway? Why had he told her the truth, even though he knew it would hurt her?

He tossed the phone on the sofa and rubbed at his unshaven cheeks. It had been a long night, which would turn into an even longer day filled with complicated excuses and plans that would turn the town on its head.

In his spare room, he had Kit bound in a trapping circle. The amulet that had kept her immobile on the drive back to his house would only work for a short time, but the trapping circle could hold much longer. Long enough for the Council to arrive.

But he didn't make the call. He wanted to prepare the witches for what would happen. They deserved a warning at the very least, since the team of Enforcers might also have to descend upon their coffeeshop too. But he couldn't make that call either. None of them would be awake at this hour and it was likely Alexa had told them everything already. They wouldn't answer his call, just like she wouldn't. He had to wait until the morning light when he could catch them at the coffeeshop.

He dropped onto the cushion beside his phone and leaned his head back to stare at the ceiling. He had ruined everything and he hardly understood why. He had been sloppy and unfocused. When Kit ran out of the bar, he knew something was up. Her thoughts were jumping from one idea to the next, disjointed and so panicked that he couldn't even read her. And even if he could, her thoughts had slipped into her native language, one he couldn't translate.

It was likely that something in what Aaron told them about the domestic disturbance calls had upset her. But the last few hours had been wasted fretting over Alexa and their shattered relationship that he hadn't given much thought to the kami in the back room or what her final thoughts in the alleyway had meant.

Wesley slammed his fist on the arm of the sofa, the wooden frame beneath splitting under the force of the frustrated blow. What the fuck had he been thinking? Alexa would never forgive him for this. Lying to her, pretending to be just an ordinary warlock, all the while he had been looking for evidence to hurt her and her friends.

He should have called off the whole mission the minute he knew he had gotten too close. Or lied. Anything but this. There had to be a way out of this mess.

Standing, his tired legs strengthened by the resolve to finish what he started, Wesley marched into the back room. Kit sat on the bare floor in the middle of the trapping circle, her legs folded and hands upon her knees. At first, her eyes were closed as if she were in a trance or meditative state. But he knew better.

"You're going to tell me everything I need to know."

Kit's eyes slowly opened and pinned him with such a placid look it nearly chilled his bones. "Or what?"

Wesley crossed his arms. "Or I'll forget that thought you had when I caught you in the alleyway."

Her dark brows twitched with puzzlement. "Thought?"

"You were thinking about someone. Someone named Kitamura Hatsune. I want to know who that is."

"You can read thoughts?"

"Don't change the subject," he ordered. "Just answer my question."

Kit's porcelain face hardened into a scowl. "Why should I tell you anything? Your job is done. Hand me over to the Council."

"My job isn't done until I find out if you had help sneaking into the Council chambers. Is this Hatsune your accomplice?"

No answer. Kit's lips tightened, knowing that he could force them open if he wanted. In hindsight, he shouldn't have been able to force her that easily. A kami was a powerful spirit. A half-warlock, no matter how skilled, shouldn't have been able to bind her and force her to speak the truth so easily. Maybe she wanted to be caught. But why?

"How much of your story is true? What harm could it be to tell me what you really are?"

A bit of her frown loosened and he knew that he had her pegged.

It took a few moments before she admitted, "I am a kitsune."

Wesley nodded at the word. "A fox spirit." Looking at her now, and thinking of all she had done before, it made sense. Kitsunes were terrified of dogs, hence her aversion to Valerie's pet and Caleb's werewolf nature. And the way she could twist and manipulate the situation to suit her fit the bill as well. "Do you have Shawn under a spell?"

Kit's eyes went wide and she shook her head. "No. No, I do not."

"Kitsunes can be seductive tricksters. I know what you were thinking in the bar, that he could be your one ally if things went wrong."

She wasn't as surprised to hear about his ability for the second time. "And do you see him breaking down your door to rescue me? I have done nothing to him."

"And the witches? Have you won them over by innocuous means too?"

"I have done nothing here."

"Except hide from the law."

Kit's grip on her knees tightened, but she wouldn't refute his claims.

A thought occurred to him. A kitsune could have wriggled her way out of this already. She could have put on a glamor to disguise herself and fly under the radar. Yet, she wore the same face that showed on the surveillance cameras. Neither did she try to twist their minds into believing that she was innocent, which she could do. They all possessed some power of manipulation, making them dangerous and extremely hard to come by. And Kit was sitting here, in a form that would condemn her, allowing herself to be captured and interrogated.

"Something about this doesn't add up," he said. "You've allowed yourself to fall into a precarious situation. You didn't hide your face from the surveillance cameras, so you knew everyone in the magic community would be looking for you. Goldcrest Cove might be a small town, but it's not the perfect hiding place for a kitsune looking to disappear. The witches here have ties to the Council. Did you know that?"

Kit's eyes fell to the floor beyond the trapping circle. "I did."

Wesley shook his head. "But you stayed. Why would you stay if you knew the whole time that you could be found out at any moment?"

"The enemy of my enemy is my friend," she replied slowly, methodically. "Goldcrest Cove is... was the safest place I could find."

None of that made sense. "These witches are not enemies with the Council."

"Not with the Council."

Wesley narrowed his eyes. "Enemies with me?"

A smile spread over her lips, one that was intended to disarm. "Not with you. Never with you. You are Alexa's Twin Flame. You can never be her enemy, no matter what you do."

He didn't want Alexa in this conversation. Didn't want to even think about her as other than just another witch in this town. He closed his eyes and took a deep breath. This was a trick. Kit was just trying to distract him.

"Who is the enemy of the witches that is also your enemy?" he asked.

More urgently, Kit sat up on her knees. "I know you care for Alexa, more than you will tell anyone else. You are wasting your time with me when you could be with her. She needs your protection."

"Who is your enemy?" he demanded, letting his voice rise to threatening heights.

"Alexa loves you! And if you love her in return, you will go after her! You must protect your Twin Flame!"

The room began to shake with the force of his anger. "Tell me who this enemy is!"

The kitsune fell silent and sat back on her heels. She was getting nowhere and she knew it. Wesley wouldn't talk about Alexa or Twin Flames. He didn't want to hear it. That was the second time he had heard that he and the witch were soulmates. The terrifying part was that he might have begun to believe it was true.

It would explain his ability to read minds. It could have been his dark magic. That didn't emerge until he first met Alexa. And it would account for his impossibly strong pull to be with her, and how devastating he knew it would be to leave her.

He paced the length of the room, waiting and thinking. How to approach this from a different angle so she would cooperate?

"Is it someone on the Council?"

No answer.

"Is it someone who lives in this town?"

Still, the kitsune remained mute.

"If you don't tell me, I can't help you."

Dark eyes snapped his way. "You are not interested in helping me. You want to give me to the Council to face a trial I cannot win."

"I haven't called the Council to come and get you."

That earned him some surprise. He revealed a bit of his poker hand all in an effort to earn her trust, if that was worth anything. He wanted to know this enemy and if there was any connection between these seemingly unrelated things. The kitsune, this second accomplice, and her choice to waltz right into a den of witches. It all meant something.

"Tell me your story," he said gently, "and I can see what I can do about taking care of your enemies. Let me be their enemy too, so we can be friends."

Wesley was crossing a fragile line here. Aligning himself with a wanted criminal might be signing his own decommission papers. He could be kicked off the force. He could be tried for aiding a felon. But hadn't he been doing that all along? He had the information to put the witches on trial as well, and he did nothing. He had been aiding and abetting their operations for days and he did nothing. One more infraction might not have worsened his case.

But Kit didn't answer him. Not in the way he wanted. "Tell me how you feel for Alexa, and I will tell you my story."

He ground his teeth and looked away. It would have been a simple thing to confess it all. To just let it all go and admit the truth he had been avoiding. Saying it all out loud could either stoke the fires or render his feelings of the power to control him any longer. He would never know which one until he finally said it.

"I care about Alexa."

Kit smiled, an odd thing for a prisoner and assassin to do. "Is that not enough for you to spare the witches? I heard what you told her. You want to give them to the Council, just as you will give me to the Council. But how can you betray someone you care for?"

"I never said I would give them over to the Council."

She leaned forward. "Is that not your mission? To find out they have been charming the humans and turn them in?"

The muscles in Wesley's back bunched. "It is... but, just like I haven't told the Council about you, I haven't told them about the witches."

"Because you love Alexa?"

"Because my objectivity in the case has been compromised."

"Because you love Alexa."

That grin on her face became more and more annoying. "The situation is now complicated."

Kit squirmed closer to the edge of the binding circle. "You and Alexa are Twin Flames. You are meant to be together. It is okay to say that you love her."

"I've only known her for a few days."

"That is nothing. Twin Flames have loved one another since the beginning of time."

"She is not my Twin Flame," Wesley asserted, growing tired of her badgering. "I told you how I felt for Alexa and now it's your turn. Tell me why you attempted to murder one of the Council members."

Kit shook her head. "You have not told me the whole truth, so I will not tell mine to you."

If Wesley wasn't liable for the damages on this house, he would have thrown his fist through the drywall.

"I am a kitsune and I am innocent. I did not attempt any assassination."

All fight left him. "I've seen the surveillance footage. You were at the Council."

"It was not me."

"Up until now, you've given me every reason to believe that you're involved in this somehow, but you say you didn't do it."

"I did not do it," Kit insisted. "But I am involved. If you turn me over to the Council, they will not believe I am innocent. That is what he wants."

Wesley crouched down to her level. "Now you're talking about Hatsune. Is he your enemy?"

Her mouth shut like a steel trap, jaw set and unyielding. That was all he would get out of her, unless he forced it. But it was enough for him to go on.

"Where can I find Hatsune?"

Again, nothing. The fountain had gone dry, but he held the key to making it flow again. He had to speak his feelings about Alexa, or whatever part Kit wanted to hear, before she would confess any more.

"The evidence against you is damning," he explained. "If you are innocent like you say, I can't help you unless you tell me who Hatsune is and why he wants you framed for the attempted murder."

Kit closed her eyes and bowed her head but would say no more.

But he had a name. A search in the database might produce something until the kitsune decided to talk again.

Wesley stood and turned to leave when Kit murmured, "Do not give up on Alexa. Tell her the truth. She has a forgiving heart."

He didn't turn back, but his steps slowed. He couldn't afford to have his mind torn two ways. He either devoted himself to this mission or he would pursue Alexa. There was no having both. Not right now.

Alexa wasn't sure at what point that night she had decided that she couldn't keep driving around. But where could she go? She didn't want to be alone, but who could she go to without hearing some sort of lecture about giving her heart away so quickly? And who would listen?

That's when she showed up at the Hayden Mansion. Krystal's car wasn't in the driveway, but Sierra was home. She was almost always home. A stiff knock on the door woke up the light sleeper and they were together in the kitchen, pouring shots.

"He lied to me from the beginning," Alexa wept as she picked up her glass of vodka, hoping it would drown out the wailings of her broken heart.

"He lied to everyone," Sierra corrected. She listened to everything Alexa had told her. Everything from making love the night before to catching him in the alleyway.

"And Kit, too!" Alexa cried. "She's wanted for murder!"

"She probably thought she could hide out here and she'd be safe." Sierra knocked back the shot and winced at the kick it gave. "She might have never suspected that Wesley was an Enforcer."

Just the word brought on fresh tears. Alexa couldn't even bring the glass to her lips before laying her head down on the cool granite countertop. "How could I have been so stupid?"

Sierra's hand rubbed up and down her back. "We were all a little stupid. Hell, I thought it was neat to have a warlock in town for once. I was excited too. None of us would have thought he was an Enforcer."

"Oh, don't say that word!" Alexa sat back up, trying in vain to keep her composure.

"Sorry... All we can do now is try to repair the damage."

Damage. What damage had he done except to her heart? "He made me think that he cared about me. That he loved me. I bet he's not even my Twin Flame. It must have been some random guy that walked into the shop, just like the other girls said."

Sierra grabbed Alexa by the shoulders and turned her so they could face one another. The older witch, hair unkempt and still wearing her pajamas, took on the look of a mother about to scold her child. "Listen to me. If you believed he's your Twin Flame, if you feel this strong connection with him, then I believe he is. It doesn't matter what he did. He's your Twin Flame and that won't change."

Alexa sniffled and shook her head. "But he's a... you know. And he's here to get all of us in trouble with the Council. They'll find out about what I did last October with that guy and the second-hand charm and – "

"Don't even think it!" Sierra gave her a good shake. "You aren't going to get in trouble and neither will Krystal or Valerie."

She pointed a weak finger at her. "But you knew about the coffeeshop too, right? Krystal told you."

Sierra gravely nodded. "Yeah, she told me. And my mom knows too. I don't know who else, but I can promise you that we will be safe through all of this."

"What about Wesley? If he's my Twin Flame and it's his job to bust witches for using magic on non-magic folk, then we'll still have to shut down the shop."

"No one is shutting down the coffeeshop." Sierra pulled out her phone. "I don't care if it's three in the morning. I'm calling my father."

Alexa gasped and lunged for the phone the minute it came out of her pajama pocket. "You can't! Then he'll find out too!"

The older witch held the phone high above her head, and with the differences in their height, there was no way Alexa was going to get it back. "I'm not going to tell him everything. I'm going to ask if he knew about Wesley coming here. He might be able to find a way out of this for us."

"You think he would do that?"

Sierra only shrugged. "It's worth a shot."

She left Alexa alone in the kitchen while she talked on the phone with her father, one of the Elite Council warlocks. If anyone could get them out of this scrape, it was him. But she didn't have any faith in that. If the Council gave the order to spy on the coffeeshop, then what more could he do since Wesley could prove them guilty?

Holding back another bout of tears, Alexa took the shot of vodka and threw it back with practiced skill. The liquor scorched her throat and warmed her chest, but the pain didn't go away. She grabbed for the bottle to pour her another, but couldn't bring herself to down it in the same way.

Alexa slumped on the kitchen barstool. How could she have been so naïve? Not just with Wesley, but with Kit, too. She had been the one to convince her that she possessed the Gift of Influence. Maybe that had been a lie, just to butter her up for something. They had both conned her into trusting them, and now she was left empty and right back where she started.

This despair clawed at her gut until she thought she couldn't bear it. What hurt just as much as the betrayal was the knowledge that they had all been right. Wesley didn't belong to her. She had flung herself off the deep end and allowed herself to believe there was more to his kindness than what was on the surface. He probably laughed at her the whole time. He just wanted an easy fuck while on the job and preyed on her vulnerability.

All of it had been just one big con to get her to say something condemning about her friends and the coffeeshop they owned. At least she had never openly said anything like that. Her one consolation was that she had kept their secret. But never again would she be fooled.

With a burst of courage and defiance, Alexa stood from the stool and marched to the back door. The cold wind chilled the moisture on her face.

Alexa fished out the moonstone from her pocket, the one she had been cherishing since that first night together in Wesley's home. He wanted her to have something that would help her magic, that would lighten her load and make her feel like she could start fresh and forget all the heartache that came before.

A lot of good it did. She hated the sight of it now and the way it caught the light of the back porch lantern. With one good chuck, the rock flew through the air, whistling before burying itself in the snow. She didn't want to be reminded of it.

When she closed the door and doused herself in the heat of the kitchen, Sierra came back from the living room.

"My dad didn't know anything about Wesley being here," she said. "But he's going to call up the head of the Council in the morning to find out. I didn't say anything about why he was here, just that there was an Enforcer in town."

The word didn't sucker punch as hard as it did a few moments ago. Alexa nodded and scrubbed at her cheeks to get rid of the last tears.

"Are you going to be okay, honey?" Sierra asked sympathetically as she set her phone down on the counter.

With a wounded heart, Alexa nodded. "Yeah, I think I'll be okay now."

What the other witch didn't know was that she made a vow. A vow that she would never fall so hard again. Never would she let a man destroy her like this. If more Enforcers came to Goldcrest Cove, they wouldn't find her a weak link. She wouldn't be so open and pliable. Not anymore.

Her heart was officially closed and under construction until further notice.

Nothing. Not one thing on a Kitamura Hatsune. Not even from the Japanese Council database. Perhaps it was an unknown alias.

Dawn broke through the living room window, the cool blue of the morning combating with the harsh LED lightbulbs. He had gotten no sleep the night before, but Kit had dozed off in the binding circle. He'd get no more information out of her until she awoke.

Maybe it was the exhaustion or the frustration from coming up empty handed, but Wesley began to wonder if it was worth the trouble. Kit claims she didn't do it, but she was involved somehow. That would have been enough months ago if he had been the first Enforcer to track her down and find her. Something had changed. He didn't see things so black and white anymore. Shades of gray began to blur and confuse him. Just like the coffeeshop. The girls were breaking the law, but for a good purpose. Did that make them bad? Or did it present the case that all rules should be bent every now and again?

If he could have gone back in time and told himself not to go to Goldcrest Cove, he would have. This town and everyone in it had done nothing short of fucking with his head.

The doorbell rang and he jumped. No one knew where he was, except...

Wesley rushed to the door and swung it open. Alexa stood on his porch, eyes red and puffy as if she had been crying, her expression rigid, lips puckered in a scowl. He was too relieved to see her, the mix of anger and sorrow in her face mattered little anymore.

"You got my messages?"

She only nodded and he let her inside. Her flowery perfume met his senses and he wanted nothing more than to take her in his arms and pretend none of this ever happened. Before he could even get close enough to touch her, she held him back with a simple sign for him not to come any closer.

"Where's Kit?" she asked, voice quiet and broken.

"She's taken care of," he replied, trying not to let any of the worry enter his own voice. "I haven't hurt her and I promise that I won't."

Alexa wouldn't look at him, but let her gaze wander around the living room and kitchen. He agonized over her silence and decided that he couldn't waste another minute.

"Listen, I know I hurt you. I know I broke your trust. I never meant for it to get this far. But the minute I saw you, I... I lost my head. I've always been so cool under pressure, but with you, I can't think of work or missions or anything else but you and being with you."

She gave him a hard look, but anger stole her voice.

"I know about what you and the witches do at the coffeeshop," he hurried on. "But I'm not going to tell the Council. I'll lie and tell them that there's nothing illegal going on in Goldcrest Cove. I understand why you charm the drinks and I see what good it does. I know about the single mom and the daughter, the one that was in there the other day. I think if I hadn't seen what you do and only knew the facts from a report, I wouldn't have seen it the same way."

He stepped closer, testing her limits, but she wouldn't shy away.

"Since I met you, I see everything so differently now. I used to think I understood people and their intentions, but I know now that I didn't understand the half of it. You did that for me, and... I can't bring myself to hurt you or your friends."

Wesley swallowed hard and drew dangerously near to her, feeling himself pulled in by her essence and soul. He needed her and hadn't realized just how much until he let it all go.

"I love you, Alexa... and I know you love me too and I don't want to ruin this. I want to make it right... Please, say something."

Desperation drove him to slip into his aura vision, but he saw nothing. Alexa only continued to stand in front of him, staring with daggers for eyes and arms crossed. Not a hint of color and not a peep from her mind.

Wesley straightened and shot out his hand to grab her shoulder. Only, just like her aura, nothing was there. Her image vanished like a mirage and he was alone again.

He shook his head and slapped his cheeks, wondering what the hell had just happened. Had he been dreaming? Or was this something else? It all felt real. Her smell, her voice, her essence. And yet, she wasn't really here.

Realization set in and Wesley sprinted to the back room. The binding circle was completely empty. He let out a booming curse and slammed his hand on the doorframe. Kit must have created Alexa's illusion to distract him while she broke the circle somehow. That circle was one of the strongest he knew. How could she have slipped out of it so easily?

She could have been anywhere by now. At least he knew what she was and that could help him track her down. But he couldn't do this alone. It had been sheer dumb luck that they happened to be in the same town together. Tracking like this, he needed help. And if he couldn't call on other Enforcers, he had to resort to other means.

He checked his watch. Perfect Books and Brews should have been open by now. There, he'd find the only help he was liable to get in Goldcrest Cove. The real question was if they would be willing to give it at all.

Chapter 14

Alexa was actually thankful that the coffeeshop was busy that morning. This kind of traffic was unusual for a Tuesday, but she rolled with it. Anything to keep herself busy and her mind off of Wesley, Kit, and the whole business. It felt like a bomb was waiting to go off and they were all seconds from the fallout. Every moment, Krystal and Valerie waited for word from the Haydens or expected Enforcers to storm through the doors.

She and Sierra had told them everything just before the shop opened. Perfect Books and Brews had stayed open through a serial killer's murder spree, when the dead rose from the graves, and they would stay open while the Council was ready to drop the hammer on their operations.

Still, nothing came. The other two witches remained on pins and needles, but Alexa knew better. Wesley didn't have a case. He never saw them charm a coffee and she never told him. The others confirmed that they never spilled the beans either, and while Kit might have had an idea about their operations, they weren't sure if she would give them away. They had tried to hide her, after all. The kami owed them something in return.

But who could they trust anymore? Who was friend and foe in this town?

While Alexa's faith in humanity was shaken, she did find some allies. Every other person who came up to the counter asked Krystal if Alexa was feeling well.

"Is she sick? She doesn't look so good."

"She seems tired."

"Did something happen with her mom?"

The citizens of Goldcrest Cove and the loyal customers who had known them for years all noticed the change in her. Alexa wore muted colors instead of her bright pastels. The smile that brightened everyone's day was displaced by a sour frown that added years to her face. But she couldn't bring herself to be the way she was before. She needed time to hurt and heal. Her friends understood that, and gave her space.

Much to her astonishment, they didn't scold her or say "I told you so." They had a right to say it. They had known all along that Wesley wasn't the one for her, that he might have just been playing her. Anyone else would have gloated over their superior gut instincts. Instead, they rallied around her, comforted her, and consoled in what way they could. She never expected it or even asked for it. She had a safety net all along and had almost forsaken it for the love of a man who had turned into a traitor.

Through it all, murders, necromancers, and Enforcers, they'd had one another's back. Alexa wasn't sure how she could have ever doubted it.

The bell over the door jingled to life one more time, but none of them would have expected to see Wesley striding across the lobby. Alexa was frozen. She had never thought she would see him again. He had his assassin and his mission was done. Why was he still in Goldcrest Cove?

Krystal finished up with her customer with all the politeness she could muster before glaring at the new arrival. Valerie was already taking off her apron and worked to tie her hair back into a ponytail.

"This mother fucker doesn't know when to take a hint, does he?"

Alexa's stupor was broken by the threat of an all-out brawl in the coffeeshop. She jumped in front of Valerie and did her best to block the way before Krystal stepped in with a quick charm to make Valerie stay put.

"I don't want any trouble," he told them.

She couldn't even turn to face him, but listened to the ensuing conversation while she stood guard over the feistier witch.

"You sure found it, jackass," Krystal replied. "Alexa told us everything."

"I had a feeling she would." There was a pause and she could feel his gaze rake down her stiff back. To hear his voice, to know he was near, brought on all the feelings she had sworn off. She still loved him and she despised herself for it. After all he had done to them, she should hate his guts, but all she wanted was to run into his arms and say all was forgiven, even if it wasn't.

"I came to explain myself and ask for help."

"You really are a dumbass, then," Valerie spat. "You think we would help you after you tried to incriminate us?"

"Please, let me explain."

"This isn't the time or the place for that," Krystal said. "We have a store full of customers and this isn't a conversation for them to overhear."

"You're right. Can we talk in private?"

"I don't even want to give you the time of day. You're upsetting Alexa and you have no business here. I suggest you leave."

Finally, she turned and bravely faced the man who broke her heart. "No. You can't leave." The tremble in her voice might have come off as anger, but Alexa couldn't stop shaking as her blue eyes met his. "You owe us an explanation... You owe *me* an explanation."

No one denied her correction. Out of all of them, he had injured her the most.

"Can we talk in private? In a back room maybe?"

"You aren't going anywhere with her," Valerie retorted. "Whatever you say to her, you can say to us too."

Wesley glanced over his shoulder to the crowd and it was then Alexa noticed how ragged he looked. Everything about him screamed "tired and fed up". She looked to the same crowd of customers and had an idea.

"Just wait a minute," she told them.

Even if her Gift of Influence wasn't dark magic, she could still use it somehow. She forced her intent into the open, that all the humans would leave the shop. The witches and warlock watched her steady look of concentration. One by one, the customers rose from their chair for various reasons, and walked out their door. Most received some urgent text or call asking them away. Others simply downed their scalding coffee and left.

Within just a few moments, the place was empty except for the four of them.

"How did you do that?" Krystal asked.

Now free to talk of magic in the open, Alexa replied, "It's what I was telling you two before. My dark magic... Or, whatever I thought was my dark magic."

"So, it's true." Wesley looked as if he could have been blown over by a stiff wind.

Hope sputtered in her heart, but she snuffed it out. "I said it's what I thought my dark magic was."

Wesley made to take her hand, but Krystal ran interference.

"Say what you want," she ordered. "You're clear to."

A muscle in his jaw clenched and he reined himself back from the counter. "I am an Enforcer. I was sent by the Council to see if you three were using magic on non-magic folk. They knew about the strange things that have been happening and they grew suspicious when Caleb settled here. They just needed to know that everything was on the up-and-up."

Krystal folded her arms. "And, as you can see, we haven't broken any rules or –
"

"But you have."

The three witches started at the statement.

"You have no proof!" Valerie contested.

"I do have proof." Wesley gestured to one of the tables. "I saw it in action. You charmed the coffee of that single mother. A fortune charm, I think it was. The Council sent me, because I have a unique sensitivity to magic when it's been used. It's how I knew you were a half-witch even without your file."

"Files?" Krystal nearly shrieked. "You have files on us?"

"On all the witches. Amber, Taylor, Sierra, and even Devin and Caleb. I knew everyone before I even came to Goldcrest Cove."

Valerie grabbed at her amethyst pendant and made to take it off, mumbling curses and threats under her breath. It took all of Alexa's wiliness to keep it on. Even if Krystal had her trapped in place, Valerie's dark magic was powerful enough to reach Wesley from across the lobby.

"All right, fine!" Krystal seethed. "You know we charmed a coffee, but you have no idea about what we really do and why we do it. You've only been here for, what, a week? You don't know a thing about us."

"I know enough. I know about the rash of murders last October and that you had something to do with that. I know about the necromancer, the demon, and everything in between..." He looked pointedly at Alexa. "I have my dark magic too. It came when we first met... I can read your thoughts."

Her lips parted, the wind knocked from her. Read thoughts? So, he knew everything. He didn't even need her to speak to know her innermost feelings.

They were all stunned, unable to speak. Only listen.

"It came on suddenly at first. I could hear the thoughts of everyone in the room, but I trained myself to focus and pick out one mind among many. I've picked up bits and pieces from everyone, including Aaron and Shawn. Pieces of the puzzle came together after a while and..." Wesley took a breath. "I know you blame yourself for those murders, Alexa. You charmed the priest's coffee, but it got out of hand and infected a man in his congregation who was too susceptible to its affects. But it was a second-hand charm. You couldn't have known what would happen."

Tears pressed against the edges of her eyes, but she wouldn't allow them to spill down her cheeks as they had before. Wesley's words, the words of her Twin Flame, should mean nothing to her now. He'd have to work a lot harder than that to win back her trust.

"This is why the law is in place," he continued. "To keep bad things from happening to people who don't deserve it. Magic is powerful, but it has to be used wisely."

None of them said a thing. They all knew this lecture by heart, and after twenty-something years of it being drilled into them by witches older and wiser, they still ignored the rules. Wesley wouldn't make a difference.

"So, now you know." Krystal's voice was laden with all the coldness he deserved. "When does the rest of your squad come to cart us away?"

A spear of ice pierced Alexa's spine. When, indeed.

"They aren't. I haven't called them and I won't."

One surprise after another. The witches looked to one another, a silent question if the others believed him.

"I understand why you do the things you do," he went on. "Do no harm. That's our creed. And you don't do harm. You don't intend to. Meddling in the humans' affairs can get messy all too quickly, but you've managed to keep it quiet up until recently. I admire what you're doing here and I'm going to tell the Council that I didn't find anything."

They all blinked in astonishment. This wasn't what they had expected out of Wesley. Alexa half expected this to end in tears and binding amulets and a "Permanently Closed" sign stuck on the front door. Instead, it seemed they were safe.

"We're in the clear?" Valerie clarified.

Wesley nodded. "You're in the clear."

"And what about Kit?" Alexa questioned, sifting through the emotions to touch on the deeper issues at hand. They would have time for feelings later.

He grimaced. "That's what I need your help for."

"What? The kami slip your cuffs?" Valerie retorted.

"Not a kami. A kitsune. But, yes. She did."

"A kitsune?" Krystal gasped. "Really?"

"She confessed that much to me this morning." Wesley went on to tell them everything about the attempted assassination at the Council Chambers and how he knew Kit was involved, but innocent. "I read some of her thoughts and I have a real reason to believe that she didn't try to kill the warlock, but all I have is a name and a theory."

"Is she in trouble?" Alexa asked, her hand anxiously placed at the hollow of her throat.

"I think so, but she won't let me help," Wesley explained. "I think she's being set up for the murder, but I don't know why. I also don't know where she could have gone."

Valerie, now settled back from her fury, folded her arms. "And how can we help with that?"

"Kitsunes and kamis can't be tracked through scrying, which is the main way that Enforcers can find them. That's probably why they're having so much trouble finding the assassin. When I asked her why she would willingly hide out in a town of witches that could turn her in, she said, 'The enemy of my enemy is my friend'. She wouldn't explain what she meant, but the enemy isn't the Council and it's not me."

Krystal shrugged. "We don't have any enemies."

"Maybe she's talking about the real assassin," Alexa offered. "Maybe he's the common enemy, which makes us friends."

Wesley nodded. "I think so, too. She trusts you and I think she would have come to you for help if she ran from me."

"We haven't seen her," Valerie said. "We thought you would have taken her away from here already."

"I should have, but like I said, I don't think she's guilty and the Council will look for any reason to sentence her to death."

"The surveillance footage would be the only evidence against her," Krystal added.

"And the only thing that could save her would be your witness," Alexa told Wesley. "You read her thoughts, after all. You know someone else did it."

"It would be even better if we found the true assassin, so we can get a confession from him and clear her name."

The other three could agree on that much.

"When did she escape?" Valerie asked.

"Just a few hours ago. I've tried to get a pin on her. Sometimes magic folk will leave a trail of magic in their wake after they use it, but I can't pick up on anything."

"I went to my apartment before coming to work and she wasn't there."

"Is her stuff still there?" he asked, voice pitched with urgency.

"She didn't have anything, remember? Just her dress." Alexa's mind went back to the gem under Kit's pillow, but didn't think it was important to mention. It was likely she had it on her when she was arrested anyway.

"Have you checked with Devin or Caleb?" Valerie asked. "Devin could put out an APB on her for the county and Caleb might be able to track her scent using the pillow she slept on."

Wesley waved off the idea. "I don't want to get too many hands in this before we know how deep the hole goes. This might be bigger than anything this little town can deal with."

Krystal propped a hand on her hip. "You said so yourself. We've dealt with psycho serial killers, demons, and necromancers. Now we have an escaped kitsune and you think we can't handle it?"

He tread softly forward, his words slow and precise. "Whoever this Kitamura Hatsune is, he was willing to sneak into the Magic Council and frame Kit for the crime. She's gotten into something and we don't know exactly what yet."

"All the more reason to work that much harder to find her," Alexa stated. "Have you checked with Shawn? He might have heard from her. He was closer to Kit than any of us."

It was as if a lightbulb had turned on in Wesley. "No. I hadn't thought of him. Kit did think last night at the bar that he might have been her only ally if things went wrong."

"Things have definitely gone wrong," Valerie smarted.

"Shawn should be at the school?"

Krystal nodded. "Should be."

Wesley turned and made his way toward the door. "I'm going there now. If you see Kit, call me and try to keep her occupied."

Alexa wasn't thinking when she pulled off her apron and hurried after him. "I'm coming with you."

They all made some plea for her to stop, but she had her mind made up.

"If something happens – "

Alexa wouldn't let Wesley finish the idea. "Then something will happen and we will deal with it. Kit is my friend and if she's in trouble, I'm going to help."

A smile, the first she had seen since everything fell to pieces, graced Wesley's perfect mouth and her knees wanted to buckle. "Your friends don't deserve you. You know that right? You're far too loyal."

Alexa frowned. "More like far too trusting. I care too much."

"That's not a bad thing," Krystal said, one hand on Alexa's arm as if that would stop her. "Promise you'll look after yourself." The shifting look to Wesley said enough.

She nodded and together they stepped out onto the cold sidewalk. The door closed behind them just as a large party of customers approached the coffeeshop.

"Alexa, I – "

She held up a hand. "I'm not ready to make nice with you just yet." His Pontiac was parked on the curb and she wouldn't stop until she reached the passenger's side. "You really hurt me and I've got to get over that. So, for now, let's just focus on finding Kit and getting this over with. When you've got your man, we'll part ways and forget this whole mess."

Alexa refused to look up and stared at the door handle, waiting for him to unlock it. Instead, his hand braced on the top of the car and she could see the plume of mist coming from his mouth.

"Forget? I don't want to forget."

She shut her eyes against the wave of feelings that wanted to swamp her.

Not here, Wesley. Not right now. Just give me time.

Just as she suspected, he must have been reading her thoughts. He moved away and toward the driver's side before the door unlocked.

"Do me a favor," she said as she buckled in. "Stay out of my head."

He started the engine and heat burst from the vents. "I'll try."

"Try hard."

Never had she thought she'd be sitting on these leather seats again, drinking the aroma of his cologne and willing her heart to stop slamming against her chest. Alexa took long, deep breaths to sooth her raddled nerves. This was just business. Get the job done, so they could move on and have closure. The coffeeshop was safe, but her heart was back on the chopping block and another person she cared about could have been in mortal danger. Would this ever get easier?

So much for having a forgiving heart. Wesley had never seen this side of Alexa. Never even thought it existed. He had done more than break her trust. He broke her spirit.

The drive to the school was far too silent and awkward. If things had been different, he would have taken this time to explain himself, more than he had to the other witches. Alexa deserved more heartfelt words than he could fathom, but she didn't want them.

But she still wanted him. That was clear by the sparkle of golden aura within the blazing black hate he saw in the coffeeshop. That alone gave him hope. Maybe they weren't a total lost cause after all.

Then again, what good was that? He still had a mission. He was still an Enforcer. Even if he could make it up to her somehow, what would their relationship look like? He'd never be in Goldcrest Cove, but always on call somewhere. She'd be lonely and miserable. To be honest, he would too. Just being this near to her again made him burn with a need to touch her, to make all the pain go away. How could he erase the heartache that he, himself, had put there?

Getting passes to see Shawn was the easy part. Navigating through the crowded hallways of the school was harder. It hadn't been too long since Wesley had been like any of these kids, going to class and worrying about the next exam or if their crush would ask them to the dance. Times were easier then, especially for half-magic blooded people like him and Alexa. They could hide their identity much easier than those witches who still grappled with not letting their magic accidentally slip during a lecture.

Alexa hadn't even looked his way since they got out of the car, her focus and strides evident of her need to get this over with. Single-minded determination for one thing only. Saving her friend. That much, he could admire. She would have made a great Enforcer, if she were a man. Hell, the way she looked right now, she could have done it all as a woman and half-witch to boot. He almost had trouble keeping up with her.

They came to Shawn's classroom and found him standing just outside of it, eyes skimming over the heads that passed by and greeting those that scampered through his door.

He didn't spot them in the throng of students until they were nearly beside him. He smiled at first, but upon seeing their severe expressions, thought better.

"Hey, guys! Something wrong?"

"We need to talk," Alexa began, taking the wheel straight from Wesley's hands. He might have been offended if he didn't understand her better than that.

Shawn thumbed into the classroom. "I've got a lesson starting in a few minutes."

"This will only take a couple," Wesley said. "It's about Kit."

That got the teacher's attention. A student made to pass him by and he waved her down to ask her to take care of the class while he was gone. Then, he led Wesley and Alexa through the thinning crowd toward the copy room just a few doors down. He shut the door and they were alone. The roar of teenage voices dimmed to a murmur.

"What's wrong with Kit?" he asked, a bit of panic rising in his voice.

"Have you seen her today? Or has she contacted you?" Alexa countered.

Shawn shook his head. "Not since last night when she ran out."

"She's missing and we…" Wesley picked apart his words as carefully as possible, since Shawn didn't know the whole truth of the matter. "We think she may be in a bit of trouble and we're trying to help."

His eyes widened. "What kind of trouble?"

"It's a little complicated," Wesley said.

"Is Devin helping you with this?"

Wesley saw Alexa glance his way for half a second. "We're trying to handle this 'in house', so to speak."

Shawn nodded. "I get that. I don't think the cops can put out a missing person's report this soon anyway. What do you need to know?"

"Did she ever mention a guy named Kitamura Hatsune to you?"

"Never. Is he the one making trouble for her?"

Alexa sighed. "We don't know yet. Did she ever mention some place special? Some place she might run to?"

Shawn shook his head. "Never even talked about her hometown with me. Bad memories, I guess. So I just left it alone."

Wesley filed that bit of information away for later and asked, "Do you have your phone?"

The teacher pulled it out and without asking permission, Wesley took it from his hand.

"What are you doing?"

"Calling her. She'll see your name on the caller ID and she's more likely to answer for you than any of us."

Shawn balked. "Why? She's rooming with Alexa."

There was no way to explain what he had read in Kit's mind the night before, but Alexa was quick to cover for him. "She really likes you, and we tried calling before, but she wouldn't pick up."

A smooth lie.

Wesley navigated through Shawn's phone, ignoring the chain of text messages between him and Kit, and fished out her number to call. It rang three times and then clicked.

"Shawn?"

Wesley gave a nod to the others to confirm it was her.

"Kit, don't hang up."

"What did you do to Shawn?" Her accented voice slipped into a string of angry Japanese that he didn't understand, but could tell by the tone that they weren't friendly words.

"Listen... Listen to me! I haven't done anything to Shawn. I need you to calm down. We just want to help. Where are you?"

"I will not tell you."

Wesley's nostrils flared. There was only so much he could say in Shawn's presence. "You can't run forever and if you're in trouble, your friends want to help. You said yourself that we could be your friends in this mess. Let us be that for you."

"How can I trust you?"

He frowned. There wasn't any good way to answer that. She couldn't. Neither could Alexa. Unless they made the choice to.

Perhaps Alexa could already sense that this phone call wasn't going as planned, because she snatched the phone right from Wesley's ear and pressed it to her own. "Kit, it's Alexa... Yes, I'm here with Wesley. I don't blame you for running, but he's telling the truth. We just want to help, but we need the whole story..."

Her eyes lifted to Wesley's with speculative wonder. "Yeah, I can meet you... I'll tell him... Okay, just give me about ten or so minutes and we'll be there."

She hung up the phone and carefully handed it back to an impatient Shawn. The bell rang in the halls, announcing the beginning of the next class. "What did she say?" By the urgency in his voice, she knew he wasn't nearly as concerned for his students in that moment.

"She wants to meet me at the park to talk."

"Great. Let's go." Wesley was two steps toward the door when she grabbed his arm.

"She wants to meet me alone."

He shook his head. "Not happening. I'm going too."

Alexa stamped her foot. "You can go, but she wants to talk to me alone."

He narrowed his eyes and tried to ignore the way her lips puckered in a cute way when she was playing stubborn. "Why?"

"How should I know? Just be glad she's willing to come out of hiding to see me."

Shawn intercepted once more. "Are you two going to fill me in on the details or...?"

"Not right now, but we will," Wesley assured. "Once this is all over, we'll have a long talk."

Alexa's brows arched high into her forehead. "Wesley," she hissed in aggravation.

He ignored her. "It's just too much to go into right now. We'll keep you up to date on Kit as much as we can."

The human blew out a breath and wagged his head. "Like I'm going to be able to focus on teaching history with all of this going on."

They all left the copy room and Alexa, still not on board for what Wesley just promised, gave Shawn's arm a comforting squeeze. "Just know she's in good hands and she'll be fine."

His smile was half-hearted and none too certain. "I'll try."

With the same long, confident gaits that carried them into the school, they made their way toward the exit.

"You can't tell Shawn about us," Alexa whispered to Wesley, the only other sound in the halls being their heavy footsteps.

"I didn't say I would tell him about us," Wesley corrected. "I said we would explain everything. I have no intention to. A quick charm will help him forget the whole affair and as long as no one else lets it slip, we're in the clear."

"Clever." The note of praise in her tone made him smirk.

"I've built my life on being clever."

"Right. I almost forgot."

The fresh disdain wiped that smirk right off. "I wish I could make you forget more often."

Alexa pointed a stern finger at him. "Don't you dare try to charm me into forgetting all this too."

It was likely that even if he wanted to, he couldn't. Not because he couldn't bring himself to do it, but because the wounds he had inflicted were far too deep for any charm to undo. He could numb her pain, but never completely get rid of it. Only time and love could do that. Both of which he felt they were running short on.

Chapter 15

The quiet in the car made her even more unnerved than she had anticipated. Alexa thought she wanted the silence, wanted him to just leave her alone and let her deal with the thoughts and feelings that couldn't be patted down.

But the reality that he was with her, occasionally looking her way while she tried to hold it all together, made it all infinitely harder to resist him. Her heart kept pulling, willing to close the distance despite everything they had just been through in the last twenty-four hours.

She should have hated him for eternity for lying to her and betraying her trust. Then why the hell did she still want to kiss him? To feel his hands on her body and know that he was real and all hers. She thought if she could just ignore him and focus on the task of finding Alexa, it'd be fine. It wasn't, and she was ready to burst out of her skin if something didn't happen.

The drive to the school was the same as the short drive to the park. Excruciating. The minute he threw the transmission into park, Alexa grabbed for the handle of her door, but found it locked. She continued to vainly jerk, but it still wouldn't budge.

"You're going to break it," he mumbled.

"Then let me out!" The only way to relieve this pressure building between them was to get out of his car and run for the gate.

"No. Not until we get some things clear between us."

Oh, Goddess. Here it comes. Alexa pressed her fingers between her brows, feeling a headache coming on.

"You don't have to say anything," he said. "Just let me talk."

Alexa lifted her gaze to stare out the passenger side window until every hint of his visage was out of sight. If she had to listen to him, she didn't want to have to look at him too.

"What I did was wrong," he began, "but it was my job. I came to Goldcrest Cove, not looking to get attached. It was just any other mission. It was supposed to be a quick few weeks of coming here, finding out what I needed, and going back to the Council with my report."

She rolled her eyes and gave the slightest shake of her head. Not get attached. Just business. He could use those lines all day long, but it didn't change what he had done to her.

"And I wasn't supposed to draw attention to myself. I wasn't supposed to make friends or get a job or... or fall in love. But I did and that made everything complicated. I was supposed to be an observer, but I became too involved. I've been on the force for years and never have I done something so reckless as going on dates or job interviews or... or doing what we did the other night. It was unprofessional and if my commanding officer finds out how I've totally gone against protocol, I could have my rank stripped from me."

Her mouth twitched with the need to smile, but she forced it back. It was the confession he slipped in that provoked it. It was a similar one he had made in the coffeeshop when he talked about his dark magic emerging. It all meant that she hadn't been quite as crazy as she thought. They were Twin Flames. He did love her... Unless he was lying.

How could she honestly believe anything he said? She was in the same boat with Kit. Right about now, she wished that she had some sort of mind reading ability too. Then, she remembered what she had done the night before.

Risking her composure, she looked to him, holding firm to her glare. "Are you lying?" she demanded to know, forcing her will that he tell her the complete and unfiltered truth.

Wesley adamantly shook his head, a look of desperation creasing his handsome face. "No. It's all true. No more secrets. No more lies or half-truths." He reached into the inside pocket of his jacket and pulled out a bi-fold leather wallet-like piece. He flipped it open to reveal the golden engraved badge of the Enforcer.

She had never seen one before and found herself staring, studying the etched symbols that meant so much to their kind. Moon glyphs crested above a heraldic shield that meant courage, loyalty, and light. The latter being the same glyph tattooed on her ankle, a concept she had always aspired to. It seemed they had much more in common now as the real truth emerged.

"I used to take so much pride in this. I worked hard for this. I studied night and day and trained my ass off for this." He tossed it into the cup holder. "But right now, I hate it. I hate it, because I know once all of this is over, I have to leave and I don't want to. This town and the people in it... it's like nothing I've ever had before and I want it. I thought all I wanted out of life was impossible missions and the glory that came with success. But meeting you gave me a new vision of how my life could really be. How fulfilled and happy I could be if..." Wesley let out a frustrated burst of breath. "If things had been different between us and fate hadn't brought us together, I wouldn't be so damned torn up about this."

Alexa cringed and looked away, fearful that he would see the glimmer of unshed tears in her eyes. She didn't know what to think. Maybe she had ruined his happiness just as much as he had ruined hers. That might have been a comforting thought, but it was petty and mean to wish that the man she loved would be crushed just like her.

"I hurt you. I know I did and I won't try and act like I had to. I didn't have to. I could have walked away so easily in the beginning. I didn't have to ask you out to dinner or back to the house. I didn't have to do any of that, but I wanted to. Part of me might have thought I needed to, but it still would have been easier to walk away on the first day than it would be now. That's my fault and I'll take the blame every time for it."

She heard him shift in his seat. "All I'm asking is forgiveness. Not right now, because I don't expect you to give it immediately, but maybe when you're old and grey and still beautiful, you'll remember this sorry son of a bitch and not hurt so much."

A pause settled between them, expectant and trembling with vibes that she didn't want to accept. Hope and love. She wasn't ready to forgive or even think of a day when she was old and without him. That hurt more than anything else at the moment.

"Can I go now?" she asked flatly. "Kit's probably waiting."

It took a moment before he hit the control button and unlocked her door. Alexa didn't jump out as quickly as she would have moments ago, before his speech. The weightiness of her own thoughts kept her from moving too fast up to the gate and down the sidewalk either.

If all Wesley had said was true, that he loved her and wished things were different, then what did that mean for them? He said himself that he couldn't stay, and Alexa never expected him to. He was cut from the same cloth as Devin in that respect. Once a cop, always a cop. They took an oath to protect and serve. But was Wesley willing to walk away from that? Could he give it up for her? He also said that badge meant nothing to him anymore. It was what kept them apart.

Alexa shook her head, blonde hair tossing in the cold wind. She couldn't ask him to give that up, even if they purified all the bad blood between them. Long before he asked for forgiveness, she might have been ready to give it. But they couldn't forget what he had done and what he was. He might have absolved part of his sins against Krystal, Valerie, and the coffeeshop, but not completely. There was no going back to the way things were.

"Baby steps," she told herself. It was what her mother had always said when Alexa came home in a fit, because she couldn't master a certain spell or charm. "Take it one day at a time."

But how many days did they have left? They were Twin Flames, so they would always gravitate toward one another. That would never change. But his time in Goldcrest Cove was waning and Alexa had a feeling that things were going to get even more complicated once she had finished talking to Kit.

That was, if she could ever find her.

The minutes ticked by and there was no sign of the kitsune. It wasn't until she passed by a vacant bench that she heard the whisper.

"Alexa... Over here."

She turned toward the sound of Kit's voice, but only saw the bench piled with old snow that had puckered and deformed overnight. She spun, trying to find the source, but no luck.

"Walk toward the bench."

With hesitant steps, she did so and felt it. A cool, filmy texture against her skin. One more step broke through the invisible shield. Inside the illusion, Kit sat on a snowless bench, leery and edgy like she hadn't just put a glamor over their meeting spot.

Alexa, glad to see that she wasn't hurt or in any immediate danger, rushed over and hugged her neck. "Thank, Goddess! You're okay!"

Kit allowed the hug, but her usual excitement in returning it was missing. Alexa sat back and saw not only edginess now, but a weariness of body and spirit.

"Whatever it is you're running from or fighting, we can help you."

The kitsune shook her head. "It is not that simple."

"Then explain it to me. That's why I'm here." When Kit still seemed unsure, Alexa took her hand and squeezed. "You trusted me enough to meet me here. Trust me enough to tell me what's going on."

After some time and more than a little debating on Kit's part, she finally conceded. "I am sure Wesley told you that I am a kitsune. A fox spirit."

"He did."

"I am over four hundred years old. We – kitsunes – can live for a very long time, but we are not immortal. We have our limitations. We are depicted as benign tricksters and aides to witches. As belief in us began to fade, so did our powers and influence. We became weak and defenseless. Not how we used to be. There are only a few of us left to remember the old ways." Kit's eyes dropped to the frozen earth beyond her feet. "For a time, we traveled together. We feared attack from other spirits. For many years, I traveled with four other kitsunes. One of them was named Kitamura Hatsune."

Alexa, engrossed in the story, nodded and said, "Wesley told me about him."

Kit gave a weak smile. "He was my best friend. It did not last for long. Our group was hunted down by demons. I thought I had been the only one to survive, but I discovered that Hatsune had lived, but just barely. He believes that I was to blame for the attack and he has hated me ever since."

It didn't take long for her to put the pieces together. "Is Hatsune trying to hurt you?"

The innocent kitsune nodded. "Over the years, I have been one step ahead of him. I have never stayed this long in one place. It has been, as you say, a cat and mouse game. I came here, because I thought Hatsune would stay away, since there are many witches here. There was a greater chance that he would be found out, just as I would be. I thought I was safe, but I was wrong. He came anyway."

"How do you know Hatsune is here?"

"I knew it the moment Aaron came to the bar last night. He talked about the calls made to the police and I knew that Hatsune had come for me."

Alexa frowned. "What does Hatsune have to do with the domestic disturbance calls?"

Kit looked up to her. "All kitsunes have the Gift of Influence. They can use it for good or for evil. Hatsune uses it to cause trouble wherever I go. He wants me to be blamed for the trouble. He knows if he can make enough trouble with his magic, then the Council will investigate, find me, and blame me for it."

"So... Hatsune was the one who framed you for what happened at the Council Chamber. He was counting on them going on a manhunt to find you."

Kit nodded, her nose going rosy with impending tears. "And if they made the connection to what he has been doing in Goldcrest Cove, Hatsune knew that I would be found and executed."

Her heart bled for Kit, but it cheered as well. "But Wesley knows you're innocent. If he knew about Hatsune and we – "

The kitsune made a slashing motion with her hand. "No. He can know nothing."

Taken aback, Alexa asked, "Why? We can help."

"No one can help. This is my fight and Hatsune was... is my friend. I asked you to meet me, so I could tell you why I have to leave."

As if Kit would get up and disappear right then and there, Alexa held tighter to her hand. "You can't leave! Like you said, the Enforcers will be looking for you. If we can catch Hatsune and make him confess – "

"He will not confess. He is more powerful than I am and will use his Gift to dissuade his accusers. There is nothing left for me to do but to face him and end this running."

Alexa blanched. "How do you plan to face him?"

Kit lifted her chin proudly. "He will stop at nothing until he has my head. So, we will fight."

"But you just said that he's more powerful than you."

"He is, but I see no other way. I must do what I have been putting off for years and end this."

Alexa shifted on the bench. "Hear me out. Let us help you. We know about Hatsune, we know his power and what he wants. We already have an edge on him. We can catch him and be prepared for whatever he might throw our way."

Kit gravely shook her head. "It is still my fight and my fight alone. We live our lives by a code of honor, though you may not understand."

Alexa gave her a look. "By the way it sounds, Hatsune has no honor. He's willing to trick and deceive into getting you killed! That's not right."

"You see that it is not right, but he sees it as a means to an end. He is after revenge and he believes he is just in doing it. Nothing can persuade him otherwise."

Her throat tightened and she felt like crying because of the unfairness of it all. Damn them and their rules of honor and justice. Where was the justice in any of this? "How do you plan to do it."

A cunning smile curled over her mouth. "I have something of Hatsune's that he wants. Every kitsune's soul is contained within a jewel we keep with us at all times. I have his. I stole it from him months ago, and perhaps that is what has led him to take such desperate measures against me. I took it as leverage, but I can also use it to lure him out of the shadows."

Alexa remembered the shiny jewel under Kit's pillow. Was that hers or Hatsune's? All this while, Alexa had thought Kit was the true victim, innocent and blameless. But now it seemed that she could be just as devious as her enemy.

"When are you going to do that?" she asked, dreading the reality of the answer.

"Tonight. It must be tonight. I will leave Goldcrest Cove with his soul jewel and hope that he follows."

This was wrong. All wrong. Kit shouldn't have to go through this alone and Alexa knew she couldn't just sit by and watch her friend be slaughtered, if it were to come to that. And she knew Wesley wouldn't accept that either. He had a mission to bring back the assassin.

"I have a way we can help, but not really help."

Kit tilted her head. "What do you mean?"

Alexa chose her words carefully, knowing that any hint of her true intentions could ruin the idea. "You're determined to fight Hatsune on your own. I get that. Let's help you set it up. We can use his soul jewel to summon him directly to you."

Her nose wrinkled. "Hatsune will not be summoned so easily by three witches."

"What about six?" Alexa hinted. "And a powerful Enforcer warlock? This is just as much our fight as it would be yours. He's the one who attempted to assassinate a Council member. Any injustice done to our kind automatically makes it our problem too. We have our own honor to uphold, you know?"

Kit seemed to think it over for a moment and when she still seemed uncon-vinced, Alexa continued, "You told Wesley that the enemy of your enemy is your friend. We're your friends. Let us take care of our mutual enemy. Together."

"I do not want anyone to be hurt because of me."

Alexa settled a comforting hand on Kit's shoulder. "I know that feeling. Believe me, I do. But you have to understand that I can't walk away without knowing you'll be all right in the end. And Wesley can't walk away without his guy. Dead or alive. We're invested in this now, so we have to see it through."

The struggle was plain on Kit's face. She wrestled with her pride, her honor, and her sense of independence. Four hundred years of tradition had to be bent just a little and it must have taken all her courage and strength to finally nod and say, "Okay. We will work together."

Chapter 16

W esley could have throttled her. Why would Alexa go and make promises that were close to impossible to keep? When she had come back to the car and told him the whole story of Kit and Hatsune, he could admit that he felt the stir of obligation to help. But she had taken it another step further. She managed to convince Kit that they would help trap Hatsune, so they could have their final battle.

It wasn't so much the fact that she had made the promise. Wesley might have done the same if it were just up to him. However, her plan involved coordinating with every witch in town. Five other witches had to be rounded up, told the story, and debriefed. These sort of missions took days to prepare with the Enforcers, but Alexa wouldn't have known that. With the right team, this might have been a breeze, but they didn't have the time or luxury of calling up the Council for help.

Summoning a spirit, kitsune or otherwise, took a lot of magic and skill, which none of the witches would have been prepared for. There was the conjuring itself and then maintaining a hold on the spirit long enough for Kit to do what she needed.

Wesley's head was still spinning with the many details of the thing. Even as the witches arrived to the woods on the outskirts of town, he still felt as if they weren't ready. They had the materials, he had versed them in the incantation, but he had no confidence in this. No confidence in himself.

Part of that could be linked with Alexa's persistent coolness toward him. They hadn't spoken about his confession in the car. They discussed nothing else beyond the immediate trouble with Kit and Hatsune. If she wanted it that way, he chose to respect her and not bring it up. But it was almost all he could think about, apart from the summoning ritual preparations. Once again, his mind was torn between his Twin Flame and his mission.

He wasn't sure when it happened. Whether at the coffeeshop or outside the park, or maybe the minute the idea of Twin Flames was presented to him at the bar. Whenever it was, it happened all the same. Wesley accepted that he had found his Twin Flame and it was Alexa. Even if he overlooked his intense, consuming love for her, he couldn't ignore the emergence of their dark magic at the same exact time.

It had been cruel fate all along that brought them to this place. He loved her, he wanted her, but he couldn't have her unless he gave up his entire life's work. Did he love her more than the Enforcers? Did he want to spend the rest of his life with her? The resounding affirmative should have been enough for him to dial up his commanding officer and tell him that he was done. Still, he didn't dial. Not yet.

There was just one piece of this fairytale missing and he wasn't going to throw away his one and only potential distraction from heartache if that piece didn't fall into place. Alexa hadn't forgiven him. She barely even looked at him. It didn't matter what he wanted if she didn't want him in return.

He watched them from a distance, all six witches and the kitsune laying down the ritual materials to form a wide, sweeping circle where they would summon Hatsune. The thin layer of patchy snow upon the dead earth created a great conduit for the magic, the stands of trees perfect for buffering the sound of the battle from the outside world. Under the stillness and black of night, the plan should work. Still, he had his doubts.

The girls talked and smiled to one another, giving reassurances to those who needed it and making the mood light in spite of the coming battle.

His eyes continued to drift to Alexa, whose beautiful face was marred by worry he shared and thoughts that only he could hear.

What if this doesn't work? I can't stand to see Kit killed. What if Hatsune really is too strong? What if we can't arrest him when it's all over?

His feet began to move of their own volition, taking him to her side before he could implement any common sense. She didn't want to be bothered with him. Didn't want to have anything to do with him until this was all over.

There was still one more thing to do before the ritual. Something they both needed.

Alexa glanced his way while she continued to sprinkle the herbal mixture along the inside of the summoning circle. She said nothing and barely acknowledged that he was there until he blocked her path.

"I need you to take this." He pulled out a small burlap sachet that clattered with stones. "It has a few different crystals in it, but they're going to help with focusing and channeling your powers into the ritual."

She looked to the little sack in his palm and he willed himself not to tremble. "You said no one needed to carry a bunch of crystals all the time."

"You don't, but for this, it's going to help. We only have the power of six here and we'll need you at full strength."

That one nugget of truth, the one he had kept from her all along, prompted her to meet his stare. "Six? More like six and a half."

Wesley shook his head. "No. Six... I have my own bundle here." He patted his jacket pocket. "If we both carry these, it'll magnify our strength. It's only a little, but it will help."

Alexa's lips parted as her mind caught up with the math. No words were said. All that passed between them was an understanding, empathetic energy that soothed a bit of the brokenness within him. With a slow, shaking hand, she took the pouch from him and held it to her chest as if it were the most precious thing she owned. But was it the crystals that she treasured or the secret they now shared?

"Are you almost done?" Krystal asked as she neared completing her half of the circle with her own bag of herbs.

Alexa blinked and Wesley stepped aside to allow her to finish. He had done what he needed to do and perhaps it would help to mend the charred, fragile bridge between them.

He let out a groan as he watched her walk away, regretting once more that things had gone so sideways for them. How did he expect things to be? Did he somehow anticipate her falling all over him after he told her the nasty truth? If he did, he was a bigger idiot and asshole than he had ever thought.

When everything was in its place and all witches took their respective positions around the circle with Kit in the center, Wesley briefed them all one last time on the proper enunciation of the chant and where they needed to focus their powers.

The summoning circle would act as a trap. Once Hatsune was in, they would close it and create – ideally – an impenetrable cage of magic that would keep both kitsunes inside while they settled their business. It was decided earlier that day that the witches would not interfere unless Wesley gave the signal. And he would only give that if he saw the situation far too dangerous for them or for Kit.

Despite what Alexa might have feared, Wesley wouldn't let Kit be killed. Hatsune would be apprehended and she would testify against him. That was the only way this would end, no matter what it took.

Kit, soul jewel in hand, gave the nod that she was ready to face her nemesis, and Wesley initiated the incantation at the head of the circle. With arms just barely lifted from their sides, hands open and fingers spread to weave together their energies, the air began to hum with magic. Static electricity arched between them all as a thin mist materialized around the circle.

Their voices droned and grew louder as they could all feel their magic pulling together to make this work. Wesley looked to Alexa across from him several yards off. Her eyes were squeezed shut, her mouth curling around the words with such determination that he couldn't help but be proud of her. She threw all she had into this for the sake of her friends and the safety of her town. She had such heart and compassion. More than he had ever seen in anyone. He was ashamed to be her Twin Flame, because she deserved better.

As their magic began to plateau, Wesley felt it. The kitsune was drawing near. Kit hadn't been kidding. The power from Hatsune was massive. Either they were much stronger than he had thought, or the kitsune didn't resist the summoning. That should have shot up red flags, but he didn't call it off.

A form manifested in front of Kit within the circle. It began as little more than a dazzling haze. Then its lines hardened and the fuzzy image came in sharp and clear. A tall man stood in the snow, lean body straight and tensed. His oriental eyes narrowed upon Kit, who cut just as defiant a figure as he did.

The moment they knew Hatsune was completely within their power, the witches and warlock clamped their hands into tight fists, sealing the kitsune within the circle. Their mouths went still as they all tried to catch their breath. But the deed wasn't over yet. They got him there, now they had to keep him. Let Kit have her revenge, but the detainment amulet in Wesley's pocket would be used the moment it became convenient.

The two stared one another down as the wind streamed around them. A new energy pervaded the scene. Hatred. Absolute and utter hatred for the wrongs committed and lack of closure.

"What is this?" Hatsune demanded in a deep, booming voice that echoed through the barren tree limbs. "You get witches to summon me?"

"You tried to turn the world against me," Kit said, her words dripping with all the malice she had saved up over years for this moment. "You have wanted me dead, but never tried to kill me yourself. Here is your chance." She stretched out her arms. "Take your retribution, if that is what you want."

Hatsune let out a belly laugh. "Who ever said I wanted to kill you? Where did you get that idea?"

Kit's aura burnished a harsh red. He didn't need his special vision to tell that much. "Do not pretend with me! You have haunted me for centuries!"

"You must have me confused with another kitsune that you betrayed. I have no quarrel with you."

The witches looked to one another, puzzled and disturbed by what Hatsune had to say. But Wesley could see through it. He knew the kitsune's thoughts and that he was only bluffing. He could see flashes of the things he had indirectly done to make Kit's life a living hell. It was a wonder she decided to wait this long to confront him.

"He's lying," the warlock declared. "Don't let him psych you out."

Hatsune's gaze darted to Wesley and both of the men went rigid as they sized one another up.

"I will not fight you here," their enemy announced. "It is not honorable."

Kit's stance shifted as if she were ready to charge him. "Sneaking in the shadows for centuries is not honorable either. And yet, you have made it into an art."

"It is not honorable that you have brought help to make up for your disadvantage against me. You could not possibly contend with me on your own, so you coerced the witches to believe you."

Wesley, again, spoke up on their behalf. "We all agreed that this is not our fight. We're only here to make sure it's fair."

A wicked smile spread over Hatsune's face. "You can assure that if we fight, it will be conducted fairly."

Why didn't he believe the kitsune? He let a pulse of his magic pass through the invisible cage around the battleground to secure it further and he could feel the witches do the same, though each one of them looked to be dishing out all they had to keep the kitsune contained.

Hatsune turned to Kit and began to speak to her in quick-fire Japanese. She replied back in kind, and though he couldn't understand a word of it, nothing they said to one another was kind. Face twisted into sneers and tones rose to a furious pitch.

Glimpsing to Alexa through the whole exchange, he could tell she caught snippets here and there and none of it was good.

Just when he began to wonder if this was the kitsunes' idea of a fight, their argument reached its zenith. Both shuffled back and two bursts of light blinded the clearing. When the sheet of white cleared from their vision, Kit and Hatsune were gone. In their stead were their true forms. The form of a kitsune.

Foxes the size of small horses gleamed and glittered like the brilliant full moon. Eyes like shiny lumps of coal glared, muzzles bared sharp fangs that glistened with saliva. Fur as white as the snow their paws dug into began to bristle and shiver as the last of their shift ebbed away. They were nearly identical. The only way that Wesley could tell one from the other was the number of their tails.

Hatsune, who was the older of the two, possessed seven long, bushy tails. Kit only had four, and that fit with what Alexa had told him earlier. Their age correlated with their tails, and their tails gave them more power.

They circled one another, snapping and snarling like seasoned fighters. In less time than it took to blink, they were suddenly on one another, rolling and tearing into kitsune flesh with growls and beastly roars. Never would he have guessed that the quivering, abandoned girl they found in the street could be capable of such ferocity.

Part of him felt like he should have been filming this somehow. So little was known about the kitsunes, since they were a dying race. Who else had seen them in their true forms and in combat, no less?

Even if he wanted to film this, his hands were tied with the binding cage. The moment they shifted, the strain and pressure to keep all that magic contained pulled upon his reserves. They all showed their struggle, especially Alexa. But they needed everyone to hold it together. One moment of weakness and Hatsune would seize that opportunity.

Wesley turned on his aura vision to monitor the scene. The kitsunes beamed a menacing red as they continued to roll and rip one another apart like fighting dogs. The girls were holding steady, except for Alexa. A trickle of blood seeped from her nose as she winced and cringed. Her legs nearly buckled a few times. If he were closer, he would have supported her. He could have held her hand and lent her his strength. Anything to keep her from suffering.

A yelp and whimper curtailed the fight. Wesley looked and saw one of the kitsunes in the snow, fur matted and bloodied from the battle. He tried to count the tails, but many of them were buried beneath its heaving and seizing body. The standing victor, blood dripping from its jowls, stood over the weakened kitsune. All tails stood erect and Wesley felt a pang of anger as he counted all seven of them.

Have to escape. Have to leave. She will die... Don't want to see.

Hatsune turned and sized up each of the witches who valiantly stood their ground against the formidable spirit. Ebony eyes skimmed them over and Wesley knew what they were doing. Just like an animal needing to escape its prison, it was looking for a weak spot. He found it when he turned to see Alexa barely standing.

All seven tails twitched with anticipation and Wesley had a choice to make.

The amulet was in his pocket, but Hatsune wasn't weak enough. Nor would the necklace fit around the beast's neck. They weren't planning on this. He had to act, but that would mean breaking the cage. No one else would know a spell strong enough to take down the kitsune.

But he didn't have time to form another plan. Hatsune leapt for Alexa. The witches screamed. Those closest to Alexa were the first to break the circle and try to shield her.

Wesley diverted his powers from the broken cage to Hatsune. Without even taking a step or laying a hand on him, the kitsune changed course in mid-air, falling backward and deeper into the circle. Hatsune scrambled to his feet and looked to his attacker. Blinded by rage and feral instinct, he charged for the warlock.

It happened so fast. Arms encircled her shoulders and drove her to the ground, but all Alexa could see was the silvery white mass of fur rushing upon Wesley. Alexa screamed and reached out, resisting her friends that tried to hold her back.

Wesley was knocked down after a burst of green magic momentarily slowed Hatsune enough that the blow couldn't be lethal. She hoped it wasn't anyway.

Moments ago, the fatigue had been enough to make her dizzy. Everything ached, her blood was on fire, her vision blurred and she could taste blood in her mouth as she continued to extend her magic. It was too much for her, but she continued to push. Now, she felt as if she had nothing left. Powerless and exhausted.

But seeing Wesley fall to the snow and eyes shut, seeing Hatsune's jaws open wide to close around her Twin Flame, suffused her with a new sort of magic. Her dark magic.

In a second, the world stood still. The wind stopped blowing, no one moved a muscle. Not even Hatsune, who was inches away from killing Wesley. Alexa burned with the magic, felt it run hot through her nerves and along her skin.

She didn't even have to think it. She only needed to feel it and want it. Fury boiled over until it was all she had. Hatsune would not get away with hurting her friend or attacking Wesley. If she had the strength to kill him herself, she would have. Never had she wished death and suffering upon someone, not even if they deserved it.

Kit, who had been struggling to hold onto life, finally opened her eyes and stood. Hatsune, resisting every step, backed away from Wesley's body as Alexa willed it. Kit shook out her fur and the two were facing one another again. Only, Hatsune would not defend himself. He stood completely still and waited for the death blow. In a matter of a minute, it would all be over. They would win and everything would be as it should. Kit just had to take the shot that Alexa had opened for her.

"What's happening?" Amber asked, looking from Alexa to the kitsunes.

"She's using her dark magic," Krystal replied, half in awe and half in fear. It had taken all seven of them to detain Hatsune, but she could control his movements alone with just her will power.

But one look from the wounded kitsune struck her to the heart. This wasn't the way Kit wanted it. This wasn't the honorable way. This wasn't honest or glorious. It was manipulation. She was forcing everything to go her way, when Kit made it explicitly clear that this was not the witch's fight.

Alexa shook her head frantically. It was hers now. Hers because Hatsune had threatened Wesley. But there was still no honor in it. It was cheating. Angry, vengeful tears streamed down and curled around her chin. Her friend, a bloody and tattered mess, continued to silently implore her to let go. Just this once.

It took more strength to hold herself back and let go of it all than to take control in the first place. She dropped her hands and sank into the arms of her friends, whom she realized were Sierra and Taylor. The other three had stayed in formation around the circle, though the binding cage was useless now.

Hatsune took quick advantage when Alexa dropped her hold. He pounced upon Kit and they recommenced their vicious kitsune battle. Fangs sank into flesh and claws slashed deep.

"Someone has... has to get the amulet." Alexa's voice was just as weak as she was and she hated it. The others were tired, but even with the bundle of crystals, the summoning ritual had taken so much out of her.

Sounds became distorted as she struggled to hang onto consciousness. It sounded like the other witches were talking, but she couldn't make out their words. Her vision blurred, fading in and out. Alexa blinked hard to see Krystal and Amber running for Wesley while Valerie drew dangerously close to the feuding kitsunes.

Alexa saw this and tried to push herself up.

"They have a plan." Taylor's assurance sounded muffled, but confident.

She swallowed back a wave of nausea as she saw Valerie slip off her amethyst crystal and toss it into the snow. In one brave leap, she lunged forward and grabbed for a kitsune's tail. The air in the clearing became heavy with dark magic, suffocating like a heavy blanket. Valerie was trying to wear down Hatsune by sapping his energy.

The kitsune that had been grabbed reared back and swiped at her, but another creature came into view. A black blur of fur pounced upon Hatsune. Alexa gasped at the sight of Caleb. Where had he come from?

Kit scampered to the sidelines and licked at her wounds. Valerie continued to hold onto Hatsune's tail, her negative energy draining upon his powers and strength like acid would eat through metal. All the while, Caleb snapped at his neck and shoulders, equal in size and brawn to the kitsune.

A face appeared close to hers, one that was familiar and comforting in her childhood years.

"Was she hurt?" Catherine Hayden's voice might have been one of the most welcoming sounds she had heard all day.

"No," Sierra answered her mother. "The summoning was just hard on her."

The two began to argue, mostly about why the older hadn't been informed by the younger about what was going on. Alexa leaned around the motherly figure, looking for the one who had inevitably followed.

Sure enough, she caught a glimpse of a tall, broad-chested man across the battlefield near Wesley. Gordon Hayden stood beside Krystal. They exchanged some words and then his youngest daughter stepped away. Through the thrashing mass of furry bodies, Alexa couldn't see them well, but the tawny glow of fire was clear enough. It cut through the dimness, lighting up the whole clearing as it shot from the witches' hands and strengthened the circle they had outlined earlier.

The heat of the fire brought a bit of vigor back to her and she found the strength to sit up completely, with only a little help from Taylor.

"Where's Wesley?"

"They're taking care of him, honey," Catherine replied. "We came as soon as we could."

"How did you know where we were?" Sierra asked.

The woman shot her a look. "I'm your mother. I'll always know where to find my girls."

"You scried for us, didn't you?" Taylor's amused voice seemed so incongruent with the fiery den of battle that surrounded them.

"I did, but that's beside the point."

"We have to get to Wesley."

The three witches kept Alexa from crawling to him as she intended. He might have been all the way across the circle, so far from her with a werewolf, witch, and kitsune warring between them, but she had to be with him and see that he was okay for herself.

"Just rest now. It'll be over soon."

That might have been an understatement. With Valerie and Caleb wearing Hatsune down, and Krystal's ring of fire towering high and strong around them, there was no way the wanted criminal would escape now. Kit had given over the fight to the others, satisfied that she had won her own small victory over her rival. It might not have been to the degree she wanted, but she escaped with her life and dealt as many blows as she could.

The seven-tailed kitsune dropped beneath Caleb's full werewolf form and lay motionless just long enough for Gordon to approach. His lips muttered a charm and he pulled out a familiar amulet.

Gradually, the kitsune began to shrink and morph back into the human guise under Gordon's magic. The tail slipped from Valerie's hands and she went scrambling for her amethyst pendant in the snow. Caleb, however, wouldn't budge or let up his guard until Gordon had secured the amulet around Hatsune's neck.

They had won. It was a close call, but they won. The adrenaline that had kept her awake suddenly dropped, leaving Alexa groping to her last stores of energy to stay awake. The last thing she remembered before blackness consumed her was the faint and unfocused vision of Wesley rising from the snow with Amber's help.

Chapter 17

"The morning after I arrested Kit, she escaped."

Gordon laced his fingers over his knees. "Did you cast a binding circle?"

Wesley nodded. "I did."

"And she still escaped?"

Sitting before Gordon and Catherine Hayden would have been an honor in any other situation but this one. With Kit and Alexa convalescing upstairs and Hatsune in one of the most complex and powerful bindings he had ever witnessed in the downstairs study, Wesley's attention was split between giving his report and straining his senses for any brewing trouble.

His lips parted as he tried to order his thoughts and maintain professional eye contact with the Council member. "Yes, sir."

"How did she escape?" Catherine asked. From the moment they met, she had been nothing but compassionate in a motherly sort of way. Now, the stern facet of her title emerged to intimidate him into telling the truth.

That was the last thing he wanted to give. He knew this blemish would go on his record and potentially ruin his career.

"She distracted me and I believe it broke part of my concentration on keeping the binding intact."

"How did she distract you?" Gordon questioned. "From your profile, you're not the sort to get distracted easily."

"She created an illusion to draw my attention away from her."

"What kind of illusion?"

Wesley worked hard to maintain a placid look on his face. "She made me believe that one of the witches came to my house to talk to me."

"Which one?" The ghost of a smile on Catherine's lips told him that this part wasn't truly that important to the mission report, but more important to her personally.

The pause was just long enough for him to hear the footsteps of their daughters upstairs, probably still tending to Kit's wounds.

"Alexa Boyer."

That name had blessedly stayed out of his report until this moment. He had only ever referred to the girls as "the witches" and left that detail obscure for the record. He didn't want to drop names and put anyone under suspicion. Especially her.

Gordon sat back in his armchair. "Why would Kit choose Alexa? She had her pick. She could have made any distraction. Why Alexa?"

For the first time, Wesley stumbled. "I don't see what that has to do with the bigger picture of how things turned out."

"It matters to me." The drop in Gordon's voice snapped Wesley back into line. "Why would Kit choose Alexa?"

Wesley's muscles tensed as he fought to stay still on the sofa. "Kit must have been under the belief that Alexa and I were intimate with one another. She said things during the interrogation to suggest it."

"And since she successfully distracted you, I'd assume she was right." The clever, soft smile had finally blossomed on Catherine and Wesley chafed under it.

"I had... become close with the witches during my investigation."

Gordon's frown countered his wife's pleasantness. "You understand the implications of that, don't you?"

Wesley nodded. "It compromises my position. It could suggest that my report and findings are spoiled by bias."

The older warlock, dark thick brows slanting with severity, let out a deep sigh. "We'll revisit that. What happened when you discovered Kit had slipped your circle?"

The suspense would get the better of Wesley before the evening was through. "I went to the witches to ask for their help in finding Kit, because I suspected that she would be hiding out with them."

"You told them you were an Enforcer?"

Once more, caught in his words. "They discovered it on their own."

Gordon leaned over and rested his elbows upon his knees. "You mean that you allowed them to find out you were an Enforcer when the entire core of your mission was to remain incognito."

He would lose his rank. He could see it already. He would be drummed out of the force and have nothing to console him when it was all over. No job, no Alexa, nothing.

"It was an accident. A rookie mistake. However, I used it to my advantage and the witches were willing to help me find Kit."

Either they were willing to save his error for another time or Catherine was living up to her reputation as a peacekeeper and moving on with the report. "How did you find Kit?"

This much he wasn't too afraid to mention. "Kit had become intimate with a human teacher. We went to him and used his phone to call Kit. She answered and – "

"You involved a human in your investigation to find a kitsune?" Gordon's ire refused to be banked, even by his wife's touch upon his shoulder.

"We were running out of options. The human only knew that Kit was in some sort of trouble and that convinced him to let us use his phone." Wesley hardened, hoping that force met with force wouldn't turn into an explosion. "As I was saying, Kit answered and met with Alexa to discuss a plan of action to confronting Hatsune."

"You permitted a witch – actually a half-witch – to carry out a part of the investigation that was your obligation?"

Wesley's blood simmered at the thought that Alexa's breeding would have anything to do with her qualifications to help in the mission. It never stopped him. "Kit refused to meet with me, but she and Alexa are friends. She refused to speak with anyone else but her."

Gordon pinched the bridge of his nose and let out a tired breath. "Go on."

"Collaborating with Kit, we used Hatsune's soul jewel to summon him to the spot outside of town. The witches and I served as... referees, for lack of a better term, for the fight that Kit wanted."

"Why not just arrest Hatsune when you had him trapped?" Catherine asked, taking the lead from her husband before his fuse burned out.

"Kit was adamant about having this final confrontation with her enemy. Something about honor and retribution. Alexa told me they have been rivals for centuries. Hatsune has created more than enough trouble for Kit to drive her to these extremes."

"That's why he posed as her and infiltrated the Council Chambers."

He nodded to the Council witch. "That's why. The moment the fight became too much for Kit, we were going to arrest him."

Gordon looked up. The chandelier trembled at his booming words. "You endangered a witch, forcing her to do more than what she was capable of, and then failed to put the kitsune under arrest, so the others would have to clean up after your mess."

Wesley wouldn't answer that. He wouldn't dig his grave any deeper than it already was. If that's the way Gordon wanted to see it, then there was little he could say to change it.

"He didn't force anyone."

They all three turned to see Krystal at the parlor room archway, hair not so tidy in her ponytail. They had little time to rest since they came home from the battle.

"All of us wanted to help Kit," she continued. "He warned us how hard it would be, but we all pitched in anyway. Alexa knew the risks. He can't be blamed for what happened."

In truth, he could. The Council would see him as the one in charge. He was responsible for the whole affair. It had been his fault that Kit slipped through his fingers in the first place, as Gordon so kindly pointed out.

Catherine gave her daughter a tender look. "No one is blaming him, honey. We're just trying to sift through all the details."

"Dad's trying to blame him." Krystal's hands balled into fists at her sides. "You're trying to look for someone to be held accountable. It's not just about Wesley. We all played a part."

Gordon rose to his feet and pointed a firm finger at his daughter. "I allowed you to have your say about the werewolf last December. I should have arrested him instead of pushing his registration for residency through the Council. I won't let you persuade me in this too."

The fireplace wasn't even lit and the temperature in the room spiked, sending a surge of heat down Wesley's back. Krystal's dark eyes flashed with stubbornness she could have only inherited from the man she glared at now.

"I'm only telling you the truth. You can't put all the blame on Wesley."

Gordon gestured angrily toward the Enforcer. "He took an oath to protect at all cost and he failed to do that."

"And I have a responsibility to my friends."

"He's not your friend. He was here to find evidence to give the Council cause to shut down your coffeeshop. You do know that, right?"

Krystal squared her shoulders. "Of course, I did. He may not be my friend, but Alexa is."

"This has nothing to do with Alexa!" Gordon thundered as he pointed in the direction of the stairs. "Just like the werewolf had nothing to do with Valerie. You cannot, and will not, change my mind on this. Wesley will receive whatever punishment the Council and his commanding officer thinks is just for his infractions and that's final. I will not sugarcoat this or try to pull strings to save him the trouble."

Catherine stood and put a hand on her husband's arm. "They're Twin Flames, sweetheart. Just like Caleb and Valerie were."

Gordon looked to his wife with mock alarm. "Oh? And this is supposed to change everything? Well, by all means! Since they're in love, we'll just forget about the shattered rules and ignored protocol! Anything for the sake of damned Twin Flames!" He ambled away from his woman and leaned his hands against the mantle.

"How did you know?" was all Wesley could manage. The ominous threat of his punishment was blown straight out of his head.

She passed him a comforting smile. "Honey, I know a lot of things. Like the fact that Alexa would want to see you right about now." Her eyes cut toward his exit as his cue.

Wesley cast a hesitant glance toward the livid Gordon, then to Catherine, and then to Krystal. He hadn't won them over and it was likely that he wouldn't. There was no getting out of this, even if the witches tried to defend him. It was a lost cause. If only the Haydens hadn't come... Then again, if they hadn't, who was to say that they would have showed up at just the right time with the right muscle to help take out Hatsune?

He strode out of the parlor and climbed the stairs. Sierra was with Kit in one of the girls' bedrooms. The kitsune had been torn up pretty good, but her healing abilities were compensating for much of the damage. Bedrest was prescribed by Catherine, the same as was given to Alexa.

His Twin Flame had been given the guest bedroom at the end of the hall upstairs. With each thud of his boots on the rug, he mulled over all that had transpired. Not just downstairs, but over the last few days.

So much in so little time. He failed a mission and inevitably lost his rank as an Enforcer. But he also found love. He found something more to live for than just himself. And for that, he decided something rather important. He regretted nothing, save for the way the truth finally came out. Because of that, within the last few days, he lost everything, even the love he had just found.

The door was cracked and he pushed to open it further, peaking into the room lit by a single lamp on the dresser. Alexa, the covers drawn up over her shoulders, faced away from the door. By the steady rise and fall of her body, he thought she was asleep.

He stood, leaning in the doorway, watching her and the way the warm glow of the lamplight curved around her blanketed figure. In sleep, she was safe and beautiful. In sleep, she couldn't be mad at him or hate him so strongly. If only it could have stayed that way.

Maybe it could. He could just slip away and leave her to her dreams. There wouldn't be the awkwardness of saying goodbye, not like she had wanted that in the beginning. He could leave and walk off into a future he didn't want, but keep this last image of her in total peace.

It would break his heart. He knew he'd never be the same. But because he loved her, it might have been best.

Wesley took hold of the knob and made to close the door just as the tiniest of voices made him freeze.

"Don't go."

He waited, breath stilled in his lungs and body on fire from her request. Soon, Alexa rolled over, the blankets and sheets whispering around her. Bleary, tired eyes looked up to him with childlike sadness. How could he say no to that?

Instead of closing the door, he pushed it open enough for him to slip through. He came to her side and dug his hands into his pockets. He fingered the Howlite crystal, wishing it could take away all of his nervous energy just this once.

In one move, she did what the crystal couldn't. Her arm slithered out from under the covers and reached for him. Without a second thought, he took her hand and folded it between his own, kissing her knuckles as he sat himself on the edge of the bed. Her skin was cold to the touch, but he could sense her strength building. He wished that his presence had something to do with that.

"How do you feel?" he asked, minding to keep his voice hushed for her sake.

Her lips pulled into a tiny smile, one that made his heart leap in his chest. "Like I've run a thousand miles."

"Using that much magic will do that to you."

Her thumb rubbed over his. "But you're not this tired."

Wesley focused on her fingers, the way the skin stretched over her bones and knuckles. Hands that did so much for those she loved and so little for her own self. "I've trained hard to get to the point where it takes a lot to wear me out."

"Does... Does anyone else know?"

"Maybe a few, but only because they had to know. You're the only one I've told personally."

"That makes me feel a little better... Did we get Hatsune?"

Wesley then spent the next few minutes telling her what had happened after she passed out. How Gordon and Catherine were deciding his fate downstairs and Kit was on her way to recovering.

"What will you do?" she asked, a flicker of panic in her blue eyes.

That was the question of the hour. What could he do? What options were left to him? "If they don't kick me off the force for botching up these missions, I'll have to leave."

Her grip tightened, which he wasn't expecting. "And if they do?"

He gazed into her eyes, searching for the answers. In them lay his whole world. His new reason for breathing. "I'll have to figure something out."

Alexa edged closer. "Why not stay? You said yourself that you liked Goldcrest Cove."

Wesley smiled and continued to stroke along the back of her hand. "I like more than just the town, you know."

Her pale cheeks reddened. "I know."

And that was the rub of it all. "I can't stay if I can't have that too."

Alexa closed her eyes and he hoped that she understood. He needed an answer. He needed to know where they stood now. Just because she blushed a little and held his hand didn't mean that all was mended. He needed to hear those words.

"I... I hope they don't kick you off the force."

The heart that had skipped earlier might as well have been struck with a sledgehammer. She wanted him to leave? She wanted him to continue to be an Enforcer, even if it meant he would have to go away?

"You've worked hard to get to where you're at," she continued weakly. "I wouldn't want you to lose it all because of me... I used to think I had it bad, because I was only a half-witch. But you're a half-warlock and kept it a secret all this time. I can't imagine how much you've gone through. I wouldn't want you to turn your back on what you've accomplished... I love you too much to be selfish like that."

Wesley had no words. She understood. For the first time in ages, someone understood. She understood his struggle and could appreciate it for what it was. An achievement. But it was nothing compared to her. Because she loved him in return, he was ready to march downstairs and tell Gordon Hayden that he was officially done with the Enforcers. He would make a life here in Goldcrest Cove and be with his Twin Flame.

It seemed simple and his heart no longer tugged two ways. Alexa was everything.

Yet, he didn't get up. He didn't hurry downstairs like he could have. He stayed by her side. Something in him wouldn't let him leave and he wondered if that had more to do with Alexa than his own will power.

He pressed his lips to her hand and breathed in the scent of her skin.

"Promise me if they'll give you a second chance, that you won't waste it?"

Wesley started to shake his head. He'd throw it all away for her, but she wouldn't let him. He could recognize that dark magic now. The kind that forced her will upon someone else. She was using it against him, so he would return the favor.

I know he'd be miserable here. He would be bored and feel useless. I can't bear to see him like that. Goddess, how I love him. I can't see him sad, but I don't want to live without him either. When will this get any easier?

"It can be easy," he whispered. "I can stay. I want to stay. I want to be here with you."

Alexa shook her head, eyes watery. "You don't mean that."

"I do. I've never been more serious about anything."

Silence rang in his ears as Alexa struggled with her next words. "Let's just... Let's just wait. Let's see what happens. I don't want to think of all that right now. I just want you to be with me. Right here."

That much he could do and that much he could give her. He bent down to slip off his shoes before swinging his legs up onto the bed and lying beside her. It took a moment for them to get comfortable again, arms and legs intertwined as if the world would blow them away at any moment.

Their foreheads touched and all was right again. Like in the ritual to join their powers, he could feel their magic and souls weave together to become one again. He closed his eyes, the exhaustion of the long day finally catching up with him.

He let sleep take him. Because in sleep, they could both forget about the unknown and the future that awaited them.

Wesley stood in the center of court, chin up and at ease with his hands behind his back and feet planted evenly. Three dozen pairs of eyes stared down at the Enforcer in his dress uniform, brass buttons shining in the harsh light around him. He had stood under these lights for three days now, answering questions and giving his testimony, just as he had done with Gordon Hayden in Goldcrest Cove.

By the grim faces surrounding him, he wasn't confident about his prospects. He knew this would be the end of his career in the force. He knew nothing else but the world of policing magic, and he was about to be expelled from it forever. That was just fine with him. The minute his sentence was passed, he would be in his car and zooming back to Goldcrest Cove. Back to Alexa.

"Wesley Griffith," rang the booming vice of the head councilman, "you have stood before us during this trial, completely adamant of your own innocence. And yet, you agree that you have failed your prime mission." The old man with graying hair peered down at the report in front of him through half-moon glasses. "You were to investigate Goldcrest Cove, Massachusetts, for any sign that magic has been practiced illegal and under dangerous circumstances." He set the report down and picked up another. "You stated on the first day that you found no evidence of this. Is this true?"

With the patience that only a soldier possessed, Wesley declared, "Yes, it is true."

The councilman looked down to the accused. "And yet, we have accounts of numerous occurrences where magic may have indeed been used to violate the most sacred and vital rule of our order. Magic cannot be used to interfere in the lives of non-magic folk. You deny that such a violation has occurred?"

The muscles in Wesley's shoulders tightened as his hands clenched around one another. "I found no evidence that magic was used to harm or directly interfere with the lives of the citizens within Goldcrest Cove."

His accuser pointed a bony finger at him. "You are playing with semantics. Did the witches of Goldcrest Cove use their magic against humans?"

"Not against them, no sir."

"So they did use magic on humans?"

"No, sir. ."

"So, then... They used the magic indirectly?"

Wesley knew he was on the record. He knew what power he held to condemn or save the witches. What he said here would define their future. His future. If he were a lesser man, he would have told them all the truth and saved himself. But he was better than that. Alexa showed him that he could be better than that.

"The magic used in Goldcrest Cove was used to better the lives of the witches. If I understand which reports you speak of, I can account for them. The murderer caught last Samhain had directly threatened the life of Sierra Hayden, a daughter of a council member present today. His interference in the lives of the witches warranted their involvement. Using their magic to put away the murderer made the town safe from his crimes. In the case of the demon that terrorized the townspeople, employing the services of a necromancer, the witches were also directly affected. A member of their family was brought back from the dead, disturbing her rest and once more, warranting the attention of the witches within the town. They used their magic to banish the demon, with the help of Enforcers and a werewolf who exchanged his services for the right to reside within the town. Again, they made the town safe from the demon's influence and used their magic to do it."

Wesley looked to Gordon who sat just a few seats down from the speaker. "And more recently, in the case of the kitsune who had attempted to assassinate a council member, the witches used their magic to help capture the escaped criminal. The kitsune has confessed, in this same courtroom, to his crimes and that he had not only harassed the witches of Goldcrest Cove, but the non-magic citizens as well. If it weren't for their help, the kitsune might not be in our custody now."

With a deep, fortifying breath, Wesley finished his speech. "The witches of Goldcrest Cove have only ever used their magic for the betterment of their community. It just so happens that they've been using it to take down dangerous criminals who would be a bane to the council and magical community. If they had not stepped in on all three of these accounts, the Enforcers would have more chaos on their hands than they could handle. The law states that magic cannot be used on non-magic folk, but I state today, in front of the council and for the record, that such a law, in its simplicity, gives much leniency to the definition of what constitutes an abuse of magic. The witches are innocent. If I have failed in my mission by proving them innocent, then I have indeed, failed."

To say the words aloud made his chest and guts constrict. His wounded pride, however, was a sacrifice he was willing to make for the town and witches he had come to love and care for. He could die a contented man, knowing that he had kept his honor and conscience.

The councilmen and women around the court began to whisper to one another. He could make out nothing, but that didn't matter. He knew what would come and he braced himself for it. He knew that this would be the very last time he wore this dress uniform.

The speaker slowly stood and straightened his aging back, the ancient robes of their order draping his shoulders. "With complimentary reports and testimonies from your commanding officer and Councilman Hayden, this court has reached its verdict."

All went silent, the air pregnant with the fallout that would come.

"Since Goldcrest Cove seems to be a hotbed of conflict, it is our decision that it needs greater protection. It is not the place of the witches to serve as the only line of defense for their town. This is why The Force has enlisted warlocks for centuries. And since there are no warlocks in Goldcrest Cove, the council must step in to rectify this imbalance."

Ice ran through Wesley's veins. Enforcers descending on Goldcrest Cove? The girls would be found out in a heartbeat.

"By the recommendation of several others, the council has decided to station you, Wesley Griffith, in Goldcrest Cove for the remainder of your service as an Enforcer. It will be your sole mission to protect its inhabitants from the influences of magic, uphold the supreme law of magic, and police any violations of this law. The council will endorse your station there, compensating for a portion of your expenses just as it does when any Enforcer is sent on a mission." The councilman picked up a thicker set of papers from his desk. "In regards to your implied negligence in both your mission to investigate the town and in apprehending the kitsune, the council has decided to absolve you of any guilt assumed with these charges. The results justify the means. However..." The councilman narrowed his eyes upon Wesley again. "You will be under strict observation for the next six months. If one incident should occur in Goldcrest Cove that you fail to take care of, the council will reconvene and the transcripts from this trial will be reviewed again as potential evidence toward negligence of duty. Am I clear, Mr. Griffith?"

The strength in Wesley's knees were sapped away. This was not what he was expecting. Far from it. The council was sending him back to the place he truly wanted to be and would even pay to keep him there. He'd be with Alexa under orders from the council and keep his job as an Enforcer.

He glanced to Gordon and the smug look on the warlock's face wasn't lost on him. In the end, he had something to do with this. Wesley didn't doubt it.

He looked back to the speaker and nodded. "Yes, sir."

The council closed out the trial and Wesley was escorted out of court, all while his mind raced with plans. There were so many opportunities for him now. He could keep his job at Torn Sails Bar if he wanted. He could decorate his house and make it a real home. He could go to Perfect Books and Brews every morning for coffee and see the witches every day.

And best of all, he could be with his Twin Flame. Together, they were one and he couldn't live without her. Being separated for so long showed him that more keenly than anything. He now knew what his mother suffered and was determined never to suffer the same. Even if he lived in a cardboard box with no job, no friends, and no magic, he would still choose to be by Alexa's side. For once, he knew his future and it was in Goldcrest Cove.

They weren't given much time in the end. Gordon and Catherine were to return to the Council Chamber with Wesley and Hatsune for final processing. Krystal told Alexa how she had tried to defend Wesley in the same way she had begrudgingly defended Caleb months ago. It was some consolation to know that her friends still cared for her sanity. But it hadn't been enough. Mr. Hayden was still fuming and spitting flames the last hour of their visit.

Life returned to something resembling normal. Kit, the newest addition to their strange coven – or pack, as Caleb referred to it – worked with them in the coffeeshop. That, in itself, was an adjustment for all of them. To have a kitsune, an ancient and powerful spirit brewing espressos alongside them seemed surreal. In all reality, it shouldn't have been. According to the lore of the kitsune, they were aides to witches. To have one in Goldcrest Cove only made sense.

Besides that Kit had one very good reason for staying in Goldcrest Cove and it was a high school teacher by the name of Shawn. They had become so engrossed in one another that they all wondered if the two were Twin Flames themselves, if such a thing existed for a kitsune and a human. One day, Shawn would have to learn the truth, but for now, the three witches loved to watch them smile and talk to one another in Japanese – presumably flirting.

Business picked up enough that they needed the extra hand to make drinks. Soon, they were back to their old figures again, but with the reduced wait that all the customers had wanted.

Shawn, thanks to a charm, had forgotten the whole business. As far as he knew, Kit wasn't in any trouble and they were all the same bunch he chose to hang out with nearly every day.

Excuses were made for Wesley's absence, saying that his mother wasn't in good health and he needed to go take care of her. No promises were made about his return, so no one asked. Alexa was glad for that. If anyone so much as mentioned his name, she felt a cry coming on.

It had been easier than she thought at first. She was able to go to work the day after he left. He texted a couple of times to let her know when he had arrived in New York. What she didn't anticipate was the final fallout. The total cut off of communication that followed in the days after he left Goldcrest Cove. She sent a couple of texts, trying to check in and pry out of him the verdict from the Council about his rank as Enforcer. Not a peep. It was as if he had never existed and these messages were going nowhere. Was this his way of severing their ties? Did he think this was better than the slow, agonizing goodbyes?

After a while, she stopped sending them. She tried to stop thinking of him and waiting for him to come back, because he clearly wasn't. Krystal and Valerie tried to console her, knowing all too well what it was like to be separated from a Twin Flame. Even Amber gave some useful tips. Stay busy and never touch his memory unless she was ready to be broken again.

Day eight of his absence sent her over the edge. She couldn't even roll herself out of bed for her morning ritual. It didn't seem to matter. Nothing mattered. The half of her soul that she had kept safe for the day when it would be rejoined with its other half was finally shattered. Her heart continued to beat, but it felt nothing. There was a hollow in her spirit, a dull ache behind her eyes, and a throbbing in her head that made her too ill for much of anything.

Kit understood that morning and stayed with her, saying little. In times like these, it was better just to have a friend sit with her in the dark, rather than trying to drag her out into the garish sunlight.

"Are you going to work?" she asked.

Alexa cracked open her eyes to stare at the rough and uneven floorboards. "I don't know."

"Do you want me to call Krystal?"

She glanced to the alarm clock on her nightstand. "Not yet."

Kit nodded, sitting on the floor and leaning against the bed rail. "Do you want me to read your horoscope?"

On any other day, she might have accepted. But hope wouldn't come from the stars. Not today. She shook her head.

"Do you want me to light some incense?"

"My head hurts."

"Do you want any crystals? Some tea?"

Alexa shook her head again. The one thing she wanted, the only thing she needed, was miles and miles away in another state doing Goddess only knew what. Why hadn't he called? Why hadn't he texted? Didn't he feel the same as she did?

This is what death by a broken heart felt like. She was sure of it. Nothing else in the world could hurt her this deeply and completely.

Alexa squeezed out a few tears and sniffled back the sorrow she wished she could hide. Each passing day became harder and harder. When was it supposed to be easy to forget him?

Kit, like a dutiful friend and roommate, stood to shuffle toward the window. They were both still in their pajamas and Alexa was sure that if she didn't go to work, the kitsune wouldn't either. On her table by the window sat the half-used box of tissues. The third one she had bought in the last week.

When she didn't come back to the bed right away, Alexa looked up to see her friend pulling aside the curtain to peek outside. The snow had begun to thaw all around town, leaving the sidewalks icy in the morning and trees bare along Johnson Avenue. The rumble of cars told her that the townspeople were already up and moving about. Nothing out of the ordinary.

Then why did Kit have this satisfied look on her face?

Her nerves jolted to life with impossible hope. "What is it?"

Kit grinned and jerked her chin toward the window. "See for yourself."

Alexa was afraid to. What if it wasn't what she was thinking? What if it was something completely different? Would it break her down even further to come so close to a positive thought and be dashed to pieces?

Still, with aching joints, she climbed out of bed and suffered the cold floor chilling her bare feet as she joined Kit by the window. There, parked on the curb, was a familiar classic muscle car. A black Pontiac Firebird. Its owner leaned against the passenger door, arms folded over a black leather jacket and blonde hair teased by the wind.

Life and energy flooded through her limbs and before Alexa could realize what she was doing, she had run out of the apartment and down the back stairs to the antique shop below. The cold was nothing. The ice that numbed her feet wouldn't slow her down. Not even when she slipped a few times and nearly crashed to the concrete.

All she could think of was getting to Wesley. And when she was there, in his arms and wrapped in his warmth, the tears came like gushes of raindrops down her face. She breathed in the spicy scent of his cologne through her joyful sobs. His fingertips dug into her ribs as he held her close, neither willing to let go for anything.

"I thought you were never coming back," she whimpered against his shoulder. That's when she pulled away and smacked at his chest. "Why didn't you call me!"

Wesley only chuckled, the deep, rumbling sound she missed so much. "I wanted it to be a surprise."

Her eyes went wide. "A surprise? This?"

"More than this." He reached into his pocket and pulled out a folded letter. "I have new orders. Read them."

He let her down onto the sidewalk, her toes insensible to the cold. Her shaking hands unfolded the paper and eyes poured over the contents.

"Wha... What does this mean?" Through the military jargon, she thought she knew, but she needed confirmation. It was too good to be true and she half thought she was dreaming it all up.

"I'm staying. With all the activity in Goldcrest Cove, the Council decided that having a permanent Enforcer in the town would be beneficial. Since I already know the people, they chose me."

Breathy mist clouded the space between them.

"So... You're still an Enforcer? They didn't drum you out?"

He shook his head proudly. "Nope. The Council saw that my choices were for the benefit of the mission to catch Hatsune and absolved me of any guilt."

"What about your other mission? I mean, the one against the coffeeshop?"

"I reported that the witches of Goldcrest Cove were completely innocent of any accusations and Mr. Hayden backed up my testimony."

Alexa snorted. "That's a shock. He didn't seem so agreeable the last time he was here."

Wesley shrugged, but the twinkle of mischief in his eye made her giggle. "I think his wife had something to do with that, but he'd never admit it. The important thing is that I'm here. And I'm here to stay."

Stay. Her Twin Flame was back for good. Heedless of who might have heard her, Alexa let out a squeal of delight and hugged his neck, feeling their souls stitch back together. This was how they always should have been. Two flames as one. Forever.

Epilogue

C atherine would have loved to take credit for this. She had seen it all in the beginning. Well, perhaps not everything, but a good majority of the events over the last four months had been foretold to her through her scrying sessions. All the dangers, the struggles. Her girls had braved it all and here they were, triumphant and with their Twin Flames.

They had all gathered to celebrate on the last new moon before the wedding, throwing a small party at their home for their closest friends. In the parlor, she could see them all as clearly in her crystal as if she were there in person.

Ostara was upon them and soon, her youngest daughter would be married. Krystal had fallen in love with a non-magic man, but she could never regret fate. The Mother Goddess had seen what she needed and given her Devin Daniels, a cop who could teach her that life wasn't all about work and duty. Perfect Books and Brews had been her daughter's life for the last five years and little could come between her and her business. She hadn't let go of the coffee shop, but she had trained herself to take the time to enjoy life outside of its walls. And in turn, her daughter had something to teach him. True bravery was shown when he accepted her dark magic gift of fire when fire was the very thing he feared most. They complimented one another so well that Catherine couldn't have picked a better partner for her daughter.

Her eyes scanned the room and found the werewolf, Caleb Lancaster. Perhaps the only odd bunch out of the group, but once more, destiny knew better. Of all her girls, she never thought Valerie Lloyd would compromise her rebel soul for love. But it took another rebel soul for her to see that she could be loved and belong after all. She had practically raised Valerie and taught her the path of magic, welcomed her into the fold like one of her own. And yet, Catherine always sensed that hesitance in her to truly let herself be part of it all. Caleb coaxed her from that thick shell. Maybe it was something of his instinct to connect with a pack that made her finally understand. Now, he was part of their coven, and they were his pack. Though Valerie still had much to learn about her dark magic, the amethyst around her neck would curb the outpour of negative energy. But looking at her now, smiling and sitting in the lap of her Twin Flame, no one would guess she had any negativity left.

And then there was sweet Alexa Boyer. Catherine found herself misty-eyed as the story of fate unraveled before them in so many unexpected ways. She, more than the rest, had struggled with her magic. Being a half-blooded witch wasn't easy. No one would ever lie and say that it was. But Wesley Griffith came into their lives and showed them what perseverance and dedication could do for one whose blood wasn't of pure magic. She was sure that none of the other witches in the parlor knew of his secret. Only his Twin Flame, the lively sprite of a witch who loved with all her being, knew his truth and accepted him. Together, they embodied the true meaning of Twin Flames. Two halves joined to become whole again. Alexa, with all her spirit and sparkle, would unknot the tightly bound order within Wesley. And he, in turn, could train her as no other could. Catherine and

Gordon had tried, but neither of them could have known how desperately Alexa struggled. Now, she could finally know the full scope of her power and refine this Gift of Influence, as she called it. With her dark magic came the need for great control over her desires. But as Wesley navigated his own dark magic, he could read her thoughts and give her what she wanted before she would ever have to force her will upon someone else. They would complement each other perfectly in the coming years.

Around the room, there were others. Shawn Stokes was there with his new love, the kitsune they called Kit. There was still much for the Goddess to reveal through them, but Catherine could see the embers of their flames begin to crackle and sputter to life.

Aaron Wright, Devin's partner on the police force, talked with the quiet and meek Taylor Morrow. While the witch and human weren't meant for one another, Catherine knew this to be fact, their friendship was undeniable. She only hoped that time would be kind to the non-magic human. He had already been disappointed with the loss of Valerie. He deserved someone to match his boldness and vigor. But blessed was the witch who would never suspect the turn that fate had in store for her.

Her eldest, Sierra, stood with Amber McCain against the wall. Instant friends, they would need to cling to one another in the approaching months. Catherine sighed at Amber's bright purple hair and fiery spirit. Her time was drawing near and the stars would play their cards once more for the witch who had tried to outrun her destiny. Sierra, tall and confident in her station, would also be tested. Catherine had marked the day and would make sure that her daughter wouldn't be alone for the trials to come.

Yes, they were all coming into their own. This year of change and turmoil would be the most difficult of their lives, but Catherine was their witness and guardian. She would never let them fall, never let them do this alone. Not as long as she still had magic in her veins.

Catherine smiled to them all as they toasted and chattered to one another about wedding plans.

"Are they having a good time?" Gordon asked. His heavy hand settled on her shoulder. He couldn't see what she saw in the crystal, but they shared few secrets anymore.

Catherine only nodded. "They are. Blessings be upon them all... My lovely witches."

About the author

Sheritta Bitikofer is an author of paranormal and historical fiction. She lives for the deep, engaging stories that enthrall readers from cover to cover. As a wife and mother of eclectic tastes, she can be found roaming Civil War battlefields, haunting her local coffeeshop, or relaxing with a plate of chili cheese fries.

Follow her for upcoming novel releases

www.sherittabitikofer.com

The Native

The Irishman

The Scholars

The Convicts

The Soldier

The Outlaw

The Deviants

The Unsinkable

Keeper of Light

Bulletproof

The Nexus

Bewitching Brews

Bewitching Fire

Bewitching Darkness

Bewitching Hearts

Wolves in the Open

Highland Howls

Silver Screen

Mourning Moon

The Decimus Trilogy

The Beast of Verona

Amber Ashes

Saving the Beast

Redemption Duet

The Rose

The Lion

Standalones

Escape

Clouds

Passions

By The Book

Also by Sheritta Bitikofer